FIRSTBORN

STARCRAFT™

THE DARK TEMPLAR SAGA

BOOK ONE OF THREE

FIRSTBORN

CHRISTIE GOLDEN

POCKET **STAR** BOOKS
New York   London   Toronto   Sydney

An *Original* Publication of POCKET BOOKS

 A Pocket Star Book published by
POCKET BOOKS, a division of Simon & Schuster, Inc.
1230 Avenue of the Americas, New York, NY 10020

This book is a work of fiction. Names, characters, places, and incidents are products of the author's imagination or are used fictitiously. Any resemblance to actual events or locales or persons, living or dead, is entirely coincidental.

ISBN-13: 978-0-7434-7125-1
ISBN-10:   0-7434-7125-3

This Pocket Star Books paperback edition June 2007

10   9   8   7   6   5   4   3   2   1

POCKET STAR BOOKS and colophon are registered trademarks of Simon & Schuster, Inc.

Cover art by Glenn Rane

Manufactured in the United States of America

For information regarding special discounts for bulk purchases, please contact Simon & Schuster Special Sales at 1-800-456-6798 or business@simonandschuster.com.

This book is dedicated
to Marco Palmieri and Chris Metzen,
with heartfelt appreciation for their support
and enthusiasm, and to all the players who
have kept the Starcraft flame alive.

PROLOGUE

TIME WAS NOT LINEAR. FAR, FAR FROM IT.

Time wrapped in on itself, converged and entwined and embraced events and feelings and moments, then danced away into separate gleaming, shining, precious strands that stood alone and resonant before merging again into the vast stream.

The Preserver rested and dreamed, and time wove itself in and around and through her. Memories fluttered through her mind like gossamer-winged insects: a word that shattered centuries, a thought that changed the course of a civilization. Individuals whose insights and aspirations and even greed and fear turned seemingly inalterable tides of destiny into something new and fresh and hitherto inconceivable. Moments where everything teetered precariously on a crumbling brink, where something as intangible as an idea would send everything hurtling into oblivion or pull it back to safe, solid ground.

Each thought, word, deed, life was a mere drop in

the vast ocean of time, constantly merging and separating to merge again. The concept would challenge some minds, the Preserver knew; but her mind had been destined to hold such contradictions as things being separate and having no separate identity. Grasping such elusive concepts was what she was born for.

Over all these thoughts of words and lives and ideas floated a terrible urgency and fear. Time was not linear; time was shifting and changing. But there were patterns that floated to the surface, their interwoven strands so clear and strong that even the dimmest minds could grasp them. Inevitability? Perhaps. Perhaps not. Again and again the pattern appeared in the swirling waters of time and destiny and luck, submerging and manifesting with a cold precision that made even the Preserver quail.

All the knowledge she held was precious; every memory, every sound, scent, sensation, voice, word, thought. All were vital to her people.

But *this* knowledge, of the pattern that had happened so often before and was about to happen again—ah, this was what made the Preserver more than important to her people.

It was what made her indispensable.

She opened to what was out there, every second that ticked by in its nonlinear, unique majesty challenging her to close in on herself, to not expose herself to the pain of the debris caught in the swollen river.

She could not allow herself such luxuries.

Not when the horrific knowledge of what had come before, and what was certain to come again, polluted the waters of time in her psyche.

She summoned her energy, and sent forth the cry.

CHAPTER 1

IF THERE WAS A GOD, JACOB JEFFERSON RAMSEY had never seen Him, and was somewhat dubious as to His existence. But Jacob Jefferson Ramsey knew there was a Satan. Because most certainly there was a Hell, and it was called Gelgaris.

A few years ago, archeology was a rather musty but respected profession, rather like an old, leather-bound encyclopedia one dusted off from time to time with embarrassed pride. The Confederacy had allotted grants on a stingy but regular basis, and Jake Ramsey, a rather musty but respected archeologist, had been awarded a decent share of them. Over the years, he'd sat happily in sand, whistled while slogging through mud, and cracked weak jokes while encased in a protective environmental suit in places that had no atmosphere. He'd been sunburned, windburned, and just plain burned; frozen, frostbitten and critter-bitten. He had weathered all difficulties with a cheery optimism that often annoyed his teams as much as it inspired them—frankly, probably more.

But this place . . .

Jake and his team had been stuck out here on a place that Darius Grayson ineloquently but nonetheless aptly described as a pimple on the butt of the universe. For two years with little funding, fewer supplies, and tempers that grew shorter by the day, the thirty-two archeologists and one originally perky and now sullen intern had labored on this rock with little to show for it.

That, Jake was convinced, was why he hated this place so much. Surely it was that and not the subzero temperatures at night and the blood-boilingly hot temperatures during the day. It was that, and not the practically microscopic insects that managed to find every crevice in one's body and set up housekeeping therein.

Yes, Jake told himself, *that's why this place is hell*.

The ceaseless wind buffeted him as he grimly made his way from the rockcrawler, a functional but barebones vehicle, back to the tiny shelter that served as his living quarters and communications center. It was only a few meters but that short walk, whether it was freezing as now or blazingly hot as at noon, always felt as though it was ten kilometers. He staggered and swayed in the vicious wind like a drunken man, keeping his goggled eyes fastened on the image of the shelter growing infinitesimally closer. They donned the suits about three hours before sunset, when the temperature plummeted faster than their spirits, and Jake was convinced the suits were faulty. Every damn last one of them. Because he sure as hell always felt cold in them. There was a brief period of about ten minutes twice a day when he felt neither too cold nor too hot, and Jake found that he lived for those moments.

The wind howled like . . . like something that howled. He was so tired that he couldn't even grasp a simile. He extended a gloved hand and finally—*finally*—touched the door, turned his body to block the wind as much as he could to prevent his fingers from wavering, and attempted to punch in the key code. He couldn't see the pad; there was too much frost on his goggles. They were just as faulty as the suits. Muttering, he removed them, squinted against the cold and wind, entered the code, and shut the door on another frigid night.

The glare of the lights, which had come on automatically when the door opened, was painful after the darkness of the Gelgaris night. Jake narrowed his eyes for a moment and dropped his gloves on the floor as he moved into the shelter's warmth. He blinked.

"Ah, crap."

One of the tiny, glowing blue decipedes (he often wondered how they survived when nothing else could, but that was a question for an entomologist) had crawled its ten-legged way into his eye seeking warmth—again—and he took a moment to dig it out and squish it between callused fingers before he decided to depress himself even further and see if there were any messages. Usually there weren't. Jake had had few enough people he called friends before the zerg devoured Mar Sara and the protoss came to finish the job. Now, he expected nothing. But some of his crew still had family they kept in touch with.

Jake had noticed, though, that as time passed, everyone on his team got fewer messages.

He trudged over to the vidsys, an out-of-date tangle of dinged metal, wires, and lights, divesting himself of the frost-covered protective armoring that encased his body as he went and running fingers through his sandy brown hair before realizing they still had luminescent bug guts on them. Ah well, nothing the sonic cleanser couldn't blast off, along with a few layers of skin Jake supposed he didn't really need.

A red light was flashing on the console.

Jake blinked his blue eyes, not sure if the flashing red was real or a pleasant hallucination caused by the late, unlamented decipede.

No, it was there, blinking cheerily as if it were on a Christmas tree back in one of the better neighborhoods of Tarsonis, back when there was a Tarsonis. . . .

Worry flooded him. The last time they had had a message, Leslie Crane's mother had died of a massive stroke. Leslie, of course, had been unable to travel back to pay her final respects, or be with her shattered father; the ferry ship wouldn't return for them for another eight months.

Jake took a deep breath and steeled himself for the

worst. Then, he punched the annoyingly bright red light.

The Dominion insignia flashed on the screen and Jake raised an eyebrow in surprise. Ever since they'd had their butts handed to them on a platter, the Terran Dominion had been somewhat less than dominating. He'd heard that Mengsk had been busying himself with rebuilding, and clearly the insignia on the screen was evidence that they'd done so to the point where they could send out official messages.

But why the hell would anyone in the Dominion want to send a message to Jake Ramsey or anyone on his team?

The screen went dark for a moment, then the visage of a young man appeared. Blond hair curled over the top of the high collar of a military uniform. It was past regulation length, marking the youth as either a military poser or an exception to the rules. Steely gray eyes, elegant features, and a calm bearing mitigated looks that made the young man almost too pretty to be called "handsome." Jake grimaced, bracing himself. Anybody looked that good, he was going to be full of himself.

"Good day, Professor Ramsey," the young man said in a rich, smooth voice. "My face may be unfamiliar to you, but my name will not be. I am Valerian Mengsk, son of our glorious Emperor Arcturus."

Jake's eyebrows reached for his hairline. Mengsk had a son? He thought of what he'd seen of Mengsk on the holos. Mengsk didn't have this boy's physical perfection, but Jake recognized the poised, polished demeanor. Apparently the fruit didn't fall far from the tree. Exception to the rule then, not military poser.

Valerian smiled. "I'm sure you're surprised to hear this, as my father has made no public announcement. For the time being, I don't really exist . . . though I assure you I do, and the funds and supplies and opportunity I'm about to offer you are equally substantial. I suppose you are wondering why I am contacting you today."

"Yeah," Jake drawled, as if he were actually talking to the impossibly perfect boy instead of listening to a prerecorded message. "The thought had crossed my mind."

The door opened and a blast of icy air swept in. A harsh male voice uttered an oath as its owner tripped over Jake's discarded gear.

"Damn it, Jake," came an annoyed female voice, "will you quit leaving your stuff all over the floor!"

Jake didn't take his eyes from the vidscreen, but beckoned to Darius and Kendra Massa, who hurried over to watch with him.

"You and I share a great passion," Valerian continued.

Kendra, who was all of twenty-four and who often lamented the lack of attractive men on the digs, chuckled.

"I'd like to share some passion with him," she said. "Who is this guy, Prof?"

"Valerian Mengsk," Jake said. "Arcturus's boy."

"You're shitting me," Darius said with his usual eloquence. Jake shushed them both.

"We have a passion for the works of the past," Valerian said, pronouncing the word "past" as "pahst." Somehow, the affectation suited him. "For the evidence left behind of civilizations long forgotten and lost to time and wind and dirt. For structures unearthed, and treasures—not chests of gold of yore, but real, true treasures of knowledge—recovered. My father has not been idle during recent months. We are rebuilding the Dominion, and both he and I have vowed that it will not be simply a rule of might, but one of art and sciences as well."

Darius made a comment that made even Jake, who had known the other man for ten years, blush.

"Shut up, Darius," Jake muttered. Something inside him was stirring, something he thought had been killed and buried long ago, squashed as thoroughly as he had squashed the decipede. Was it hope? Valerian's intense gray gaze bored into his, as if they were in truth regarding one another. He realized that his heart was beating rapidly in anticipation of Valerian's next words.

"Not so long ago, a strange construction—completely different from anything we've ever seen before—was discovered on the planet Bhekar Ro. I'm sure the incident is familiar to you."

Indeed it was. They had heard about it even in this godforsaken hellhole. A fierce storm had unearthed a building—if you could call it that—that no one could get their heads around. When a kid had accidentally activated something deep inside the artifact, it had sent out a signal heard by all three sentient races. A dreadful battle had ensued, with terran, protoss, and zerg all coveting the glorious, beautiful thing for themselves.

The kicker that no one had foreseen came when a completely new life-form exploded out of the construct. It was a sort of . . . energy creature that had absorbed zerg and protoss, but for some reason unknown to anyone had expelled humans alive and well. Many a night Jake had lain awake pondering this, wishing he knew more. He'd developed a theory. Published papers on it. Thought not-very-nice things as he heard rumors that more and more archeologists other than himself were discovering more artifacts that were neither protoss nor zerg, but something new, something other, something . . .

Jake blinked, coming back to the present as he realized that Valerian was still speaking. He'd have to watch the message again; he was sure he'd missed some of it in his shocked reverie.

"It has come to my father's attention that more artifacts are being reported. We cannot say for certain why, at this time, the artifacts are coming to the surface, only that they are. He in his wisdom has decided that they should all be explored, and knowing my great love of archeology he has placed me in charge of this program."

"Heh," muttered Darius. "Great love of archeology—right. Bet he's never squatted in sand up to his ass trying to—"

"Shut *up!*" Jake snapped. It was definitely awakening inside him, like the strange creature that had sucked up zerg and protoss—this thing called hope—and it was almost painful. Like a frozen limb coming to aching life.

"Because this is so important to us, I can offer you things that you haven't had in some time, I expect. Full funding. The latest equipment and technology. And because this is so important, you should know that I have spent some time reviewing various lists of names that have crossed my desk," Valerian said. He let his lips curve into a slight smile as he spoke. "Your work on the Pegasus dig has not been forgotten, Dr. Ramsey. If you are interested, I would like to make you part of this team."

Darius clapped Jake on the back, and Jake permitted himself a smile. He'd been awfully proud of what he and his team had accomplished on Pegasus. Pity no one on any important awards committee had been able to appreciate the significance of what he'd done.

Valerian leaned forward and spoke with quiet urgency. "I would like you to join me in uncovering the secrets of this *third* alien race. What we learn could help all humanity, Dr. Ramsey."

"It'd certainly help us," Kendra said in a low voice. She was staring at the vidscreen now with all traces of playful lust gone, her brown eyes wide with the same emotion that was now surging through Jake. "Full funding. . . . My God, you think that means working plumbing?"

Jake barely heard her. Valerian was finishing up. "If you wish to join me, then contact me at once. I hope you do. There is a code at the end of this message; please enter it if you would like to accompany me on this glorious adventure. A final word of caution: Since I am not operating in an official capacity, please tell no one outside of your team about the nature of your benefactor. I'll remain an anonymous donor. Even the people you will be interacting with know me only as Mr. V . . . someone who has the ear of the emperor."

He smiled gently. "I suggest you hurry. Should you decline, there are many, many more who would be more than happy to take your place."

The screen went black. For a long moment, Jake Ramsey stared at it, seeing in his mind not the shiny black screen but an image of a towering alien temple that had been discovered on Bhekar Ro.

The whole thing had been dreadfully botched from an archeological standpoint. Hell, it had been botched from anybody's standpoint. All three races, battling it out bloodily in the skies and on the ground. All the zerg and protoss on the planet taken; most of the terran ships destroyed. It had been months before anyone had thought to go look for them.

The knowledge that had been lost! It made Jake sick. Very little concrete information had survived. The achingly beautiful construct that had housed the creature had been pulverized. All its secrets had been lost with it. The marines barreling in had had orders to take or destroy the construct, not to inspect or analyze it. Hell, they'd even tried to nuke it, only to see the thing devour their energy like candy. As a result, there had been few holograms made and little data taken.

Just enough to be an archeologist's wet dream. Curving walls made of a material no one had ever seen before. Gems and colors and swirls and textures. Ancient, no doubt, but looking as fresh as if it had been crafted the day before.

So many questions. Would the military be involved? Who would get final say over the project? How was it being funded, and did anyone have any special interests?

"Jake?" Darius's booming voice actually made Jake jump. "You going to respond to the man or stand there staring? And wipe the drool off your face."

Jake's hand automatically went to his mouth, and Darius laughed uproariously. Kendra grinned. Jake blushed and smiled. He wouldn't have been surprised to learn that he *had* been drooling.

He took a deep breath, entered the code, and began the journey.

CHAPTER 2

VALERIAN MENGSK, TWENTY-TWO, BEAUTIFUL, AND brilliant, and, he mused, likely a bit arrogant for knowing it, settled easily into the en garde position. Bare feet were steady on the wooden floor; his body, tall and lithe, was draped in the traditional fighting garments of the keikogi and hakama. He grasped the hilt of the four-hundred-year-old sword with a familiarity born of years of practice. The weapon, elegant and beautiful and deadly, was like an extension of himself. Valerian had ceased long ago to think of it as anything else.

Candlelight glittered off the bright blade. In the background, soft music played and the fragrant wood in two large fireplaces crackled as it burned. Valerian held perfectly still in what was known as the horse stance, muscles coiled in preparation for movement, holding the position with the patience of the predator, the tip of the sword held at an imaginary opponent's throat.

With not a twitch to telegraph his movements, he exploded into action.

Valerian moved through the elaborate, graceful poses of the forms with speed and precision. Block, strike, whirl, slice, duck, roll, leap, and again and again, the blade making a sharp sound as it cut air, his breathing coming more quickly with exertion but still regular and steady.

Finishing, he flicked fictitious blood and gore from the blade with a quick, almost arrogant gesture, whirled it over his head, and inserted it into its scabbard. And then, he was motionless as a statue again, his breathing under absolute control so that no adversary would sense that weak moment of inhalation. Sweat gleamed on his brow, catching the firelight as his sword had moments earlier.

He executed a formal bow, and it was over.

Valerian returned the sheathed sword to its stand. He turned to the small table set with old bottles and glasses and made his selection. The port was old, and so was the decanter that contained the brown liquid and the small glass into which he poured it. Both suited him.

He held up the port, examined it as the liquid caught the light, inhaled its fragrance, and took a sip. His father liked ruby ports; Valerian preferred tawny. It was one small way that Valerian could continue to separate himself, at least in his own mind, from the towering presence of his father. He supposed his rebelliousness was not unique. The children of all great individuals constantly strove to step out of the shadow of their parent. Some of them failed, becoming names that were remembered only as bits of trivia, swallowed by history as their unique light and gifts were swallowed by their parent's legacy.

Valerian vowed that would not be his fate.

He took another sip, the syrupy liquid coating his tongue and slipping easily down his throat, and touched a few gently glowing buttons on the wall. A large section of the paneled wall rolled upward and a sleek black platform rolled out. Valerian sank down into a soft leather chair and settled in to watch.

Three-dimensional images came to erratic life on the platform. He had seen this at least a hundred times, and that was a conservative guess. He knew every badly lit shot, every awkward angle, every jerky close-up. Playing before him now was all of the documentation anyone had of the alien creation of maddeningly unknown origin.

The light from the moving images flickered on his face. He watched intently, recalling the first time he had seen this. The sounds of men, protoss, and zerg screaming in agony and gasping their last breaths had bothered him not in the slightest. He had eyes only for the artifact, and the hunger within him could not be sated by these imperfect images. Valerian was like a starving man being passed a cracker and a cup of water. All it did was make him crave more.

Valerian had always been fascinated with ancient civilizations. When he was very little, he would go outside to play—with two soldiers toting weapons as escort—and dig for relics in the dirt. Every time he would occasionally stumble across something odd, he would carefully "excavate" until his bemused mother had quite the collection of strange-shaped rocks, fossilized wood, and the shells of small creatures.

Arcturus—when Valerian had actually seen the "great man," which had been exactly twice until recently—had belittled him and told his mother that she was raising a bookish, effeminate weakling. As he matured, Valerian had been able to prove, even to his skeptical father, that while he might indeed be bookish, he was not effeminate and was no weakling. Starting at age eight, Valerian had had trainers in weapons both ancient and contemporary. He was a master swordsman and martial artist, and moved easily and effectively in full combat gear with a gauss rifle.

Cultures that blended war with art were his favorite. Valerian's great passion was for ancient weapons. He liked them because they were beautiful, carefully crafted, and old; Arcturus approved of the collections because they were things that could kill people. It was a place where the two men could happily meet and agree on something, and consequently, it was the focus of most of their conversations.

In the time since Arcturus had decided that it was safe to bring his son and heir off a backwater planet, the two had spent more time together than they had in Valerian's entire life. It was an uneasy alliance; two such different personalities would never get along smoothly. But they shared the common goal of developing an empire again and its eventually being handed over to Valerian, so peace was largely maintained.

Both men were poised and powerful and feline: Arcturus the muscular lion of the plains, Valerian the sleek, silent panther of the jungles. They saw things differently, but had sufficient common ground that there were few disagreements.

And when word began trickling in of yet more alien temples—for so Valerian was fond of thinking of them, the image reminding him of bygone days of great civilizations—they had agreed that they were worth investigating. Mengsk Senior, of course, had been sufficiently impressed by what had transpired on Bhekar Ro to want to either contain or use the power of the temples. Valerian had been like a boy with a crush on a beautiful girl—dazzled, enraptured, wanting to get closer, to learn more, to touch and explore.

He'd convinced his father not to begin with the marines this time, arguing smoothly and persuasively that their unique skills were needed elsewhere, in the rebuilding of the Dominion, in the quashing of uprisings.

"Out of the question" was Arcturus's first volley.

"We know that the artifacts are truly dangerous only to protoss and zerg," Valerian had said.

"That boy who first activated the one on Bhekar Ro was consumed and later spat out," Arcturus had replied.

"True," Valerian had agreed without missing a beat. "And we know exactly what he did to trigger that kind of reaction. The artifact is alive, in a way; it appears to have certain psychic abilities. If we study an empty one, one which the strange creature has abandoned, we can learn things about it without taking that risk."

Arcturus frowned, his heavy dark brows drawing together and looking like massive caterpillars on his forehead. "What's the point of examining an empty one?" he had said.

"Obtaining the knowledge on how to handle one that's *not* empty," Valerian had replied. "Think what we could do with an intact one . . . if we understood how it worked." When Arcturus remained silent, his son shrugged his shoulders, settling back into the butter-soft leather sofa. He forced himself to look disinterested. His heart was hammering; he wanted this project more than he had wanted anything else in his life. Wanted it with an intellectual passion that Arcturus, whose cravings lay in quite another area, could not possibly understand. But he knew he could not be seen by his father as wanting this too badly. That would be a sign of weakness. Although their bond had gotten stronger over the last few months, Valerian always felt as though he was walking a tightrope. Arcturus's intelligent gray eyes were always watching him.

"You must admit it's worth a try," Valerian said, reaching for a small piece of exquisite dark chocolate and popping the expensive morsel into his mouth. Around the confection, he said, "And it's unlike you to be unwilling to sacrifice for the good of humanity."

Arcturus smiled. The words "the good of humanity," they both knew, was private code for "the benefit of the Mengsk dynasty." Once, Valerian imagined, when his father was young and passionate and burned with the flame of righteous fury, the phrase actually meant what it said. His father had not always been a cynic, his mother had told him. Arcturus had taken up arms against a Confederacy that had in the most cowardly fashion laid waste to an entire planet. He'd willingly left a comfortable life for the uncertain one of a so-called terrorist, one with no ruby ports or fine chocolate or antique swords or comfortable surroundings to break the monotony of fighting and fleeing and strategizing. That things had turned so that once again Mengsk was wealthy and surrounded by luxury had been good fortune, but there had been many a time when such an outcome was not at all certain.

Secretly, Valerian still admired that man. Sitting on his mother's lap, he had seen his father largely only in vids, only as others saw him—passionate, intense, charming, deadly. "That's your daddy," his mother had said. "You're going to grow up to be just like him."

Except he hadn't.

Valerian had reached adulthood with only his mother and hard-faced soldiers for company. They moved constantly to avoid being found, to avoid being murdered as his grandparents and aunt had been before him. Once, when he was three, it looked like they had found a safe place, a hidden, fortified base deep within the Umojan Protectorate. They had remained there in safety for five years. Then had come the night when Valerian's mother had roused him from a deep slumber, her hair disheveled and fear in her eyes. She'd bundled him up, imploring him to be silent—"Not a word, not a whimper, Val my darling"—and they had fled minutes later. Valerian recalled the bright light of weapons fire in the night and the sounds of fighting, remembered falling as he ran and hitting the earth hard to be scooped up by a soldier who didn't even break stride. Val was handed off to another soldier, and the one who had picked him up turned back to keep fighting. With the benefit of hindsight, Valerian eventually came to realize that the nameless, faceless soldier had died for him and his mother. For no one who wasn't on the escape vessel would have survived.

Valerian squeezed his eyes shut and clung to his mother while the vessel rocked as it came under fire. But the pilots Mengsk had hired were good ones, and they managed to escape.

"Mommy?" Valerian had asked, shivering, his eyes wide, his heart racing, "Will Daddy ever come for us?"

"Yes, honey. He will. One day."

Valerian lay awake for hours, his head in his mother's lap, her hands stroking his bright golden hair. He heard her weeping, trying to stay silent, trying not to frighten him more than he had already been frightened that night. He feigned sleep so she would think she had succeeded. That night and for a long, long time afterward, he held on to the image of his father as a great warrior fighting a great, good fight, one Val didn't quite understand but which his mother always told him was so important that it forced Arcturus to be away from them.

But the man before him, while still hard with muscle and keen of mind, was not the young rebel of Korhal.

And neither, Valerian had thought, *am I.*

"I suppose it is worth a try," Arcturus had agreed. "We can at least make the effort. If that doesn't work, we'll try something else." The emperor had raised his glass. "For the benefit of humanity, then," he had toasted, and grinned.

The next several weeks were both the worst and the best of Valerian's life. The worst, because the reports were coming in of more and more artifacts "of unknown origin" being discovered, and he could do nothing about it yet. The best, because he was finally getting to do what he had always dreamed of—learn things no one else had learned about alien artifacts. The little boy who had poked around in the soil about his home had grown into a man able to put that dream into action. If only he could be physically among them as they entered the temple!

He'd fought for that too, but had lost that particular

battle. Arcturus had put his foot down. He would not have his son and heir anywhere near the artifacts or temples until they had been proven well safe, and, he stated bluntly, probably not even then. It had been one of their worst arguments ever and had ended with chairs literally being overturned. In the end, the fact that Arcturus was still in charge won out, and Valerian was forced to yield.

Valerian frowned at the recollection of that argument. He sighed, took another sip of the tawny port, and continued to watch the grainy, jumpy hologram.

He would see how his father reacted when some amazing discovery was made. He smiled at the thought of seeing Arcturus Mengsk rendered speechless. It was a pleasing image.

"Sir?"

The voice belonged to his assistant, Charles Whittier. A young man in his twenties with a shock of bristly red hair that seemed to refuse to want to be tamed, Whittier stood in the doorway looking a bit nervous. Valerian thought nothing of it. Whittier always looked a bit nervous.

"What is it, Charles?"

"Professor Jacob Ramsey is here to see you, sir."

"Ah!" Valerian smiled. "Excellent. Show him in, please." He reached and paused the hologram. It froze, blurry and seductive.

Whittier disappeared, reappearing a moment later with the good professor. Valerian rose, his sharp gray eyes assessing the man quickly and thoroughly.

Professor Ramsey stood over six feet, but that was the only truly distinguishing characteristic about him. He was of medium build with pale blue eyes, crow's-feet from too much sun, sandy brown hair too brown to be blond and too fair to be brunet. He had that slightly rumpled, somewhat sunburned, and a bit used-feeling and distracted air about him that Valerian had come to associate with archeologists. Tall or short, thin or stout, male or female, they all had a similarity that Valerian could spot immediately. There was no mistaking an archeologist for anything other than what he was.

Jacob—the information Valerian had on the man indicated that he usually went by "Jake"—seemed more rumpled and distracted than most, however. His blue eyes darted about, trying to take in more luxury in this single room than he had probably ever seen in his entire life, before finally alighting upon his bene-factor.

Valerian smiled and stepped forward, hand out-stretched. "Professor Ramsey," he said with a warmth that was unfeigned, "it is very good to meet you at last."

Ramsey grasped the outstretched hand. "And you . . . Mr. V." As Valerian expected, the archeolo-gist's hand was callused and strong, the nails torn and splintered. That was a good sign. Valerian had learned that although all archeologists were supposed to be wearing gloves, the best of them tossed them aside at one point or another, wanting, needing, to touch with their own hands the things that they could handle without causing damage. He suspected he would have been one of those. His own hands were callused, not from digging in the dirt as he had done when he was a youth, but from grasping ancient weapons. He saw one of Ramsey's eyebrows lift at the firmness of the young Heir Apparent's handshake.

"Sit down," Valerian said, gesturing toward the sofa while he went to the small table with the port. Ramsey hesitated for just an instant before smiling and obeying. His suit, no doubt the best he had, looked faded and out of date amid the opulence of the room.

Ramsey's eyes quickly went toward the hologram and widened slightly. He was obviously more interested in the poor-quality hologram of the alien temple he'd seen several times than he was in observing a room so luxurious he would probably never see its like again. Valerian permitted himself to hope that this man was the one.

"A congratulatory cigar is perhaps in order." Valerian opened a carved mahogany humidor. "Care for a smoke, Professor?"

"Uh, thank you, Your Excellency, but no, I don't smoke. And please, call me Jake."

Valerian smiled and closed the humidor. "Only if you will call me Valerian."

Jake blanched. Valerian's smile widened. "Come now. As I said in my message, we share a great passion. Titles will only obscure communication about this topic we so love."

"Very well, Valer—Valerian." Jake stumbled over the name.

"So you don't smoke. Do you have no vices, Jake, or may I tempt you with port?"

Jake laughed a little in surprise. "I do indeed have vices, I fear. And I'll take the port. Thank you."

Valerian refreshed his own glass and poured one for Jake. The other man hesitated for a fraction of a second before accepting. His eyes were on the crystal, and Valerian didn't have to be psychic to read Jake's thoughts: That single glass probably cost more than the funding of his first archeological excavation.

"To the discovery of wonders," Valerian said, lifting his glass. Jake clinked his against it, very carefully. Both men took a sip, then Valerian put the glass down and pressed a button on the table. Charles Whittier entered a moment later, carrying a small leather case which he handed to his employer.

"Thank you, Charles. Jake, this case contains several data chips. One of them contains resumes I'd like you to read. These individuals came highly recommended and I think you'll find that they'll be valuable additions."

Jake hesitated, then said, "Sir . . ."

"Valerian."

"Valerian . . . I've worked with my current team for years. I find them completely reliable, hardworking, and intelligent. I've no desire to let any of them go, and frankly no reason to."

Valerian nodded. "I appreciate your loyalty. Rest

assured I've investigated them all thoroughly, and I'm not asking you to dismiss anyone. But take a look at the people I'm suggesting you add. I'm sure you'll agree with me once you do."

He smiled. Jake nodded. They understood one another.

Good.

"There's also some classified information you need to peruse prior to your departure. This is for your eyes only."

Jake shifted in the depths of the couch. "I prefer not to keep anything from my team. Like I said, I've worked with them for years. I trust them."

Valerian smiled. "Of course. But there are some things I *am* going to ask that you keep to yourself until such time as I decide it's all right to reveal them. This is not a standard dig, as we both know."

Jake seemed to want to protest. Valerian continued. "Surely you of all people can appreciate the import of what we're doing here. And, if your last excavation site was any indication, I'm equally certain you will appreciate the funding you're being given."

Color rose in Jake's face but he did not deny the truth of the comment.

"You've caused a bit of a stir recently with your theory on that," Valerian continued, nodding at the hologram. "You'll forgive me if I say that I've heard the term 'crackpot' used to describe you more than once."

Jake set down the port. "Not to be disrespectful,

but did you really fly me in all the way from Gelgaris simply to add to the insults?"

Ah, so there was a backbone there after all. That was good too, as long as it wasn't too rigid a backbone.

"Of course not. In fact . . . one of the reasons you're here is that I agree with your theory."

Jake's blue eyes looked startled. "Really? I think you're the first."

"It's the only logical conclusion, isn't it?" said Valerian, warming to the subject. "This . . . temple . . . is certainly not zerg. And from the little we know about protoss architecture, it's not protoss either. Yet it exhibits some features of both. And it wanted protoss and zerg, not terran. We as a species don't interest it. Or, as some of my colleagues think, we as a species are superior to it. Either way, the pattern is evident—I believe, as you do, that the evidence points to the conclusion that the aliens who created this temple are the common ancestor of both zerg and protoss. It's . . . it's got a certain feel about it." His eyes went back to the holo.

"Your Ex—Valerian—I am very, very pleased you agree with my theory. But there's no evidence that this building was a site of worship, so there's no reason to call it a 'temple.' And relics don't have a 'feel' to them."

"Some would disagree with you on that, Professor."

"Possibly. I know some have notions that this is a very romantic, exciting profession. But really, it's a lot of hard work and practical puzzle solving. It's a wonderful intellectual challenge, certainly, but there's little romance in it when all is said and done."

"Be that as it may, I like calling these particular structures 'temples,'" Valerian said, his voice deceptively mild. Jake's lips thinned, but he nodded. Valerian's message had been received.

"You have exactly what we need in order to make this the success we all want, Jake. You have . . . special talents as well as excellent credentials."

"I—I do?" Jake clearly thought there was nothing very special about himself at all. Valerian was pleased. No ego to contend with, then. Another point in Jake's favor. He nodded and again sipped at the port.

"You do indeed," he replied. He indicated the case. "It's all in there. Once you've had a chance to read it, I'm sure you'll have some questions for me. But I think it will all make sense. There is also a prerecorded message for your entire team. Please wait to play it until the marines have departed and before you go anywhere near the dig site. I won't keep you any longer; you've a ship to catch, after all. And remember, I'm only Mr. V to everyone else but your team."

He rose: a dismissal. Jake knocked back the rest of the port, stood, and offered his hand. He looked confused, but game, as he walked out of the room. Valerian followed him with his gaze for a moment, then again turned to regard the frozen hologram.

The discovery of wonders.

He touched a button, and watched it again.

• • •

The *Gray Tiger* was dented and dirtied by hard flying over the last few years, but the captain assured Ramsey and his team that the scarred battlecruiser was completely spaceworthy. Ramsey eyed the young man up and down, uncertain as to whether the messenger confirmed Jake's fears or proved his own point.

He was tall and thin, with greasy blond hair and eyes of an indeterminate color, and looked about as dented and dirtied as the vessel he captained. Beneath what Jake hoped wasn't oil and feared probably was, his skin was as pale as if it had never seen the light of day. His eyes had dark smudges beneath them. He introduced herself as Captain Robert Mason.

"The *Gray Tiger* is the best ship around," Mason said. "I've flown a lot of 'em in my day, but this one's a keeper."

Jake again glanced at the vessel, expecting at any moment to hear the pop of a rivet and the sigh of tired metal.

"We've done this three times already," Mason continued. "We like flying you archeologists. You're a quiet group of people, ain't ya?" Mason grinned, showing uneven, off-white teeth.

"For the most part," Jake admitted, trying not to think of Darius and hoping the big man would have the sense not to try to pick a fight with any of the crew. Then the full import of Mason's words registered. "Wait—you're telling me you've done this before? Where did you take them?"

Mason shrugged. "Hell if I remember. But we've dropped off three sets of archeologists over the last four months."

"In this ship?" Jake asked before he could censor the question. Mason's smile faded, and although Jake was happy not to see his crooked, stained smile, he decided that the glare was not an improvement.

"This ship's been flying for seven years," Mason snapped. "She's seen just about anything you care to throw at her. Just because she ain't pretty don't mean she can't save your sorry ass."

Jake swallowed hard. "Of course," he said politely.

"And it ain't like you soft boys are anything I need to worry about," Mason added, getting the final dig in before hurrying down the ramp and barking orders at his crew.

Jake had assumed that his would be the first crew sent off on this exciting journey, and it was deflating to learn that he was only number four of who knew how many. He was keenly disappointed that Valerian hadn't told him he wasn't a first choice. His credentials were sound—he knew it, even if he was being publicly dubbed a crackpot. There was a time when— well. *Times change*, he thought, *sometimes subtly, sometimes with an alien invasion.*

Jake sighed as he watched the crew in their old, retired combat suits lug the boxes of equipment onto the vessel. He wasn't overly familiar with combat gear, thank goodness. But he knew that these suits, like the ship, had seen better days. They were stained and damaged and clearly unsafe for the purpose for which they were originally intended. But they still had a use, and nothing was being wasted. Jake supposed that was a good thing.

After all, as long as the ship could get them there, that was all that mattered. He'd inspected the equipment when it was delivered and had been shocked by the quality of it. So new it virtually squeaked, so clean it practically dazzled the eye, it almost made him weep. The prefab buildings were light-years ahead of what he'd been forced to make do with on Gelgaris, and he was pleased to report to a stunned but happy Kendra that yes, they would have working plumbing.

All in all, he had little to complain about. So why did he feel so petulant?

He winced at the casualness with which the crew moved the equipment and again wished he hadn't offended the captain by insulting the *Gray Tiger*. He cleared his throat and was about to make a plea for gentler handling when he heard his name.

"Professor Ramsey?"

The voice was soft, but something about it indicated that its owner was someone who was used to being obeyed. Ramsey turned—and had to drop his gaze to meet that of a petite woman of about twenty-five. She had glossy black hair cut in a bob that framed a porcelain face. Her lips were full and soft and her eyes a deep blue, but those eyes were cool and not in any way inviting. A navy blue, form-fitting jumpsuit of some sort clung to her slim curves. A belt twined about her hips, and, incongruously, holstered two wicked looking slugthrowers.

Ramsey blinked. "Um. Yes, I'm Jake Ramsey. What can I do for you?"

The woman smiled and stuck out her hand. "It's what I can do for you that's important," she said. "And what I will be doing for you. I'm R. M. Dahl. I'm the head of your protection unit."

Jake's hand closed about her small one, almost engulfing it. The grip was surprisingly firm. "Sorry, my what?"

The tiny woman's smile grew. "Your guards," she said. "You didn't see any marines trundling around standing ready, did you?"

"Uh, no," Jake stammered. "Should I have?"

She shook her head, and her hair, like thick black silk, swayed softly with the movement. "Nope. We'll have your back in case you encounter anything hostile."

"Like what?"

Dahl shrugged slender shoulders. "Zerg, or protoss, or just a bunch of wayward terrans hiding out who don't like their privacy disturbed."

"Has any of that happened before?"

Again, she shrugged. "Once or twice," she said.

Jake fought back a smile. R. M.—whatever that stood for—was not just short, she was tiny. Fifty kilos, max. The thought of this little slip of a thing fending off a zerg was highly amusing. She seemed to read his expression, for a small line of annoyance creased her otherwise smooth, pale brow.

"I get so tired of this bull," she said as calmly as if she were discussing the weather. "I guess I should be used to it by now. You've seen the quality of the equipment that's been authorized. You think he'd send along someone to protect all *that* who couldn't do her job? You think that just because I don't have hardware in my head and don't have to pop stims every thirty seconds I can't shoot straight?"

Jake raised his hands in a placating gesture. "You're going to be around an extremely valuable and rare alien relic. I'm not sure I want you or anyone firing off weapons in the vicinity. Is this really necessary?"

"Our mutual employer seems to think so."

Mutual employer? "Mr. V said nothing of this to me."

R. M. looked around, then said quietly, stepping in to Jake, "He's the Heir Apparent. He doesn't have to tell any of us anything he doesn't feel like telling."

Jake's eyes widened slightly at the usage of Valerian's title. She wasn't bluffing, then. Still . . . "I don't like it. He let me see the resumes of the rest of my team. Why not yours?"

"Maybe because he figured you wouldn't know how to properly evaluate my resume. Or me."

She had him there. He'd all but flat out said he didn't think she could do her job. "It's not you in particular," he said, "it's—I don't want any of you." He wished the words back the second they'd left his lips, but of course, it was too late.

"Professor, you can dislike and resent us all you

like. But in the end, we'll still give our lives to save yours. Just make sure you stand out of the way and let us do it."

She turned and strode off. A few seconds later another woman and three men Jake didn't know pushed past him, most likely members of Dahl's security team, nudging one another and giving him grins whose meaning he couldn't interpret.

Jake stood alone for a moment. He couldn't help but feel he'd gotten off on the wrong foot with . . . well . . . just about everyone.

CHAPTER 3

JAKE HAD NEVER BEEN AROUND SO MANY MARINES before, and he had to admit they made him uncomfortable. An easygoing man himself, optimistic once upon a time and again now at the prospect of excavating the "temple," as the Heir Apparent insisted on terming it, of Nemaka, he realized it wasn't the extreme pleasantness of some that he found unnerving. And, having worked with his fair share of taciturn and occasionally sullen men—Darius sprang to mind in bold and vivid color—he also knew it wasn't the condescending and sometimes hostile attitude of the other, nonsocialized marines.

It was the knowledge that the nicest ones on the ship had once been capable of crimes so heinous that it made Jake sweat to even think about it.

Marcus Wright was one such. He at least looked the part, Jake thought as the big man took him on a brief tour of the ship. And it would not take a tremendous stretch of the imagination to hear that gravelly voice, hoarse from smoking cigarettes since the age of ten, snarling threats that would make one's blood run cold.

Marcus Wright, Kendra had told Jake in whispers, had tortured, killed, and eaten seven people before he had been caught.

Wright stood six foot six and was well over a hundred kilos of what appeared to be solid muscle, with buzz-cropped pale yellow hair, washed-out blue eyes, and a scar that ran the length of his face from temple to jaw.

"We enjoy transporting scientists," Wright was saying in that voice that sounded like he gargled with broken glass. He smiled, his pale blue eyes alight with delight, and oddly enough, Jake believed him. "We're trained to fight, of course. That's what we do. But I for one certainly don't mind an occasional uneventful trip."

He pushed open a door with a hand that was as large as a dinner plate. "This is the mess," Wright said. "Galley's open all the time if you're feeling a bit peckish late at night."

Jake blinked at the word "peckish" and wondered if it had come with the resoc or if that was something Wright had bandied about when preparing to dine on his latest victim. He wondered if there was enough of Wright's old personality left inside his clean-scrubbed brain for the criminal to appreciate the irony of the mess hall's being the first place he took the ship's guest. And he wondered just how good a job the resoc really did, when all was said and done.

"Thanks," Jake managed. "I'll keep that in mind."

The vessel, once a proud ship of war, had been retrofitted to transport large numbers of civilians and cargo. Walls had been erected, dividing up large bays into smaller sleeping quarters for the thirty-one members of Jake's team, although bedding was still military-issue bunks and they slept eight to a room. The team's equipment—probably worth more than the ship, Jake mused—was carefully piled up and secured in the cargo bays. Battered and rough as it was, the *Gray Tiger* could no doubt still roar when she had to. The weapons systems seemed to be up to par, from what Jake could tell. At one point Jake poked his nose into an area where combat suits, looking much less dented and dinged than the ones worn by the crew to haul the cargo, hung like slabs of meat on hooks.

Why, he wondered, did his mind have to keep coming up with images of slaughter?

"You play poker?" asked Wright.

He did play, actually; and he usually won. Counting cards came so easily to him that he had to consciously try not to do so. Considering this interesting fact, he was not about to engage in any game of chance with people who had once had no compunctions about torturing, killing, and even eating other human beings.

"Um, no, I don't," Jake stammered.

Marcus smiled gently. "Too bad," he said.

"I play," came a cool female voice behind Jake, and he stiffened.

Marcus laughed, a deep, booming sound. "Hell, I know you play, R. M.," he said. "But we don't want you at the table no more."

"Why not?" Jake asked before he could stop himself.

"Little lady likes to fool you into thinking she's all harmless and sweet," Marcus said, his voice still mirthful. "She'll take you for all you've got. You remember that now, Jake, all right? And R. M., you be nice to Jake."

R. M. feigned a pout, pursing her full lips in an expression that nearly gave Jake a heart attack.

"Now you've gone and spoiled my fun, Marcus," she said. She gave him a wink, and even that big man, that murderer, that cannibal, was not unmoved by it. "But you're right. Too bad, I was looking forward to fleecing the prof here."

She strode down the corridor, her boots ringing on the metal flooring, heading purposefully to who knew where. Both men watched the smooth play of muscles in her legs and buttocks through the navy blue jumpsuit.

Jake suddenly wished that Marcus were the one coming to be their guard, not R. M. Dahl.

"She's going to start trouble," Jake said with a sigh once R. M. was out of earshot, thinking of Darius and the other men on the team—and more than one or two of the women.

"Naw," Marcus said bluffly. "R. M. don't start trouble. She stops it."

• • •

That night at dinner, Jake had the opportunity to reflect that Valerian Mengsk's generosity toward the archeologists he had hired stopped with the equipment. He thought wistfully of the tongue-tingling port as he regarded his meal. MREs that Jake suspected dated from the dawn of the Confederacy were heated somehow—probably by a Firebat—and plopped onto unattractive gray dishware. The marines ate with gusto, shoveling the faux food into their mouths, laughing and exchanging coarse jokes. Jake poked at his pile of gray-green something with gray-brown something as a side dish. He passed on dessert, something labeled "Chocolate Surprise."

Jake didn't particularly feel like being surprised.

He was grateful for the distraction that meeting the new members of his team provided. Jake had tried to look for any reason to reject the men and women Valerian suggested, but he had to admit, their credentials were exceptional. He was even looking forward to their participation.

Antonia Bryce, Owen Teague, and Yuri Petrov did not have the weather-beaten look that Jake's team did, but after all, up until now they had had cushier assignments. Awkward introductions soon turned into lively conversations, and Jake felt a renewed sense of confidence in Valerian. Good equipment, good people—it looked like this was going to be all right.

The two assigned doctors, Chandra Patel and Eddie Rainsinger, also had perfect credentials. While archeology wasn't the riskiest job in the universe, broken legs and arms weren't uncommon, nor were infections, animal bites, and the occasional exposure injury. And who wanted to be sick a day more than you had to? The fact that Patel's eyes lit up when they talked about the alien construct was all that Jake needed. Although it wasn't her field, the good doctor clearly knew enough that she wouldn't be bored out of her skull on an assignment that could take . . . well, no one knew how long it would take.

Across from Jake and a few seats to his left sat R. M., who ate in silence, though it was clear she was following every word of the conversation. The dislike Jake had taken to her was surprisingly intense, and he wondered at it. He'd never had any problems getting along professionally with women, but something about this one rubbed him the wrong way. But that wasn't fair of him, was it? She had to do what she was told, just like he did. It wasn't her fault that she and her team of hired goons had been assigned to protect him, it was Valerian's. But Valerian wasn't here, and R. M. was, and Jake was taking out his annoyance on the wrong person.

And, he had to admit, she was gorgeous. He'd never worked with anyone, male or female, who was gorgeous, and he was worried that she might distract some of his team. *Hell, Jake,* he admitted to himself, *you're worried she might distract you.*

At that moment, R. M. turned her head slowly and looked him right in the eye. Caught, Jake simply stared. A hint of a smile curved those full lips, and they parted slightly to admit a forkful of gray-green fake food. Jake sighed and returned his attention to the conversation.

It was going to be a long assignment.

Nemaka was, frankly, a rock.

A rock with no atmosphere.

It wasn't even a particularly *interesting* rock with no atmosphere. There was nothing unique about it from a geological standpoint, and what few creatures had once evolved on it had doppelgängers on about ten different worlds. Jake had read the reports and was expecting nothing more. If it hadn't been a rock, if it had offered any kind of promise of . . . well, anything at all, it would already have been investigated and the chance for, as Valerian put it, the "discovery of wonders" would have vanished. But Nemaka itself, as a planet, offered nothing to tempt terrans, or apparently any other sentient species.

Any other, of course, except for the unknown beings who had left behind a temple.

"The const—the temple is still partially buried," he told his team as they assembled in a large bay that had once held dropships and now yawned cavernously empty. He winced a little at using the term Valerian insisted upon, but was forcing himself to practice it so it would come more naturally to him. He had gotten the captain to let him rig up a vidsys and now used the bay as a meeting area for his team. They'd had a

few briefings, and every one of them had read the
same reports Jake had (except, of course, the ones
that Valerian wanted him to keep to himself), but
now that they would be landing in the next day or
two, Jake wanted to get everyone primed and excited
about the dig.

The "briefing room" wasn't comfortable. There
were no chairs, so everyone brought their flat and/or
lumpy pillows to sit on for each session. Today, Jake
had a special treat for them. He was also slightly in
violation of Valerian's orders that he not share any of
this with his team. Jake Ramsey valued this opportunity, and respected Valerian. But his team deserved to
know what they were going to be greeted with. He let
them settle in, then nodded to Sebastien, Tom, and
Aidan, three members of R. M.'s team. They nodded
back and stepped outside the door, making sure that
the briefing was not interrupted by marines who had
no idea who Mr. V was.

"Today, I have some good news and some bad news
about the dig on Nemaka," he said. "First, the good
news. There's not a lot of visual information on
Nemaka, other than the perfunctory information that
was gathered about fifteen years ago when the planet
was discovered. Usually they're pretty shoddy records
made by disinterested marines—people who are just
doing their jobs and panning a camera around. And
such is the case here. Wait . . . that sounds like the bad
news, doesn't it?"

Darius laughed, and so did some others. Jake

grinned a little. "And so it is. But the *good* news is, that bored recorder from years past has managed to capture some images of our next project . . . at least our project as it looked fifteen years ago."

He activated the holo, and the room fell silent. Jake had seen this before, of course; he'd looked at everything Valerian had given him the first second he had a chance. It was sickeningly obvious to him that the vidcam had panned over the temple without its holder having any idea what he was seeing, or the import of it. The time that had been lost. . . . This temple could have been excavated years ago, at the first evidence of any non-terran sentient life. And the vid had sat somewhere, gathering dust, until somehow Valerian had discovered it, fished it out, and found out what it was. It was a thought that appalled both Jake and his employer.

"Oh, stop!" wailed Kendra as she saw that the idiot filmer from nearly two decades past hadn't even lingered on the strange, beautiful, glowing green thing but had instead moved quickly over it. Jake shared her distress.

"Pause," Jake instructed the slow-moving recording. He touched the console and focused on a small blur. "Magnify." The blur grew bigger. Even with this poor-quality image, Jake found his heart speeding up slightly. Fuzzy, washed out, it was still beautiful to him. He couldn't wait to see it for himself. From the soft murmurs, he knew his team felt the same way.

"That's our site," he told his team.

"Damn, but we're lucky mothers," said Darius, his voice trembling. Jake grinned at him. This, Jake mused, was why he had been able to stand Darius for the last ten years—because beneath the abrasive exterior lay a spirit that understood the power of ancient technology and artifacts. You just had to dig through a bit of crap to get to that spirit. Okay, Jake amended mentally, a *lot* of crap.

"Darius is right," Jake said, "although he's phrased it in his usual colorful way. We've got the best equipment available to us to analyze and record everything we might find. I've been told that the atmosphere generators are cutting-edge, so once things get set up, we'll have an ideal environment to work in. After so long on Gelgaris, I know you'll appreciate that—I certainly will."

He grinned at them and they grinned back. Life was a funny thing. They could now laugh at the deplorable conditions in which they had functioned for so long.

"I'm actually rather pleased that this particular temple is still mostly buried," Jake continued. "We'll be able to excavate it ourselves, which means that we can ensure that nothing damages it."

"I thought nothing *could* damage it," came a cool voice from the back. Jake's head whipped around from the vidsys to see R. M. Dahl standing at the entrance to the bay. She leaned against the door, arms folded across her chest. She hadn't shouted, yet her voice carried.

Used to giving commands, Jake realized, then thought, *Well, no kidding*.

"Yeah," said Eddie Rainsinger. "I heard that this thing was able to withstand a direct nuke—and then harness the power for itself."

Jake nodded. None of this was anything new to his team, but Dahl and the doctors hadn't heard much about it.

"That's true. And yes, our tools will probably not make any kind of a dent in it at all. Still, raise your hand if you want to take a chance at damaging this thing," Jake said.

Laughter rippled among the crowd, and of course, no one raised a hand.

"Thought so. I'd rather be the one to get it out of the earth than Mother Nature."

"Question if I may, Prof," said Dahl, stepping closer. "I don't know much about this temple or excavation, but I've done my research as part of what I need to do to keep you safe. The artifact is dangerous. As I understand it, on Bhekar Ro, someone accidentally activated it and then disappeared. What's our plan to prevent that from happening this time?"

"Well . . . that actually brings me to the bad news I was talking about. While as an archeologist I would love nothing more than to safely excavate a temple with the energy creature still intact inside it . . . the one on Nemaka is, sadly, dark. Whatever was in there is long gone. The top's been blown off the thing and it's no longer any threat to anyone. But I'm certain that there's still a great deal to be learned, and you'll have to elbow me out of the way if you want a chance to poke at it yourself."

R. M. looked a trifle put out. "I see. I was under the assumption that this assignment was going to be a bit more dangerous than it sounds like it will be."

"You say that like it's a bad thing," Kendra said, turning her head to grin at the other woman. R. M. grinned back.

"From my perspective it is. Maybe I *will* elbow the prof out of the way. Poking at the temple would give me something to do. That is, unless Jake's completely wrong and this thing has a few tricks up its sleeve."

"Not a chance. Any danger that thing poses left along with the energy creature. I'm afraid you and your team will be a bit bored, R. M." He knew his answer had been flip, as he had wanted his team to remain calm, but the woman who had been assigned to protect him had asked a damn good question.

What if they *were* wrong?

CHAPTER 4

THE FIRST TWO DROPSHIPS, CRAMMED TO THE GILLS with expensive equipment, had already departed by the time Jake and his team settled into theirs. Much of the work was already well under way, but Jake was glad that he'd be able to see some of it going up. The team's mechanics were already down there with the marines. Everyone was in a hostile environment suit and there were six spares on hand. Jake was used to the awkward, uncomfortable things, but that didn't mean he liked them.

Nemaka had once had an atmosphere, thousands of years ago. An enormous meteor had destroyed it; the crater was visible from space, almost two hundred kilometers wide. He could see it clearly now, as the pilot took them down. The field generators were a meter by a meter and a half in width and weighed over a metric ton. The marines, in their lumbering combat suits and operating SCVs—space construction vehicles—looked like children's toys, but they were performing a task that meant the difference between life and death for those who would be left behind.

Graham O'Brien, a good-looking young man with red hair and freckles, told them they'd set down close to the temple and walk into the perimeter established by the atmosphere generators. He said this while looking extremely bored.

"Will you be coming out to take a look?" Kendra asked, smiling at him. Poor Kendra, Jake thought. Stuck again out in the middle of nowhere with nobody but her familiar team. He couldn't blame her for trying one last time.

O'Brien laughed. "Hell no," he said. "This will be the third one of these things I've seen. It was interesting the first time, but after that . . ." He shrugged.

Kendra sighed.

What O'Brien lacked in enthusiasm for alien architecture he more than made up for in piloting skills. The ride was smooth and uneventful, the landing so soft it took Jake a second to realize they were no longer moving.

Everyone was trying to appear calm and unprofessional. Everyone failed. Jake bit back a childish surge of disappointment when he was not the first to disembark. He moved clumsily in his suit, turning his whole body to get his first good look at the relic that had brought him so far.

Dozens, perhaps hundreds, of crystals surrounded the artifact. They jutted in all directions, bristling like swords, catching the bright sunlight so that the gleam dazzled the eyes. But beautiful though they were, Jake had no interest in them. His attention was on the magnificent thing they surrounded. Only one side was visible, but that was all he needed to see to confirm that it was indeed dark. It looked dead, like a discarded insect carapace. No regimented design this; it whorled and turned in on itself in a labyrinthine fashion, marked by a dozen or so holes that would provide his team entrance into its heart. The top was jagged and harsh, out of symmetry with the rest of it. This, then, was where the strange energy creature had broken free.

How old was it? Jake wasn't even sure if he could wrap his mind around it. All he knew was that he would have been content to simply stare . . . if he hadn't burned so badly to touch it.

He blinked, coming out of his daze, and felt his face grow hot as he caught R. M. watching him with an amused smile.

More than anything he could ever remember wanting, he wanted to go explore that artifact immediately. But it wasn't possible. All the vehicles were in use and as the only suitable base site was several miles away, it was too far to walk. The marines were still setting up the perimeter that would constitute their habitable existence, and Jake watched impatiently as one of the generators autospiked itself into the ground and began to emit a low humming sound.

He busied himself by referencing the map he'd drawn out, locating the building sites, and directing the SCVs accordingly. He watched them trundle off and imagined what it would be like to sleep in a proper place on a dig for the first time in his life.

"It's time for the fireworks, ladies and gentlemen," came a familiar harsh voice. Marcus Wright sounded almost childishly excited. "Hold on to your hats."

At that moment, someone somewhere pressed something—Jake presumed that the techs would know all the technical terms and inform him at dinner that night—and there was a sudden, brilliant flash. Jake closed his eyes involuntarily, and opened them to a world of light blue. Above him arched a dome that was almost the color of the sky back on Earth, according to all he'd heard. But unlike Earth's sky, the protective dome glowed and slowly pulsed. He grinned. Now, it would be only four hours until the atmosphere was established, and while it would still be quite cold for several hours after that, they could safely shuck their protective suits. With luck, no one on his team would need to step back into one for another eighteen months, when a ship would come to resupply them.

It was a long four hours, but they used the time to establish the camp. Finally, Marcus's voice sounded again in his ear.

"You can take your suits off now," he said.

Jake did, and saw his team doing the same. He took in a breath of air—cold, dry, but breathable. Marcus smiled gently at him.

"You'll get used to it," he said. "Your nose will bleed a little for the first month or so, but you'll adapt."

A bloody nose was not a pleasant prospect, but it was better than what awaited anyone who stepped outside the protective atmosphere. Jake nodded, shivering a little, but filled with excitement. The team placed their suits in the storage building, taking care to hang them properly. When the last person had hung up his suit, Jake looked around at the eager faces.

This had been a long time coming. One more task to do, then they could all pile into their rockcrawlers and head out to finally see and touch and experience this amazing relic that awaited them.

The marines who had accompanied them donned their combat suits, waved, and walked back to the dropships. Marcus Wright shouldered his way through the crowd to grab Jake's hand in a bone-crushing squeeze.

"I wish you the best of luck, Professor," Marcus said with complete and utter sincerity. Jake continued to smile at him, knowing it was turning into a slight grimace from the pressure of the giant's hand.

"Thanks, Marcus," he said, and tried not to gasp in relief when the murderer released him. Ignoring the throbbing pain in his violated fingers, Jake watched the marines go, feeling the same emotions he felt every time this happened—relief and a hint of sorrow. The marines were taking with them the last remnants of civilization, and now the team was entirely on their own. In case of an emergency, they would be able to contact someone and help would be sent, of course. But considering how far away Nemaka was from any-

where else, any assistance, even if it were dispatched
within hours of a distress call, would probably take at
best days to arrive.

But at the same time, Jake was always pleased
when it came down to him and his little "family" of
archeologists. There was a camaraderie and intimacy
among them that he had experienced with no one
else in his life.

He felt like the king of the universe right now. His
team was excited. The base camp was luxurious com-
pared with anything they'd ever experienced before.
The temple awaited them. His hand was even starting
to recover from Wright's overeager squeezing. He held
his head high and strode to the communications center with a deep, calm sense of purpose. Out of the corner of his eye, he saw R. M.'s eyebrows, black and
curved as a raven's wing, lift in surprised respect at
this change in his demeanor.

Good. Maybe they could stop circling each other
now. He really didn't want to be at odds with her.

The communications center had been one of the
first buildings erected by the marines, and Jake tried
not to look shocked at the array of blinking lights,
wires, shiny blank monitors, consoles, and buttons.
Most of them, he realized, were portable, and a little
shiver of excitement went down his spine.

He, like Valerian, deeply lamented the lack of documentation that had been obtained from Bhekar Ro.
But such almost criminal negligence would never be
the case again. Jake's team had everything they

needed to thoroughly record this moment in human history for posterity.

Teresa Baldovino, their chief techie, swept her long black hair back and grinned at him. Even more than he, she was enjoying this aspect of their assignment.

"Ready when you are, Jake," she said.

He took a deep breath and nodded. She touched a button and a holo of Valerian appeared. Everyone watched intently. Only Jake and R. M. had ever met the Heir Apparent in person, and only Darius and Kendra had even seen him in the holo he'd sent to Jake. They all knew who their mysterious benefactor "Mr. V" was, though, and were anxious to get a look at him.

The prerecorded image of Valerian smiled. Damn, but the boy was charming. "Good day to you, Professor Ramsey. And greetings to your hardworking team. And hello again to you, R. M." The smile widened, becoming one of genuine friendship rather than politeness. R. M. grinned back. *Well*, thought Jake, *clearly R. M.'s relationship with Valerian has been a solid one.*

"By this time, Professor Ramsey has informed you all that the temple is dark. This does not mean that there is not a great deal left to be discovered, however. In fact, you will find that there is quite the perplexing little puzzle for you to solve. I know that you probably assume that you are the first to be working on this site. I'm afraid I led you to believe this, and for the misdirection, I am sorry. Several teams have already investigated this particular temple. But . . ."

Valerian's image continued to speak, but he could not be heard over the stunned and angry protests of Jake's team.

"What the f—" from Darius.

"What does he mean, several teams have already—" from Teresa.

"They'll have destroyed anything worth—" from Kendra.

Jake waved for silence and did not get it.

"*Hey!*"

The shout was loud, clear, feminine, and brooked no disagreement. Everyone shut up and turned to stare at R. M. Jake did too, shocked that so loud a sound could come from that small body.

"Let the professor talk," R. M. said into the sudden silence. "Continue, Professor Ramsey."

He blinked. "Um . . . thanks." He ran a hand through his sandy brown hair. What had he been going to say? He was just as disappointed and angry as the rest of them. The *Gray Tiger* crew had ferried other archeologists, he knew that much. But he somehow hadn't made the connection that these previous teams had been sent to the same temple. Valerian had deliberately led him to believe this was an unexplored site. Who knew how many careless feet had trampled through the temple?

"Look—I'm as upset as you. Maybe more so. But let's finish watching this. Valerian clearly isn't done."

He nodded to Teresa, who'd paused the vid, and she continued.

". . . already investigated this particular temple," Valerian's image was saying. "But that doesn't mean all the mysteries are solved. Far from it. There's a hollow area deep inside the temple. But we can't get into it. There is another vid with commentary from the other team leaders. I suggest you view that before approaching the temple. They have some interesting theories that you should know about. Jake . . . The teams here before you have tried just about everything to get into this area. Even, regretfully, trying to blast their way in."

Darius said something unfit for . . . well, any civilized company and turned away, closing his eyes. He looked sick. Jake knew how he felt.

"Perhaps you'll say it's just me romanticizing the profession again, but there's something very, very strange about this place. I am convinced that whatever secrets are locked in the temple's heart are profound ones. They are most certainly ancient.

"You've got a reputation for thinking along different lines than most, Professor Jacob Jefferson Ramsey. Now's the time that might come in very handy. Find a way to the temple's heart, and you'll find your way into history, my friend. There are other chips with the documentation of past digs, which you should peruse as soon as possible. I've no doubt that your team will be able to add to our knowledge as you work to unlock the mystery. Best of luck to you. I look forward to hearing from you once you have had a chance to integrate all this. For now, farewell."

The image disappeared.

"Well okay then," Jake said with forced cheerfulness before more angry complaining could erupt. "Sounds like there's still a lot for us to do. Why don't we head on out and see what's what for ourselves."

No one, not even the usually silent and rather looming men and one woman who made up R. M.'s team, wanted to stay behind. They all piled into rockcrawlers and set off. Jake noticed that R. M. and the rest of their team brought rifles with them. He was too disheartened by what he'd just learned from Valerian to protest.

They drew closer. He could now see that indeed, there was plenty of work left undone by the previous teams. Reddish-brown stone and earth still covered half of the temple, and Jake felt a sudden, illogical resentment toward it. How dare something as lowly as soil keep the magnificence of the temple from view? Ah, well. They'd take care of that soon enough. The forty-two people tumbled out of the rockcrawlers and waited, letting Jake lead the way.

Jake paused for a moment, regarding the surrounding area with a practiced eye. Sure enough, there were boot prints in the soil. Some things had been dug up and taken away. He lifted his gaze up . . . and *up*. Damn, the thing was big. It was a dull, sickly green, and inwardly he sighed. He hoped there'd be something other than this mysterious inner chamber for his team to investigate. He waved and they went forward. They negotiated their way among the crystals, Jake noting with disgust that someone less careful had stepped on and destroyed many of them. He wondered why they were so fragile. Perhaps without the energy creature, they had become more brittle? They'd find out.

He located the nearest oval, dark entrance. It was a few meters up and to the left, but the wavy surface of the artifact would provide sufficient foot and handholds. Jake reached out and touched it. He half expected . . . something, he didn't know what, but nothing happened. The thing was quite dead. He fished out his flashlight and stepped inside.

"Darius, Kendra, Teresa, and Leslie—you come with me." They were the ones he'd worked with the longest and the ones he trusted the most. He also felt they deserved to be the first to get a look at whatever was in there. "We'll do this in teams of five once I've determined it's safe."

"I'm going with you," said R. M., stepping forward with the rifle.

Jake frowned a little. Although he and R. M. had achieved something approaching détente, he didn't want to have to share this moment with her.

"The temple's empty. There's nothing dangerous in here. And remember, we're not the first to go inside." R. M. did not reply, nor did she move. She looked at him with cool blue eyes, and he sighed. "All right, come on then."

She stepped up gracefully, threading her way through the others to stand right beside him. He supposed he should be grateful she didn't insist on running point. He focused on the easy climb, reaching the entrance quickly. Hauling himself upward, he got to his feet and peered inside.

They moved forward slowly. Jake paused, turned the light on the curving walls, and extended a bare hand over them. Threads of colors, dulled now from what must have been their former brilliance, ran through the walls, emerging and disappearing in thin lines. What were they? What did they mean? He recalled Valerian saying something about solving a mystery. Such was obvious already. He was an explorer, and by God, this was probably the greatest opportunity to explore he was ever going to have.

Jake turned a corner, still trailing a hand along the way, and noticed that the walls gradually lost their smooth texture. Here, they were studded with more of the crystals that had surrounded the artifact outside, as well as other knobby protrusions.

Jake heard a thump and a muttered curse, along with a gasp. The thump and curse had come from Darius, the gasp from Leslie. "Watch your head, Darius," he said belatedly, and eyed Leslie curiously. "You okay, Les?"

She nodded. She looked . . . nervous. Jake was a bit confused. He'd known Leslie for several years now and she'd never displayed any signs of claustrophobia. Then again, this place was weird, very different from anything they'd ever excavated before. She said, hesitantly, "Anyone else feel this wall vibrating just a bit?"

R. M. bit back a smile. Kendra frowned. "You're letting it spook you, Les. That's not like you."

"Yeah, I guess. Sorry." Leslie looked embarrassed.

"It's okay, Les. It's an unsettling place. But I'm sure we'll get used to it," Jake said soothingly, giving her a friendly grin. Leslie returned it, though somewhat unconvincingly. Jake continued on.

Odd sounds punctuated the darkness now and again, probably the wind coming in from the various openings that dotted the temple. He kept an eye on Les, and was a bit surprised to see that Darius, too, was starting to look a bit unnerved. Only Jake and R. M., in fact, seemed completely unfazed by the strange relic.

It was bigger and more labyrinthine than he had expected. More than once he got out a piece of chalk to mark which turn they took. Now he was starting to wish he'd taken the time to peruse the documentation that Valerian had sent along. But the Heir Apparent's message had been so deflating, he'd just wanted his team to get to the site and—

Jake frowned. The previous excavator had strung a piece of rope across the section ahead of them, but the rope had come untied and trailed in front of him. Frowning, he reached for it, stepping forward without realizing what he was doing.

"Jake, don't—" R. M.'s warning came a heartbeat too late.

The floor beneath Jake gave way. Before he even had a chance to utter a sound, he was gone.

CHAPTER 5

JAKE HIT HARD. THE BREATH WAS KNOCKED OUT of him in a violent *whoosh* and for a couple of seconds he thought he might pass out.

"What the . . . ," he muttered as he drew air back into his lungs. He heard a groaning sound beneath him and barely had time to mutter a curse before the floor broke beneath his weight a second time. He dropped down deeper inside the temple, again landing hard. This time, he was pretty sure he'd twisted his ankle. He lay where he had fallen a moment, leery of the floor's opening a third time, but it appeared to be stable. Jake sat up gingerly. Nothing seemed broken, but in addition to the ankle he knew he'd have some bruises. He tested the surface on which he lay, and it seemed solid. Jake sat up just in time to have someone land on top of him. He yelped.

"Just me, Jake," came R. M.'s cool voice. "Sorry I stepped on you." A light came on and R. M. trained it at the ceiling. "Looks like I got here just in time."

Jake followed her gaze. There was no sign that above him anything had ever existed but the curved ceiling of this particular . . . tunnel? Corridor? Where they hell were they? "What happened?"

"Floor opened up underneath you and you fell through a second corridor," she said, coiling up a length of rope and frowning at the almost surgically sheared-off end. "I always bring rope and other tools with me. I saw you go through, I tossed an end to Aidan, and I came down after you. Then the opening closed up, and here we are."

He looked up and sure enough, there was no hole to be seen. "Closed up, huh?" How? What *was* this place?

He got unsteadily to his feet, favoring his left leg. Leaning against the wall for support, he turned on his flashlight. The corridor widened and forked a few meters ahead. Behind him, it went on for a brief distance before narrowing into impassability. Jake turned his attention to the floor, wondering if it, too, would suddenly decide to give way.

"Huh. It looks . . . different here. Greener."

He studied the floor and walls while R. M. relayed her location to her team. "Yeah . . . just dropped right through two layers. You see me on your screen? Good." She listened, then said, "Okay, we'll meet you there." She turned to look at Jake. Her gaze fell to his ankle, and she made a face.

"Broken?"

"Sprained at the very least."

"Tom's going to vector me in; they've found this

particular set of corridors and there's an exit a few turns from here. They're going to meet us. Can you walk?"

"I can hop."

She sighed. "Wait here, then. We'll come back for you with a stretcher. Shouldn't be too long." Without waiting for a reply, she turned and headed off down the left corridor. He watched her light disappear and scowled, then frowned at his ankle and shone the light around.

The minutes ticked by. Jake kept staring at the right-hand tunnel. He got to his feet and tested his ankle. It hurt, but if he was mindful of it, he might be able to make his way along the right corridor. He leaned against the wall for support and limped down.

Bravado with an injury was usually a stupid thing, but he was curious. Though it would probably peter out to nothing like the corridor behind him, at least he'd know. And he hated the thought of just sitting and waiting for R. M. and her team to carry him out.

It did not peter out. It kept going. And . . . it kept getting greener. And the surface felt different under his feet—more solid, somehow, and at the same time more yielding. He rounded a corner and came to a sudden stop. A meter ahead, the tunnel came to a dead end. But that was not what had brought him up so abruptly, what had made him freeze in his tracks, his heart racing with excitement.

The wall to his left was adorned with large glyphs scrawled in some kind of dark paint.

For a long moment he stared at the lettering, barely breathing. He did not recognize the language at all, but it was clearly a language, not random shapes on the wall. He leaned as close as he dared, taking great care not to disturb it. So many questions: Who had written this? What did it say? What was the ink? He'd start with that. Over time, some of the ink had flaked away, and a few specks dotted the oddly green floor. Holding his breath so that no wayward gust would blow the precious specimen away, he put on his gloves, removed a sterile container from one of the myriad pockets of his jacket, and carefully collected a sample. He was surprised his hands weren't shaking. He guessed all the years of training were coming into play now, mercifully seeing his through this dramatic moment. How old was the writing? What was it made of? What did it say?

"Jake, where the hell are you?" R. M. sounded quite put out.

"Down this corridor," Jake called. He started to get to his feet. "I think I've found—"

His ankle buckled beneath him. He stuck out his hand to break his fall and touched the wall opposite the writing with his ungloved hand. Light suddenly flared, almost blinding him. He snatched back his hand and saw its imprint glowing faintly. Light snaked out from his fingers and formed a rectangle that glowed brightly for several seconds, then faded.

Jake stared at it. He'd never been much into the whole mind-reading mumbo jumbo, or the so-called

romance of what he did for a living. He trusted in
what he could see, and examine, and touch, not what
his emotions or imagination told him. But at this
moment, he felt a shiver run through him. What the
hell had they stumbled onto?

R. M. stepped down the corridor just in time to see
the light begin to disappear. "Huh," she said. "Looks
like you found a door."

An hour later, Jake, his foot attended to, wrapped
mummylike and propped up on a pillow, sat with the
other forty-one members of his team as Teresa
attempted to contact Valerian. Jake had briefed them
and now they all wore big grins. He was delighted,
almost more on their behalf than his own. Teresa
spoke first with the Heir Apparent's assistant, then a
few moments later Valerian 'Mengsk's handsome face
appeared. He smiled, slightly puzzled.

"I wasn't sure what to think when Whittier told me
it was you, Jake. I hope you haven't run into any
problems?" Valerian glanced briefly at Jake's swathed
ankle.

"The by-product of a tumble, that's all. But I am
delighted to report that we discovered something
already. We found another approach to the center
chamber. A completely unexcavated tunnel. Teresa's
sending you some images now."

Valerian glanced over at another screen Jake
couldn't see, and his eyes widened.

"We're not sure what the writing is," Jake said, "or

what it's written in. The lab is analyzing that right now. But the most astonishing thing is what happened when I touched the wall."

He waited for Valerian to watch that as well. By this time, both he and the heir to the Dominion were grinning like little boys.

"You were right, sir. It's a door. And I bet those glyphs will tell us how to get inside."

Valerian sighed. "Jake . . . at this moment, I would gladly trade my lot in life for yours." Jake believed him. "Contact me as soon as you know anything more. Anything at all. At any hour." His eyes were bright with excitement. "Tell me. Tell me everything."

"Of course. I promise you we will document every single moment of the dig."

"Excellent. This is very, very exciting. What do you think about Professor Carlisle's theory?"

Jake had not seen the vids yet, and so did not know what Professor Carlisle's theory was. "Um . . . I'll have to see a bit more before I can say anything."

"Of course, of course. Jake, I don't know what to say. I had high hopes for you, of course, but you have surpassed them already. I am absolutely certain you will discover a way into that room."

"I'll do my best, sir." Valerian nodded, winked, and then his image disappeared. Jake leaned back in his chair and let out a gusty sigh of relief.

R. M. looked at him admiringly. "I think I'm glad you don't play poker, Prof," she said. "You're a hell of a bluffer."

Jake smiled weakly.

After dinner, they sat and watched the other vid. It was a recording of comments from the leaders of the teams that had gone before. The first was a simple archeological team. The last two had had marines with them. Jake and the others listened to the various things that had been tried by three other teams in an attempt to open the door to the heart of the temple.

Many things appalled him. Some things aroused his curiosity, including Professor Reginald Carlisle and his theory as to what might be inside the temple. Carlisle was a few years older than Jake and very solemn-looking, with dark chocolate skin, piercing eyes, and white hair. His theory was that the temple was an interstellar vessel; that the energy creature which had come forth in Bhekar Ro and here on Nemaka was the pilot; and that therefore the creature itself was of the race of unknown aliens who designed and built the temple.

It sounded pretty good. Jake thought about the floor's giving way beneath him and then repairing itself. A highly advanced vessel could conceivably be programmed with an auto-repair function. Except, Jake mused . . . why did the pilot need to "break out" of its own ship? And why would it sit there for centuries before doing so?

One thing struck him as quite odd. It wasn't anything that was said or shown, but rather something that was left unsaid. Every last one of these people had seemed to have, for want of a better word, the "jitters" by the time they departed Nemaka. Some less than others, of course—the elegant Carlisle had seemed largely untouched by it—but by the end of their time here, they'd all looked harried, with new wrinkles around their eyes and a note of strain in their voices. The facts they'd discussed, he filed away. But this . . . this would bear watching.

The day had been long, and night had fallen by the time they were done. "Get some sleep, everyone," Jake said. "We have an early morning tomorrow."

Tomorrow. The first full day on the planet. He couldn't wait.

No! It must not be lost!

Pain . . . blood, dark and thick and hot, gushing from wounds that would not be sealed. She was dying. She was dying and soon it would be lost, all lost. . . .

Leslie bolted upright, shaking violently, her heart racing. Had she screamed? The other women slept on. Apparently she hadn't even disturbed Kendra, fast asleep on the lower bunk.

She ran a hand through her sweat-stiff hair. Not sweat . . . blood, it was blood, her hand was dripping, it was black in the light, the whole bed was covered with it—

Leslie woke up, in truth this time. And this time, she had screamed.

The next morning R. M. greeted Jake courteously at the mess hall as he arrived for breakfast. She and her team had their weapons at the ready, even before they headed out to the site for the day. Jake sighed inwardly. The archeologists hadn't been unarmed on previous expeditions, of course. Even Jake had fired a weapon a time or two at an angry alien creature that surprised him at a dig. But this was different. While R. M. had stressed the fact that no one on her team, including herself, was officially military or even "government issue" as she'd jokingly put it once, they were definitely warriors of a sort, even if they were private sector mercs hired by "Mr. V." Jake felt very strongly that there was a difference between choosing to use a weapon to protect yourself or your property and choosing to use a weapon because it was in your job description. But since he had absolutely no choice in the matter, and since R. M. and her mercs were here to see that his team members remained safe while they scrabbled in the dirt, Jake supposed he really shouldn't get too bent out of shape about it.

He spotted Rainsinger pouring a cup of coffee. The young doctor looked tired. He glanced up as Jake hobbled over to him.

"I've got good news and bad news," Rainsinger said. "I stayed up late running the tests. The bad news is, the writing on the wall is less than a decade old. So it's hardly ancient."

"And my theory that the creators of the temple had left us a message goes out the airlock," Jake said. He sighed philosophically. "What's the good news?"

Eddie grinned as he sipped the bitter, sludgy beverage that passed for coffee. "The message was written in blood. Not human, not that of any known creature native to Nemaka."

Leslie had stepped up, holding her own steaming mug. "Zerg?"

"Nope. Trust me, we have lots of zerg DNA to test against in the databases."

"Protoss then, maybe," Darius theorized. "Only other sentient alien—that we know of, anyway. Whoever wrote it could have used his own blood. And that message ain't written in any terran language I studied."

"A message written in someone's own blood," Leslie murmured, her eyes distant and unfocused. "That's eerie to think about."

"And completely unfounded," Jake said, looking at Leslie. He recalled that she'd been jumpy while inside the temple. "Les, are you okay?" He caught Dr. Patel's eye across the room, and the dark-haired doctor nodded slightly, understanding the unspoken request.

"Yeah. I guess . . ." Leslie laughed. "I'm getting spooked."

"Naw you ain't," Darius said. "That place gives me the creeps too. And finding a message written in blood don't help none."

Jake's spirits sank. Darius as well? Members of archeological teams had gone a bit crazy before. The isolation got to some of them, and their imaginations started working overtime. But he'd worked with most of these people for years, selecting and keeping them on precisely because they were sane, stable individuals.

This would be a very, very bad time and place for his judgment to be proven wrong.

R. M. had walked up to him. He gestured at the rifle. "Is that really necessary?"

She threw him a glance. "Didn't hear you complaining about my services yesterday." She refilled her cup and turned. He walked with her a bit, still hobbling.

"Your services were most welcome, believe me. But they did not involve a gun."

"You've been set a task, Professor. It's to get into that room. The rest of your team is just window dressing, and despite the glow of your initial success, you and they know it. No one knows what's in that chamber. It could be very nasty indeed. You do your job, and I'll do mine. We don't have to be in conflict."

She smiled sweetly. He let her bring the rifle.

The confrontation he knew was coming happened on the third night.

Jake was fixing a snack in the mess when R. M. presented him with a detailed description of who among her team would do what. That was fine with Jake. Defense was R. M.'s department, and she was entitled to run it however she saw fit. What irked him was that immediately afterward, R. M. presented him with a detailed description of how everyone *else* in the encampment needed to behave, and when they needed to be where.

Jake had stared at the list, small hard round things

that were supposed to be cookies sitting untouched on his plate, and then to R. M.'s obvious annoyance, he started laughing.

"Listen, R. M., when and if there's any kind of a safety crisis, everyone on this planet is going to listen to you so hard you'll be able to whisper instructions. Until that time, this is not a dictatorship. There's no curfew, there are no restrictions on what people do in their off hours. Good God, where do you think they're going to go? The enclosure isn't that big!"

"That's precisely my point," said R. M, hands on her hips, smiling faintly. "It's a good thing your work is so physically tiring. People are beat by the time they hit the sack. God knows what could happen if they were bored and itching for something to do."

"These aren't children we're talking about," Jake had said with exaggerated patience. "They're intelligent, experienced, professional adults. They're—"

"God damn it to hell!" Darius's booming voice interrupted at precisely that moment from the next building. "Where did you get that ace, Rainsinger? You musta pulled it out of your . . ."

Fortunately, the rest of the comment was drowned out by someone's—presumably Eddie's—angry retort. R. M. arched a raven brow and Jake felt his face grow hot. R. M. rose.

"I better go break this up. I'll be right back. Look it over and tell me what you think."

Jake had looked it over, and even with Darius's horribly timed outburst, he decided to stand his ground.

When R. M. returned about fifteen minutes later, with not a hair out of place, he looked at her evenly.

"Darius is prone to blowups like that," he said before she could say a word. "He is also—"

"An intelligent man and a meticulous archeologist who saves his temper tantrums for his off hours. I know," R. M. interrupted him. She slid catlike into a chair. "I've read everything about you all I could get my hands on. And I've been observing all of you ever since I met you. I still think that setting some boundaries and limits would be good for everyone. If there's someone getting bored with nothing to do and itching for action, let it be someone on my team."

Jake shook his head. "No," he said. "I don't know how you're used to doing things, but here every order comes from me. And I do not regulate what my people do on their own time. They're adults. Some of them don't always act like it, but they are. I've been with most of these people for years, and we've never had so much as a fistfight. Things can get heated, but there's never been a single incident. And you should know *that*, if you really have read everything you could get your hands on."

She looked at him for a moment longer, blue eyes searching his, then nodded. "I get it, Jake. But what's going to happen when and if there really is trouble?"

"I will tell everyone to listen to you and do what you say to do. And I'll be the first to follow my own advice."

"What if there's no time? What if you're lying dead

after you've sprung some ancient booby trap in that chamber, or from an attack by some zerg who wants this thing for the hive?"

He supposed he should have been prepared for that, but he wasn't. Jake blinked and hesitated. "I suppose the team will turn to you of its own accord then."

"Not if they're not used to it."

The solution drifted to Jake like the scent of wild-flowers on a summer breeze. Sweet, and perfect.

"You're right," he said suddenly. "Let's get them used to it. I'll expect to see you on the dig bright and early tomorrow morning."

He managed not to laugh out loud at the expression on R. M.'s face. She uttered an old Anglo-Saxon word that Darius would have approved of.

"I'm a trained professional. I have a job to do!"

"You've said yourself that there's really not that much to do," Jake countered. Oh, how he wanted to smirk. "And you've expressed concern that my people might not naturally turn to you if, heaven forbid, something should befall me. Seems like getting your hands dirty along with the rest of us would solve both problems."

For a moment, he wondered how such cool blue eyes could produce such a heated glare. Then, gradually, he saw the hint of a smile curve her lips.

"Touché," she said. "Touché."

There had followed essentially a hazing on her first day; everyone on Jake's team seemed gleefully eager to have R. M., who had struck not only Jake as being slightly elitist, do the most menial tasks. To Jake's surprise, R. M. had set to her job without complaint, and by the end of the third day, the petite woman who could probably have killed Jake with her thumb was being treated as if she had always been part of the team.

Most of the tasks at this point were indeed very menial. The dirt and crystals that were not close to the artifact itself could easily have been moved by machines. But once they got within a yard of the temple, Jake insisted that the work be done with hand tools. And when they removed that layer of dirt, they went in with brushes, small hammers and chisels, and gloved hands.

After the initial flush of success, the team seemed to lapse into a chronic state of malcontent. Jake had discovered something big, but it had nothing to do with the excavation of the temple itself, and the fact that they had come late to the experience disheartened them. Though Jake had had experience in boosting flagging morale, usually such a lack of enthusiasm didn't set in until several months into a dig. To have to be combating it in the first week was an uphill battle—but he had a plan. Every day, he would take in three or four of his team to explore a different cavern. They recorded everything, with Jake providing narration about strange-faceted features of the living artifact, or subtle gradations of the flooring, or a new hue of the multicolored striations that ran along the walls and floors like blood vessels.

Another direction toward which he often chan-
neled their energies was to the earth surrounding the
area, which was crowded with fossils. Several of his
team, including Leslie, had degrees not only in archeology but also in paleontology and paleobotany, and
he was glad of the useful distraction.

Once that was taken care of, Jake would leave
them to their jobs and descend, in a rather more
orthodox fashion than his first time, by simply following the corridor R. M. had taken, to the passageway.
He would sit, alone, and stare at the wall and the supposed door, his mind racing.

He had noticed something that first time he'd
entered the temple and crashed through not just one,
but two levels. Outside, the temple was most definitely dark. It was dark greenish-brown and black,
and the crystals surrounding it were brittle. He'd
learned to recognize the areas where someone might
hurtle through as he had; they were a telltale dark
jade green. So yes, upon cursory examination, the
temple was dark. Dead.

But.

When he had approached the inner, hollow area,
the so-called heart of the temple, he'd noticed that
the areas closer in were much greener. Almost an
emerald hue, much more in line with witness descrip-
tions of the temple at Bhekar Ro.

That temple had still housed an energy creature.

Sometimes the greenness was little more than a
few spots here and there. Sometimes it was large

areas. The "door," if such it could be called, that had flared briefly when he put his hand on it was one such. It seemed that the closer you got to the heart of the temple . . . to this inner chamber . . . the more vibrant the hues of the temple became.

More than once, he would remove his gloves and touch the walls almost in a caress. Although it was a gesture that did not appear to jibe with his nuts-and-bolts approach to archeology, he knew it did. You had to touch something to know it. You had to bring all your senses into what you were doing, because the secrets hid. If everyone could tell everything from a cursory glance, there would be no challenge. He wanted it to talk to him, for it to reveal the secrets of those who created it. Tell him how to open this door that stood between Jake Ramsey and the heart of an alien temple. It was what he wanted every time he went on a dig. He wanted the relics of the past, the bits of pottery or buildings or tools, to tell him about the beings who made them.

Always, eventually, they did. And this one would too.

He just needed to figure out how to get it to talk to him.

Darius was not about to go talk to the shrink like Leslie did. No way in hell. For one thing, talking to the shrink didn't seem to help Leslie much. He'd deal with the voices whispering in his head by himself, thank you very much. And if it took a little bit of liquid courage to psych himself up to face that dark, brooding "temple" that seemed to be staring at him every time he got within viewing range of the damned thing, well, then that's what it took, wasn't it?

At least he wasn't alone. Other than Leslie, who'd been obvious about her discomfort on the first day, he'd spoken to no one else about what he was feeling. Or hearing, or dreaming. But he was starting to see the faces getting pinched and anxious. He could hear it in the clipped-off tenor of their words. The only ones who didn't seem to be affected in some way were Jake, R. M., and R. M.'s team. Hell, Jake sat down at that chamber every day, all by himself, and emerged exactly as he always had been—cheerful, patient, excited about what he was doing.

Two days ago, Darius had almost wet himself when a low, moaning sound had come from the temple. Everyone had stopped dead in their tracks and looked at each other with wide eyes. Leslie had shrieked. Just a little. Darius's mouth had been bone dry.

"It—it's crying!" someone had said. And indeed, it did sound like crying. A soft, whimpering sound, as of something in pain so deep it was beyond agony . . .

R. M. had gotten to her feet, dusting off her gloves. "Man, you are all a bunch of babies," she said.

The sound came again. Darius's gut clenched. Something in the temple was crying.

R. M. pointed to her hair, which, though short, was being tousled about her face. "It's the *wind*, you . . ." She started laughing. "Come on, people! There are all kinds of holes in this thing and it's going to make strange noises." She exchanged a look with tall, blond-haired Sebastien, who grinned back at her.

Darius had blushed furiously and returned to his task. But that night he dreamed of someone . . . some . . . *thing* . . . trapped inside the ancient temple, alone and in terrible pain.

Darius looked around. No one was close by his particular part of the dig. No one would see him remove a small flask and take a swig before replacing it in his pocket. The liquor burned a trail down his throat. Jake had authorized everyone to bring a certain amount of alcohol of their choice with them, just like he did on every dig Darius had been on. Jake, of course, didn't want them drinking on the job, but Darius knew with a sick certainty that if he *didn't* drink on the job this time . . . he'd not be able to be on the job at all.

He took another swallow, then replaced the flask. Always before, the project had wrapped up before his supply of alcohol had given out.

Always before.

CHAPTER 6

IT SHOULD HAVE BEEN AN EASY, ALMOST LUXURI-ous dig. Thanks to the same dome that provided air for them to breathe, weather was never an issue. It was a constant 21 C, with no wind or storm or snow to interrupt anything. The new people—Rainsinger, Patel, Bryce, Teague, and Petrov—were the only ones who complained about it. Jake's core team gloried in the boring sameness of every single day. After years of being largely at the mercy of the elements, the seasoned archeologists found the monotony heavenly.

But the same tension and stress that had appeared to plague the previous teams was setting in on Jake's team. Nobody seemed to be sleeping well. He suspected that more than one person had been to speak with the doctors, and not about sprains or scrapes. Unless the doctors deemed said person a danger to himself or others or a threat to the success of the mission, Jake knew he would not be informed. He respected doctor/patient confidentiality, but still, it bothered him. More than once he'd walked into the mess and heard low conversations that were silenced upon his arrival. It was frustrating.

Even more frustrating was the chamber, which stubbornly refused to yield its secrets. Jake was a puzzle master. It was what he was known for, what he'd been hired for. Someone had written something in a language no one had ever seen before, in blood from a creature that was not in any records. A code? A straightforward note? Insane ramblings? Ritual inscriptions? The equivalent of Earth's prehistoric cave paintings? At the moment, he fiercely envied Jean-François Champollion. That long-ago scholar had been the one to decipher Egyptian hieroglyphs, as strange and alien-seeming to nineteenth-century Europeans as the swirls, dots, and curves Jake regarded now. But that lucky bastard had had a Rosetta stone to help him out. Jake had only the guesses of those who'd gone before and his own instincts.

Oh, and yeah . . . there was a nice little catch. The ancient Egyptians had at least been human. This was alien writing, probably protoss if he dared to take a guess. And who the hell knew what the protoss thought like? What would be the sort of thing they'd want to write in blood?

So Jake sat at the door, sometimes using up batteries puzzling over the writing, sometimes in the darkness, trying to think like a protoss. He went over what he knew. They were elegant and graceful in combat;

the vids captured that. Disciplined. Their armor gleamed and was equipped with tools that enabled them to create daggers from the powers of their minds. They fought like robotic dancers. Surely that was a manifestation of a general cultural attitude. They didn't eat, or if they did, it wasn't the way terrans did. They had no mouths, no ears, no noses, only those large eyes. Vision, therefore, was probably their most important sense. They were fiercely intelligent and supposedly had incredible telepathic abilities.

Jake sighed deeply and rubbed his face with one hand, absently noting he needed a shave. He was highly dubious of so-called psychic abilities, thinking perhaps the rumors and stories were either made up out of whole cloth entirely or deliberately exaggerated by the government in order to keep the populace slightly tense at all times. He'd heard the stories about the Confederacy and now presumably the Dominion utilizing "Ghosts," telepathic assassins who had some kind of cloaking devices that permitted them to move unseen. *Look out, kids, there's a Ghost out there. Maybe . . . you'll never know!* Jake trusted in what his senses—five of them, thank you very much—told him, and not much else. Trying to think like a race that supposedly had mental abilities dripping out of their ears—well, if they'd had ears—was more of a stretch than he was used to. But a puzzle was a puzzle, and Jake was Jake, and he'd get to the bottom of it.

Even if it meant he had to think like a gray-skinned

alien with no nose, mouth, or ears who could read thoughts.

He'd so much rather be deciphering hieroglyphs.

His comm crackled. "Hey, Jake?" It was Teresa.

"Yeah, Teresa, what's up?"

"Mr. V wants to talk to you pronto." They'd all decided, without discussing it, that they felt more comfortable calling their benefactor "Mr. V" rather than "His Excellency" or "Valerian" or "the Heir Apparent." Regardless of what they called him, Jake's gut always got tied up in knots whenever he had to talk to the youth.

"On my way."

"Jake! Any progress?"

Jake knew what he meant. Valerian didn't want to hear about the temple, although they had started to learn some fascinating things. Valerian wanted to know if he'd cracked the code, was any closer to finding out what the hell was in that chamber.

"Well, I'm pretty sure the language is protoss," Jake said.

Valerian did not look impressed. "So you said in your second report."

Jake knew that. He barreled on. "The question is, Why would they put the writing there? And whether they knew what was inside and that . . . um . . . psychic lock was something they did or was something the original creators of the temple set up."

Valerian actively frowned. "You've said that too."

Damn. He had said that before, hadn't he? He hesitated. "Well . . . there is something. It's not about the chamber, though. It's about the temple itself."

Valerian narrowed his gray eyes. "Continue."

"Well . . . I have to say I disagree with Carlisle. I don't think this is a ship at all. It's a good working theory, but it doesn't hold up. For one thing," he said, warming to the subject, "why would a pilot take a vessel, land it, and then stay there for who knows how many thousands of years? And when he needed to disembark—why explode out from it?"

Valerian smiled. "What's your theory, then?"

"I think this building was indeed meant to contain something. But it's not a ship. I think . . . I think it's an egg. I think the energy creature grows in it until it's ready to hatch, and then breaks its way out."

The Heir Apparent looked intrigued. "Go on."

"And . . . we don't know how many chicks live in a single egg, as it were. The temple on Bhekar Ro was very green, very organic and alive-looking. Then the creature broke out and it started to go dark. This temple here is dark . . . on the outside. But in the center . . . in that chamber that I'm trying to break into . . . it's much greener."

Valerian said, "So . . . you think there may be another energy creature in there?"

"It's entirely possible, though right now it's just a theory. But it's one that fits what we know so far."

"Which is very little," Valerian said. It was a reprimand.

"Sadly, I'm forced to agree with you. But I'm spending every waking hour trying to figure this out, and my team is working diligently."

The future emperor smiled. "I'm well aware of that. And you must forgive my impatience. I know you share my burning curiosity to know what is inside. And I'm certain that once you do manage to find a way in, you'll let me know immediately. The hour doesn't matter. I want to see what you see, when you see it."

"Of course."

"Keep up the good work. And don't keep me waiting too much longer, eh? Focus on that writing. It could be that will tell us exactly what's inside. It should be easy. Just think like a protoss." Valerian winked and disappeared. The Dominion logo appeared on the screen.

Jake stared at the dark screen for a long, long time.

Nemaka had a twenty-six-hour day. For eighteen of those hours, the shield that arched above the excavators glowed a soft blue. For eight, the color darkened to indigo to facilitate sleep. Some nights it worked. Tonight, it didn't.

Jake tossed and turned, his mind racing. It had been nearly two months since he had arrived here, and he was not much closer to solving the mystery than he had been on day one. It was all well and good for Valerian to blithely say, "Think like a protoss," when no one had even the slightest clue as to how the graceful, reptile-looking things thought. He'd tried other things as well, sometimes just resorting to hunches. But he was not a protoss, and he could not think like one, and besides, others before him had tried to think the same way and failed.

He rose, grateful for the luxury of private quarters being the head of the dig afforded, and dressed. Maybe a walk around the dig would help. He winced at the noise the rockcrawler made starting up, but they were far enough away from the sleeping quarters that he hoped he hadn't woken anyone else.

Jake drove to the site almost on automatic pilot despite the darkness. This place of stalled puzzlement was not new to him. He'd visited it many a time before, and always, the answer was just on the other side of the valley. Sometimes this valley was just a dip in the road. Sometimes, as now, it seemed like a bottomless pit. Sometimes he sat there for minutes, sometimes for days. This time it had been for weeks. He needed something, anything, to jog his brain.

He got out of the rockcrawler and walked toward the temple. Beneath the eerie, artificial indigo light of the environmental dome, it loomed before him. Looking at it now, Jake supposed he could understand how it might seem frightening. Even so, his team had explored much more sinister things in their day. Hadn't they? What the hell was so unnerving about this? He wasn't frightened by the alien temple. He was pissed off at it for so smugly guarding its secrets.

Annoyed, Jake kicked at the ground, dislodging a

rock that had the nearly perfect imprint of an ancient leaf in it. The bright, harsh lights of the rockcrawler illuminated still other stones with still other leaves and shells. Jake did not worry about damaging them; there were literally thousands of them. He walked, his hands in his pockets, his shoulders scrunched up in thought, idly staring at the ground his feet traveled.

What was he missing? He was starting to get the sick sensation that somehow, he was going about this all wrong, and that if he continued down the same path he'd never, ever find his way out of this particular valley.

He glared at another leaf fossil. Usually, despite their commonness, such things intrigued him. No matter what planet he'd been on, no matter how different and strange leaves first looked, when you examined them closely, they had a deep, abiding similarity to them. His foot crunched on another stone, and a fossilized shell imprint, its chambers twining in glorious mathematical perfection in the Golden Mean ratio from its center, jutted into view. Those too were the same, mollusks that built chambers with uncanny precision. Whatever world. There were certain guiding similarities, certain familiarities that Jake took comfort in. The Golden Mean was one such. No matter how strange the world, this seemed to be universal. He—

It crashed over him like a wave.

Almost dizzy with the sudden flood of comprehension, Jake fell to his knees and grasped the chambered mollusk. There was the ratio, the same on this alien world as on Earth, as on Gelgaris, as on Pegasus, as on every planet he'd ever been to. Each chamber was just slightly longer than the one before it. One to one point six. And the leaf . . . there it was, that same purity, each vein relating to one another in the same ratio.

Jake felt nauseous, and he couldn't decide if he was sick with fear or sick with hope. Probably a bit of both. He extended his callused hand in the bright white light of the rockcrawler, noticing that the hand shook badly, and stared at it. The bone that formed the tip of his finger was slightly shorter than the second bone . . . which was slightly shorter than the one that attached the finger to the hand, but again in the same perfect ratio—one to one point six.

Frantically he tried to recall what protoss hands looked like. He knew they were quite different from human hands, but how exactly did they differ? Jake closed his eyes and tried to recall the few glimpses of armored protoss hands caught on vid. They were long and delicate. They didn't have four fingers and a thumb, they had—oh, what was it—two fingers bracketed by two thumbs. Certain marsupials and primates Jake had encountered had two thumbs as well.

He knelt on the rocks for a long moment, trying to calm himself. He knew he should go back to the base, get everyone, get the cameras, contact Valerian.

He knew he should. But he wasn't going to.

Jake knew he wasn't thought of as a "maverick." He

knew deep inside he wasn't quite gutsy enough for the title, that normally he was quite content to do things by the book. But this . . . if he was right, then he wanted the moment to himself. If he was wrong, he didn't want to look like an idiot—hell, look like *more* of an idiot—in front of his whole team and "Mr. V."

There was time enough to bring in the rest of them later if he was correct. For now, however, Jake Ramsey was going to test his theory all by himself.

He looked again for the fossilized mollusk and grasped it with hands that still shook. Clutching it in one hand and the flashlight in the other, he got to his feet, stumbling a bit, and flicked on the light. He thought he'd know the way even if he had to negotiate the curves and turns of the temple's corridors in the dark, so often had he trod this particular path. He moved quickly, his heart racing, trying not to be too excited—even if he could enter this chamber, there was no telling if anything of any interest would be inside—and failing utterly.

Jake scrambled down the ladder, dropping lightly to the floor, and turned the flashlight on the wall. As he had done dozens, maybe even hundreds of times before, he pressed his hand to the door. The glowing outline of a rectangle appeared.

But it was not the typical rectangle one might expect to see in a doorway. It was broader across the top . . . and the ratio of the horizontal lines to the vertical. . . .

How could he have not seen it right away?

Jake's skin erupted in gooseflesh.

"Plain as the nose on my face," he whispered softly. Or, rather, the hand he had held in front of his eyes. The clue had been there all along.

Thinking like a terran wouldn't accomplish anything. He'd known that; all the teams that had gone before had known that. But he'd almost fallen into the same intellectual trap they had—that of trying to think like a protoss.

Whoever had sealed this door, who had left a message in blood to the side of it, hadn't been interested in thinking like a protoss.

Whoever it was had been interested in thinking on a far more universal scale.

Jake kept his hand on the doorway, and the outline continued to glow. With his other hand, he found a piece of chalk in one of his pockets and traced the outline. As he withdrew his hand, the light faded. Jake quickly did the math and found the ratio—as he knew it would be, it was a perfect Golden Rectangle, the ratio precisely one to one point six. It was ease itself to measure off several smaller rectangles of the same ratio, one inside the other until Jake found the heart of the space. Not the center . . . the heart. The origin of the beautiful spiral of the mollusk, down toward the bottom, slightly off to the left.

Stepping forward, he made an X on the doorway at this precise spot. His hands were sweating.

"Okay, Jake, here we go."

He put his hand on the door over the X.

The outline appeared, as it always did. Other than that . . . nothing happened.

The disappointment was shocking. Why hadn't it worked? All the indications were there! Had he miscalculated? Maybe he'd better go back and get something more precise to measure this with. Maybe he . . .

And then he laughed. Whoever had put this puzzle up was a better guardian than that. Accident alone had made him touch the wall in the first place. An accident could have found someone placing his hand in the right spot as well. "No, that's not careful enough," he said to the unknown and elusive alien whose handiwork had so consumed his waking and sleeping moments. "And you are careful, aren't you?"

He needed to prove he had truly unlocked the secret—that he understood. Jake knelt and began to draw a spiral through each set of rectangles, having to stand on his toes to carry it to the top left-hand corner. There it was, the perfect spiral, known to terrans as the Fibonacci spiral, re-created in countless places on countless shells on countless worlds. And always, always beautiful.

Jake again placed his hand on the X, but this time, quickly, he put it a hand's breadth farther along the spiral's curving path. Still nothing. Grimly, he persisted. Three, four, five, six, seven . . .

And then the line he had drawn in chalk took on its own green and glowing life.

CHAPTER 7

THE LINE OF LIGHT BEGAN BENEATH HIS PALM and chased around the spiral, dancing up to the top, where it met the left corner of the rectangle. Now the rectangle's outline began to appear as it had before . . . and then the green light began to fill in the rectangle. Like a tide rising, or a ghostly child coloring carefully inside the lines, the light crept toward Jake's hand. He held his breath, fighting the natural instinct to jerk back.

Green-yellow light flashed so bright he had to close his eyes. The smooth surface of the wall was suddenly gone. He fell forward slightly, snapping his eyes open, and gasped.

The door, that barrier that had puzzled greater minds than his, that had cost him so many sleepless nights, that was ease itself to enter once you understood the mind-set that had erected it, opened into another corridor. But this one was filled with light that now bathed his face and body. Whatever lay at the end—

"Nice job, Jake," came a feminine voice.

Jake whirled, utterly taken by surprise, to see R. M. Dahl grinning at him. Bathed in the soft hues of blues and greens and purples that emanated from the tunnel, she was exquisite. Her black hair shone with purple highlights and her porcelain skin reflected every softly changing color.

But if she looked angelic bathed in this otherworldly light—which, heaven help him, she did—then she was a warrior angel. Her gauss rifle was in her hands, and she had clearly been ready to fire at anything hostile that might have been lurking on the other side. Part of him was grateful. But the larger part was annoyed as hell.

"You nearly gave me a heart attack," he snapped. "What the hell are you doing here?"

"My job," she replied. "I heard the rockcrawler start up and followed you here. I had you pegged as the type to sneak around to try things by yourself, whatever you said to Valerian. How did you figure it out?"

"You wouldn't care," he muttered. He was annoyed with her out of all proportion. He supposed it was his own guilt at, as she put it, "sneaking around." And that he could not seem to tear his eyes from the vision she presented in the glowing lights.

"I might," she said. "You can tell me later. Right now we're heading inside." She switched the heavy rifle to one hand, holding it easily in sleekly muscular arms, fished in her pack, and tossed him a vidcamera.

"And here you go. Val might overlook missing the opening if he can see what's inside."

He caught it automatically and nodded, sighing. "You're right, R. M. Sorry I snapped at you."

She quirked a raven brow at the apology and inclined her head. He switched on the vid, and turned again to look into the tunnel.

"The discovery of wonders," he whispered softly, remembering his conversation with Valerian. He stepped forward. R. M. followed.

They moved toward the light. Jake wanted to run but fought back the instinct. He frowned as they drew closer.

"You hear that?" he asked R. M.

"Yeah," she said. "Kind of a hum."

It was a much sweeter sound than she described it. It was almost musical. The corridor opened up and R. M. moved to step beside him, weapon at the ready. The sound grew louder, and the light grew bright, almost too bright to bear, and Jake lifted a hand and squinted as he stepped forward, ducking to clear the low ceiling.

His breath caught as he stepped out into a dreamworld.

The cavern was enormous. The radiant blue-purple-green illumination was coming from hundreds, perhaps thousands, of crystals that alternately glowed and glittered. Some were as small as his little finger. Others towered above him, so high that he couldn't see where they ended. For a moment he permitted himself to simply be dazzled by what he saw; then he remembered the vid, and started to move it around.

"This place," R. M. said, her voice softer than he had ever heard it. Then she, too, shook her head. "It's pretty, but it doesn't seem important enough for someone to write a message in blood about it."

"That's . . ." Jake paused, and cleared his throat, realizing it was thick and trembling. "That's what I was thinking. The crystals appear to be part of the, uh, temple, not anything artificial placed here."

The rational thinking calmed him. He had not expected to be so profoundly moved by the beauty of this place. Nor had he even expected it to be beautiful. The humming continued, sweet, lulling, and he shook his head to clear it. What had he expected? Darius, Leslie, and the others had probably expected something horrible to be holed up here. He'd have to make sure they were among the first to get in and investigate it. Wouldn't they be surprised and relieved to see this beauty, instead of whatever horror they'd cooked up in their imaginations?

He turned, examining not with the eyes of stunned disbelief but with those of a trained professional. The crystals were definitely organic. He knelt and touched the floor. It felt solid, and slightly warm.

"Well, I don't see any sign of an energy creature in here," he said. "I'm rather disappointed actually. Pretty much shoots my theory to hell. What do you think Valerian will think of this?"

"A bunch of pretty singing stones? Not much, I'm

afraid. He wanted a big payoff for a room that was so difficult to enter."

Jake moved slowly, stepping carefully over the crystals. He frowned. There was a dark purple splotch on the floor. He knelt, training the vid on the spot. Gingerly, he touched it. It was dry. He recognized it now.

"Whoever left us that message got inside," he said.

R. M. turned and tensed slightly, hefting her rifle. "Let's go find it."

The place suddenly looked much less appealing to Jake. He wondered if the protoss—for such he guessed it to be—was still alive. No one knew how long they lived, and the blood could be from a ritual rather than a life-threatening injury. But the minute he rounded a curve in the chamber, he knew.

The wreckage of a small, beautifully crafted vessel sprawled before them. It was impaled upon one of the crystals, listing badly to one side, but it had clearly come under attack while still in space. Its smooth golden surface was battered and blackened in places.

"Protoss," R. M. said. "Darius was right. Stay here, Jake. I'll move forward and check it out."

"No need," said Jake. He pointed. Almost hidden from view among the jagged crystals was a slender, crumpled body clad in long robes. He stepped toward it, his mind abuzz with questions that would probably never be answered. It had obviously crashed here within recent memory. Why had the protoss left its ship to stumble over the crystals, leave a message, then return? Why had it sealed itself inside this cavern if it was trying to get help? What was it *doing* here anyway?

"Jake—"

He'd almost reached the corpse now. The robes it wore, once a pale lavender and white, were soaked with blood.

Jake's heart spasmed.

Soaked with blood . . . not stiff with it. The blood was still wet! It was as if this creature had only just died! Was it possible it was still alive? He hurried toward it and knelt beside it, peering at it intently. He had never seen a protoss, and this was not the way he had wanted his initial contact to occur, but fate would have its way. Jake gazed at the mouthless face and its enormous, closed eyes, the slim body, the hands that were sliced open from crawling on the crystals and glistening with blood. Long, thin appendages, like tendrils or hair, trailed from the back of his head. They were neatly pulled back with a jeweled band.

This, then, was the guardian. This was the being who had protected the entrance to this place, writing a message in its own blood, sealing the cavern with a puzzle that Jake, a completely different entity than itself, had managed to solve. Jake reached out, suddenly wanting to physically touch the violated alien's hands, those hands that were aligned just like his in the ratio of one to one point six. He paused in midmove.

A single drop of blood hung, poised, about to drop

from the protoss's long finger onto the glowing green floor. It did not move. Jake blinked. What the . . . As if drawn, he reached forward and caught the blood on his hand. For a heartbeat, nothing happened. The little drop of purplish-black liquid stayed whole, somehow balancing perfectly intact on his palm like a tear-shaped gem.

And then everything happened at once.

The drop lost cohesion and spread across his fingers. The protoss beneath him bucked and shuddered. Pale blue, glowing eyes snapped open and bored into Jake's. He opened his mouth in a soundless cry. He did not move. He could not. His eyes were wide, unblinking, his heart racing so fast he felt it would explode. He was incapable of putting up even a token resistance as the dying protoss—

—*Zamara, Vetraas, Temlaa*—

—reached out and linked them with a thin, glowing, golden cord that Jake somehow knew was not visible. He stared into her glowing blue eyes, knowing that this protoss was female without knowing how he knew it, knowing that the beautiful, fragile cord he both saw and did not see was her life essence. Knowing that it was fading. Knowing that she couldn't die, she just couldn't, she had to live long enough to—

"Jake!"

The alien turned its head and affixed its dying gaze on R. M. She was suddenly lifted into the air and hung there suspended. Her rifle flew across the cavern as if snatched from her hands. Jake was only dimly aware of all of it. He stood as if made of stone, as captive to this alien's will as if he were in chains, as the opening of his brain continued.

Turmoil—blood-madness—beauty—

Tears of unspeakable empathy filled his unblinking eyes and rolled down his cheeks. He had ceased breathing.

Secrets—hope-horrors—ecstasies—

He felt the golden cord spasm one last time as his mind was filled to overflowing, crammed with things that he could not possibly comprehend, thoughts nudging and prodding and reshaping his brain so that they would fit—

The glow in the eyes died.

Everything went black.

"Read 'em and weep. Straight flush, ladies and gentlemen. Come to Mama."

R. M. spread her cards out on the table. She leaned forward and scooped her winnings toward her with a practiced gesture. As usual, she had taken the most off of Darius, who couldn't play poker worth a rat's ass. But this time, Darius didn't verbally protest. He was silent and grim, as was Kendra, as were Owen and Yuri.

Teresa Baldovino poked her head in. "Dr. Patel is ready to talk to us," she said to R. M. "Get everyone assembled."

Jake had been right, R. M. mused as she nodded at

Teresa. He'd firmly believed that if a crisis had come and he was out of the picture, they would turn to her. And they had. They'd responded immediately to her call for assistance, arriving in record time. Even the glories of the chamber didn't give the two doctors pause. R. M. knew CPR and had been able to get Jake's heart going again and keep it going until they arrived. He remained comatose, though, and the trip back had been a dreadful compromise between the need for speed and the need not to jostle the limp form.

Once back, the team had listened to her briefing without losing their heads, and had sat down at the poker table like obedient children when she suggested that a distraction might be a good idea. The vidcamera, unfortunately, had been fried. Now as R. M. went from building to building to inform the team that there was going to be an update on Jake's condition, they followed her like good little sheep to the center building where everyone could sit in comfort.

This was where they went at the end of their day at the dig, where Jake would stand in front of them and with bright eyes and animated gestures go off on a tangent about some new thing they'd discovered. As if most of them hadn't been right on the site when it had been found, right inside the dark green, looming thing that R. M. swore was watching them. The thing gave her the creeps. She had said nothing to anyone, not even her team, but she had been having awful nightmares ever since they got here. She wondered now if the protoss that had done this to Jake had been sending them.

R. M. sat in the back and watched them file in. She still wore her weapon, but no one seemed unduly uneasy about it. She was their protector, even if there was nothing she could really fight at the moment, and if she wanted to carry a weapon none of them was about to protest. R. M. was careful not to reveal it, but she was every bit as anxious for news about Jake Ramsey's condition as the rest of them were—maybe even more so. She watched attentively as Dr. Patel strode to the front of the room and cleared her throat. She was not a large woman, and looked even smaller as she stood alone in front of the gathered, silent crowd.

"I'm certain what you want to hear first is an update on Dr. Ramsey's condition," Patel said. *"Dr. Ramsey,"* R. M. noted. *Not "Jake," not now.*

"He's stable, for the moment, but he is in a coma. I've done everything I can for him here, and we need to have him taken to better facilities."

"What the hell happened to him?" demanded Darius, no longer silent. It was the obvious question, one that everyone had been waiting for hours to voice, and R. M. listened intently for the answer. Her hand fell lightly to the smooth length of her weapon.

"As best I can determine with the facilities I have on hand, Dr. Ramsey was psychically attacked," Patel said. Patel cleared her throat, and R. M., who was experienced in such things, knew that she was panicking inside. She could almost smell the fear rolling off the woman in waves.

"There seemed to be a concentration in the frontal and temporal lobes," she said, adopting a clinical tone and seeming to be calmed by it. "Damage to the frontal lobe could affect the patient's personality. Damage to the temporal lobe could disturb long-term memory functions. While there seems to be no damage per se, there has been a sort of rewiring of—"

"Rewiring? What does that mean?" Kendra wanted to know. So did R. M.

"From what I can tell, it's similar to what goes on normally in human adolescence. Except it's happening in seconds instead of in years, and in a completely unprecedented manner. Professor Ramsey's brain is changing, developing. Right now, for instance, there seems to be a great deal of activity in the region of the medial temporal lobe. The limbic system is being stimulated, and that processes emotions like fear and rage. But like I said, I don't really have the equipment here to do a thorough analysis. And I can't predict the consequences—I've never seen anything like it. I don't think anyone has."

"Terrans have been blasted by protoss psi power before," Teague said. "Don't you have documentation on that?"

Patel's nostrils flared and she narrowed her eyes slightly as she regarded Teague.

"Of course we do. And what is going on inside Dr. Ramsey's skull is nothing like that. The human brain is a terribly complex thing. There are still several areas whose functions we can't even guess at. These are primarily the areas that have been . . . tampered with."

"But what does that *mean*?" Kendra asked again, sounding forlorn.

"I can't make any kind of educated guess right now, Kendra," Patel said, sighing. "We'll need better equipment. Right now, we've got to get him to superior facilities and, frankly, into the hands of neurological specialists." She smiled sadly. "I was hired to patch you guys up when you took a tumble. That, I can do without a problem. But this is beyond my expertise. A neurologist will be able to tell much more than I can."

R. M. sighed. "All right. We'll contact Valerian."

CHAPTER 8

HORROR. ANGUISH. LOSS—ACHING, WRENCHING LOSS
—no, no, they mustn't go, they were everything, everything—
Body thrashing, skin mottled and heated with the fear
and fury. What would they do? How could they go on?
Alone, alone, so alone—
"It is your fault! You are the reason they abandoned us!
Now they are gone, gone—"
Fingers closing on rock. Hurling it hard toward the source
of the raging other. Cracked skull, spattered blood. Good, it
was good, and he sprang and tore with sharp-clawed hands
until the warm blood bathed his face—

On the bed in the infirmary, Jake's hands twitched.
His eyes darted back and forth beneath closed lids.

He wanted to kill.

"Doctor . . . may I have a moment alone with him?"
R. M. smiled hesitantly at the doctor as she stood in
the doorway. Patel looked confused.

"I know you're our security force, but it seems to me that he's in no condition to be advised of anything right now."

The voice was clipped, cool, professional. R. M. knew that the doctor wasn't overly fond of her; none of Jake's team was. They would turn to her in a crisis, as they had, but that didn't mean they liked her.

R. M. looked down. "Yes, of course not," she said. "But . . . please. Just a few moments?" She hesitated, then blurted, "He's become my friend, and the burden's on me to take care of this team now. It would mean a lot to me."

Patel looked at R. M. searchingly. She seemed dubious, but finally nodded.

"All right. Five minutes, no more."

R. M. nodded gratefully. She stepped over to look down at the prone form of Jake Ramsey, and as the door closed and Patel left, she put her hand on his.

The second that the door was closed, R. M. sprang into action. She glanced quickly at Jake's stats, then hurried to Patel's computer and placed a small object on it. The little machine whirred and clicked and began to download information at a staggering pace. Patel's report was still up on the screen, and R. M.'s blue eyes darted over the text. They widened in astonishment at what she read.

"Damn," she whispered softly, looking over at the still body on the bed. "I'm amazed you're still alive, Jake Ramsey. You and that brain of yours are tougher than I thought."

Jake's vitals were steady and regular. Although still in a coma, he was as well as could be expected. R. M. Dahl's Cupid's bow lips curved in a satisfied smile. As long as Jake stayed alive, all would go very, very well with her.

The little machine had finished its job. R. M. detached it, slipped it into her pocket, and went to Jake's side. Patel found her there two minutes later, gazing down into Jake's eyes with a false but convincing expression of worry on her pretty, porcelain face.

Teresa Baldovino's shoulders were hunched with misery as she pressed her palm against the door to the communications room. Darius glanced up as she entered. He felt for her. She had been with Jake Ramsey's expeditions for nine years now, almost as long as Darius himself, and he knew she considered Jake almost as close as a brother.

"It's so not fair," she muttered to Darius as she flopped into the chair, tapped the console, and typed in the code for *Emergency: Priority Alpha*. "Jake's been busting his butt for years on these backwater planets while other archeologists have been getting the cream of the crop in projects. He's always been willing to do the hard stuff. And now when it looks as though he's made it, that someone out there has finally recognized what he's done, this has to happen."

Her voice cracked at the end and she blinked hard to clear her eyes.

Darius cleared his throat uncomfortably. He didn't

much like the shockingly pretty but hard-assed R. M. Dahl, but he wished she had been the one to do this. He wondered why she'd asked him to. He wanted to put a hand on Baldovino's shoulder but felt too uncomfortable to do so, so he shoved his hands in his pockets and stared down at his feet.

"At least he's still alive," he offered.

"He's in a coma," Teresa said, her voice broken.

Darius glowered. "Damn, Teresa, you're more of a pessimist than I am."

Baldovino laughed shakily, then snapped to attention when the face of Valerian Mengsk appeared on the screen. He looked more disheveled than Darius had ever seen him, and Darius suddenly realized the time difference and groaned inwardly. They had roused the son of the emperor from his bed.

Valerian was generally pleasant, but he looked irritated this time.

"You sent this as Priority Alpha, Miss Baldovino. It had better be good." His gray eyes flickered behind her, saw Darius, and dismissed him. "Where's Jake?"

Darius cleared his throat. "Uh, that's why we're contacting you, sir," he stammered. "We need emergency medical transport. Jake got into the cavern and—well—something in there attacked him. We think it was a protoss . . . or what was left of one."

Valerian instantly became alert. "Tell me what happened." Again, Darius wondered why the only eyewitness to the incident insisted that he be the one to talk to Valerian. As best he could, he told the Heir

Apparent of Jake's opening of the door, of the crystalline wonderland inside, of the crashed protoss vessel and the attack on both Jake and R. M. Valerian listened intently. *Bastard looks like a big cat ready to pounce,* Darius thought.

"And the protoss? Is it still alive?"

Darius hesitated and scratched his ear. "Well, sir, that's the damnedest thing. R. M. said the thing was quite alive when they got to it, but once it had . . . done whatever it's done to Jake it was not only dead, it started to decay. Immediately. It's kinda moist in those caves. I saw the body and she was right, thing looked like it'd been dead for a few years. We've recovered it and put it in the lab, of course, and we'll get what we can from its vessel. But it's Jake we're worried about right now."

To his credit, the Heir Apparent looked genuinely distressed. "This is terrible news. Is he going to make it? What did the alien do to him?"

"Doc said something about his brain being rescrambled."

"Rewired, actually," Baldovino put in.

"Whatever. She doesn't seem to think it was a malicious attack; she thinks if it was, Jake'd be dead by now."

"I see," Valerian said. He looked distracted, then said, "Excuse me for one moment, please."

He rose and went off-screen, and for a long moment Darius and Teresa stared in silence at the empty chair, still turning slightly. Then Valerian returned.

"Sorry about that. I have just been able to confirm that the *Gray Tiger* is still the closest ship in the area. It should reach you in about two days. Do you think Jake can hang on that long?"

Teresa and Darius exchanged glances. "Well," Darius growled, "he's going to have to, isn't he?"

"I certainly hope so. In the meantime—I do not wish to sound callous, but I know you share this sentiment—please do your utmost to document everything about the chamber Jake risked so much to get into."

"Sir," Darius said, "it's gone dark. The whole temple is dark now. There ain't much there in that chamber now but crystals and the wreckage of the protoss vessel."

"I realize that," Valerian said smoothly. "But please—this could be Jake's final discovery. It should be documented. And I know your doctor is busy tending to him, but perhaps when she has a moment she could contact me? I'm anxious to hear everything about Jake's condition."

He leaned forward, punched a button Darius couldn't see, and the screen went dark. Baldovino leaned back in her chair and crossed her arms.

"That was odd," she said.

"What was?"

Teresa shrugged, her eyes still on the dark screen. "He was very concerned about Jake's welfare. More than he should be. I mean, it's not like he couldn't find someone else to carry on the excavation of the temple."

"Maybe he's gotten to like Jake" was all Darius could think of to say. "It happens a lot."

Teresa nodded her head. "Maybe," she agreed.

Valerian whirled and turned to his assistant. "Did you get it?" he demanded.

Whittier nodded vigorously. "Yes sir, I sure did. It's double-encrypted, all right. She timed it perfectly. If she'd started a few seconds earlier or later, their techie probably would have picked up on it, unless she's an idiot."

"I do not think Jake Ramsey surrounds himself with idiots," Valerian said. "Baldovino at least does not strike me as one. Play it, please."

The image was grainy and the voice was garbled. Whittier muttered under his breath and adjusted some of the controls. R. M. Dahl's cool voice began to speak.

" . . . an attack. I've checked over the doctor's notes; she may be sending you these as well, but I wanted you to know what was coming. I don't know all the medical jargon, and you'll find that in here anyway. What you need to know is that it looks as though the alien forced its thoughts into Jake's brain. The centers where memories are stored and where emotions are processed—the 'limbic system' I think Patel wrote it was, damn, it's lit up like a Christmas tree. There are also areas in the brain that are normally dormant that are now highly active. The funny thing is, Jake is in perfect health otherwise—and I

mean almost better than perfect—which tends to confirm Patel's impression that this wasn't an attack."

R. M. leaned forward, bringing her pretty face
closer to the tiny camera she'd had hidden in her lug-
gage.

"My hunch is that this alien gave Jake knowledge.
What and why, I have no clue. But the protoss didn't
want him to die, it wanted him to keep this knowledge. Keep it safe, somehow. I'm a gambling woman,
and I bet you any price you'd care to name that Jake
knows something very big."

She looked over her shoulder quickly and swore.
"Gotta run. I hope this gets to you so that you've got
the—appropriate people on the staff to handle Jake
when your guys get here. If Jake's team contacts you
again I'll try to send you an update this same way,
piggybacking it onto their signal. But the more I do it,
the higher the chance that I'll get caught."

Then, nothing.

Valerian stared, his mouth slightly open. For a long
time, he said nothing. His mind was racing with the
tantalizing possibilities. *To the discovery of wonders,* he
and Jake had toasted just a few weeks previously. He
had known there would be something marvelous
waiting for him if he could only find the right people.
He'd had a hunch Jake would succeed where the
three others had failed, and as was so often the case,
he had been correct. What information was now
locked inside the archeologist's brain? What mysteries
were about to be revealed?

What wonders were about to be discovered?

R. M. excelled at what she did. There was none better. But she lacked the imagination to properly understand. A wrecked ship and a decomposed corpse, if that was all that came of this, were valuable indeed. But Valerian hungered not for military information—that was his father's province. He hungered for knowledge. Not for how the protoss designed their ships, or what their bodies were composed of, but for what the protoss *were*.

"Sir?" Valerian started at Whittier's voice. "Sir, do you think the *Gray Tiger* has the appropriate people on board to deal with this situation, or do you want me to contact another vessel?"

Valerian sat back in his fine leather chair and steepled his fingers, thinking. The *Gray Tiger* might not have the cream of the crop for its crew, but it would do. Their duties would not exceed their capabilities.

"They should be all right. We'll have more highly trained people meet them upon their arrival and debrief them. See to it, will you, Charles?" He rose and without waiting for an answer left. There were some people he needed to talk to.

Charles Whittier watched him go and then turned back to his duties. There were many things that Valerian was comfortably unaware of, and it was Whittier's duty to see that the young Heir Apparent stayed in that state of innocence. In many ways, despite a background steeped in danger and deception, Valerian was a bit naïve and idealistic. Arcturus

Mengsk knew that. And he wanted to keep his son that way—for the present

In fact, the crew of the *Gray Tiger* would be required to perform duties which were exactly in line with their resocialization. The *Gray Tiger* would do quite nicely. Quite nicely indeed.

CHAPTER 9

UP IT WENT, THE HOME THAT FLEW, BEARING THE Ihan-rii, *the Great Teachers, the Makers, the Guardians away, away, forever away. Dozens of lithe, purple-blue-gray shapes sprang into the air in futile pursuit, clinging to starkly beautiful crystals that had edges sharp as shikmas. The home that flew continued to ascend, its inhabitants unmoved by either the begging and pleading of those who adored them or the rage and fury of those who would see them slain. Hands now slicked with blood lost their grip and the panicked beings fell to the earth, fell too far to survive, striking the ground with a sickening thudding sound that was drowned out by the overwhelming noise of the departing vessel and the excruciating mental din that threatened to tear Jake's head apart, just as the pain in his heart threatened to rip his mind apart.*

No, no, they mustn't go, they were everything, everything—

Overcome with despair, Jake fell to the ground as well, thrashing, his dark blue skin mottled and heated with blinding, smothering fear and fury. What would they do? How could they go on? Alone, alone, so alone—

Jake Ramsey's eyes snapped open, then filled with tears. His hands, covered with tape and plastic tubing, went to his face to hide it as he began sobbing for something that he had lost and yet at some level understood that he had never had.

So empty. So alone. How could they bear it with these minds?

With my mind?

Her mind?

Our mind—

Jake was lost, confused, wandering, and he began to flail frantically on the bed, kicking at the blankets that covered him, smothered him, still sobbing as if his heart had broken, keening for something that he had . . . had never had . . . could have had. . . .

Jake tore the tubing from the wall and got to his feet, heedless of the fact that he was stark naked. He yanked open the door and collided with Patel. He grabbed her by the shoulders and shook her, then released her as if she had suddenly become white-hot to the touch. Jake dropped to his knees, covering his ears in a futile gesture, for it was not sound that assaulted him.

He felt strong hands hauling him to his feet, felt the quick jab of a needle in his arm. His vision started to blur and his body felt suddenly weak.

"What happened to him?" The voice was feminine, but calm and commanding.

"God knows." Another female voice, softer, with a lilt. "Let's hope that ship gets here before . . ."

Jake knew the words. And at the same time, they were thoroughly alien to him. He knew the people, but did not recognize them. All he knew was that the power of their thoughts was like a shikma to the gut. And as conscious receded, replaced by merciful and silent blackness, Jake Ramsey had one clear thought that was absolutely, positively his own:

What the hell was a shikma?

"It is your fault, Shelak!"

Jake was clawing the soil, making gashes in it, churning it up with his anguish and torment. His head whipped up at the mental accusation. He crouched on the earth, shaking, hands and feet dug deep, and stared at the Furinax who had dared think such a thing.

"You are the reason they abandoned us! Now they are gone, gone—"

"Us? We ever served them!" It was Jake's blood-kin Raamar, answering the filthy slander in a mental retort. Raamar drew himself up to his full height, the bones strung about his neck rattling with the gesture, his hands clenching and unclenching as if they wanted to close about the Furinax's throat—

"Serve?" The Furinax bobbed its head, its nerve cords flying, a gesture of utter contempt. "You drove them away with your hounding, your pathetic pawing of them, your—"

Jake's fingers closed on a rock. He rose, took aim, and hurled it hard toward the source of the raging other. Pure ecstasy shuddered through him as the stone cracked the skull. The Furinax toppled in mid-oath, blood and brains spattering.

Good, it was good, and Jake sprang and tore with sharp-clawed hands until the warm blood bathed his face—

More waking. More forced sleep and dreams of things he knew and yet did not know. His dreams were painted in vivid hues and sounds and sensations he couldn't process, yet did process, couldn't understand and yet grasped on a cellular level.

He opened his eyes, blinked them. His mind was calm and clear. Jake gazed at the ceiling for a moment, then his gaze wandered to the little jungle of tubes crawling across him like vines. He turned his head slowly, carefully, and saw Eddie Rainsinger sitting at the computer busily typing something. Steam rose from a cup of coffee beside him.

What the hell happened to this guy? I wish I'd taken up neuroscience instead of GP. I wish I could get off this planet and take Kendra somewhere nice. Man . . . that hot little body of hers, I'd like to—

"Hey," Jake said drowsily, "that's my friend you're talking about."

Rainsinger started so violently he spilled his cup of coffee. Jake was treated to a comical moment in which the doctor was torn between immediately going to a patient unexpectedly out of a coma and wiping up the creeping brown spill that was starting to threaten the equipment. Eddie compromised by dragging the sleeve of his white jacket across the spilled coffee as he rose to hurry over to Jake. Jake chuckled a little. His throat was desert-dry.

"Welcome back, Jake," Rainsinger said, glancing quickly at Jake's stats. *Damn, look at these readings. The guy's healthier than a horse.*

"That's good to know," Jake murmured.

Rainsinger smiled down at Jake, real pleasure rolling off him. "What's good to know?"

"That I'm healthier than a horse." He licked dry, cracked lips and tried to find sufficient moisture to continue speaking. "But watch what you say about Kendra, she's like a little sister to me."

Rainsinger's smile ebbed. *I could have sworn I didn't say anything aloud.*

"Of course you did," Jake said, frowning. "How else would I be able to hear you?"

Rainsinger stared. *Oh my God. Oh my God. He can read my mind.*

Jake looked Eddie in the eye, and his own eyes widened. This was impossible. He'd been looking right at Eddie when the doctor was speaking . . . except he hadn't been speaking, had he, he'd just been think-ing. . . .

Thinking in words so clearly comprehensible to Jake that they might have been spoken out loud—

This can't be happening. No one really reads minds, that's government bull to keep us in line, it—

Running, running on strong legs that propelled him, sometimes dropping to all fours, the wet grasses caressing his nearly naked body—they were behind him, they were assaulting him with mental cries that were meant to freeze his blood, but only enraged him, he—

Jake bolted upright as a harsh cry of animal panic ripped through his throat. The restraints held him, but he continued to thrash. *I'm going insane. God help me I'm going insane—*

Eddie had hurriedly pressed a button. "Dr. Patel, report to the infirmary immediately."

"On my way. Is he awake?"

Eddie's brown eyes darted back to Jake, who looked at him with wide blue ones.

"Yeah. But—yeah. He's awake all right."

Fear. The fear was deep, so deep that Rainsinger wasn't even putting it into unspoken words. But Jake could sense it roiling beneath the surface. It inflamed his own terror and he struggled anew.

Eddie fumbled for a syringe, filled it with something, and stepped forward. Jake closed his eyes as the fear was completely replaced by drugged curiosity. Eddie was speaking inane reassurances now. He was a good doctor with an excellent bedside manner, and if Jake hadn't been able to hear his thoughts as clearly as if they were broadcast over the entire encampment, he would have been reassured. But the words from Rainsinger's mind were louder than those he spoke, and were filled with fear and hostility and apprehension.

"Hey there, Jake," came Patel's voice.

Thank God he's awake, I thought we were going to lose him.

Jake closed his eyes and covered his ears in a futile gesture. Patel's small, cool hand reached to touch his forehead. Even in this age of technology, the human touch was needed, Jake thought. He enjoyed the feeling of her hand on his skin and tried to shut out the jumble of thoughts coming now from two directions.

"Doctor, a word with you," said Rainsinger in a strained voice. He motioned toward Patel and they stepped off into a corner. Rainsinger began to speak in a low voice. Jake chuckled humorlessly. What was the point in retreating to a corner to whisper when the man in the bed could read your mind? Habits died hard, he supposed.

Jake closed his eyes. He began to concentrate on multiplication tables, trying to drown out the barrage of thoughts. Seven times one was seven. Seven times two was fourteen. Seven times—

What did that alien do to him? Could he read minds all along?

Seven times eight was fifty-six—

Should we place him in isolation? Damn it, where is that ship—

Seven times fifteen was a hundred and five—

The door opened.

"Well, well, glad to see you're awake," said R. M.

Jake's eyes flew open, and he stared at her.

He's alive. Excellent. I might be able to retire off of this one.

The coldness, the calculation, the betrayal—

Whatever Rainsinger had injected him with, it had

erased Jake's fear. But it did nothing to mitigate his anger. Jake lunged for R. M., ripping loose from the various tubes and wires to which he was connected.

"You traitorous bitch!" he cried. "You sold us out! Eddie, Chandra, stop her, get her—"

But they sprang on him, and not on R. M. He kept his gaze locked with hers, fury racing along his veins.

"I know what you've done!"

Eddie and Chandra didn't believe him. They kept talking to him soothingly, telling him everything was fine, just fine, he wasn't to worry about anything, while their thoughts betrayed them, just as R. M.'s did her. But she watched him with cold blue eyes that suddenly narrowed, and when she pulled her gauss rifle from where it was slung across her back and pointed it at them, Jake felt a sudden strange sense of relief.

"Damn it, Jake, this didn't have to be this hard," R. M. muttered. Eddie and Chandra stared at her, their mouths open. Jake smiled with a coldness that matched her own.

"You won't kill me," he said.

She looked at him and arched one of those dark brows. "You're absolutely right, Jake. But I'll kill Eddie or Chandra here without a second thought. And I think you know I will."

The two doctors looked at Jake, finally believing that he could really read minds now that their lives were at stake. Jake's head ached from the effort of juggling so many thoughts, all bombarding him at the same time, but he tried to focus on R. M.'s.

She made it easy for him, a slight smile curving her full red lips, hiding nothing from him. At this point, she knew, deception or any attempt to mitigate who she was, what she had done, and what she intended to do would not serve her. She gave him unfettered access to her thoughts, and Jake Ramsey shrank from what he saw there.

R. M.—Rosemary—Dahl had killed before. She'd done it quite a lot, in fact. She'd done it for money. And she would do it again without batting one of those lovely, thick, dark eyelashes.

"She means it," Jake said hollowly. "She has instructions to keep us alive if possible, but if we offer any resistance, she has authority to kill anyone . . . everyone . . . but me."

R. M. nodded, her shiny dark hair moving like a silky wave with the gesture. *Rosemary? What the hell kind of name is that for an assassin?* Jake thought distractedly.

"Eddie," R. M. continued in a calm and in-control voice, "I need you to do a few things for me."

The laser scalpel on the table—I could get it before she— Eddie's thoughts, brave and courageous and incredibly stupid.

Reach for it, Eddie. You'll be one less person for me to keep an eye on.

R. M.'s lips twitched in a smile as Rainsinger hesitated.

"Do what she says, Eddie," Jake said. "Please."

Rainsinger sagged, visibly defeated. "What do you want me to do?"

"Grab that gauze there and tie the good doctor's hands behind her back," R. M. said. She tilted her head slightly and spoke into the tiny communications device on her collar.

"Okay, team. Our cover's blown. Start rounding up the others in small groups. Incapacitate them and bring them to the central building. Don't attract undue attention to yourselves. These idiots might fight back, and our pay gets docked with each one we have to eliminate."

Eddie was doing as commanded. R. M. had taken a position in the room where she could keep an eye on all three of them. She watched Eddie and said, "Tighter."

"Any tighter and I'll cut off her circulation."

"You don't make it tighter, I'll shoot her in the leg to keep her from moving," R. M. said matter-of-factly. "Your choice."

Eddie swore under his breath and yanked the gauze tighter. Patel grimaced, but said nothing.

Jake winced. It was as if the pain were his own. "It really is too tight," he told R. M.

"The ship will be here in three hours. She can make it that long. Now, Eddie, if you would be so kind as to help the professor here dress. He'll be coming with me."

"R. M.," Patel said, "he shouldn't be moved. We don't know what's happened to him yet."

R. M.'s gaze flickered to Jake. "She telling the truth?"

"As she believes it, yes."

R. M. nodded. "All right."

Jake felt sick at the pleasure that Rosemary—damn it, now that he knew her name, he couldn't not know it, couldn't stop thinking about how incongruous it was—was getting from this. It wasn't a sadistic, sharp pleasure, but it was certainly amusing her. She'd been screamingly bored over these last few weeks, he realized.

He frowned. And *scared*. She'd been scared, too—as scared as Darius or Leslie, except she hadn't let anyone see a hint of that terror.

"Your job, Professor Jacob Jefferson Ramsey, is to stay alive long enough for me to deliver you into the tender loving care of the marines. Got that?"

Kill. Kill, the blood was good, it was warm and—

"No!" Jake gasped. It felt as if someone had driven an ice pick through his brain.

"You don't get that?" Rosemary said. "Shall I eliminate Dr. Rainsinger to make sure you get it?"

Jake gasped, his eyes screwed tightly shut. He managed to grunt, "Get it."

"That's my boy. Now, Dr. Rainsinger, I don't know much about pharmaceuticals, but I do believe I know enough to ask you to tell me where I can find the midazophine."

"Other side, upper left cabinet," Rainsinger said in a dull voice.

"That right, Amazing Jake the Mind Reader?"

Jake opened his eyes as the pain ebbed. He didn't

want to do what Dahl wanted him to do—read Eddie's thoughts—but all the thoughts in the room were so loud, it was impossible not to hear them.

"Yes," Jake said. R. M. was lying. She knew a great deal about pharmaceuticals. Rainsinger was the only one of the three not restrained. He was planning on jumping R. M. the second her back was turned. Jake wondered if he should warn Rosemary (damn it, he hated that name) or if he should let Eddie make the attempt. But before his traumatized brain could make the decision, Dahl had let her attention flicker to the cabinet and Eddie had sprung.

Except Jake knew that she had been expecting this, that her attention hadn't really gone to the jumble of medicine in the box, and Dahl whirled around to slam Rainsinger in the temple with the butt end of her rifle. Eddie collapsed immediately. Dahl knelt and probed his head.

"Mild concussion. He'll be fine, though he'll have a hell of a headache. Idiot. Like I'd really turn my back on any of you for a minute."

She really did think they were all idiots, Jake realized. She herself was fiercely, almost frighteningly intelligent. She was bored not because she couldn't grasp what the archeologists were doing, but because it simply held no interest for her.

"What are they paying you to betray us?" Patel demanded.

"Depends on what they get out of you," R. M. replied, though Jake got a flash of a minimum amount. It was enough to fund an expedition like this twice over. Jake watched her take out a syringe, fill it full of clear fluid, and squirt out a bit.

"I promise this won't hurt a bit, Dr. Patel." Her mouth curved up over delivering a doctors' favorite lie as she jabbed the needle into Patel's arm. The doctor hissed.

"You won't get away with this," Chandra Patel murmured, trying to be defiant even as her eyes closed and her head lolled.

Spare me the melodrama, came Rosemary's thoughts, clear as the chime of an old church bell. *Think she'd come up with something better than that old cliché.*

Because, Jake knew as she gave him a wink and strode out the door, Rosemary "R. M." Dahl had already gotten away with it.

CHAPTER 10

IT WAS NOT THE METHOD SHE PREFERRED, BUT IT worked well enough.

Rosemary Dahl sat puffing on a cigarette, her rifle resting easily in her lap, watching the hostages with narrowed eyes. Her team, whom she had handpicked and had trusted with her life more than once, had their weapons trained on the bound, cowed archeologists gathered in the central building. Good people, her team, all of them. She permitted herself a wistful longing to see one more among their number, but Ethan Stewart had embarked on a separate path two years ago. They still kept in touch, though. R. M. smiled at the pun; their relationship had been and still was more . . . personal than she had with any members of her current team. Maybe, once this business was taken care of, she'd drop Ethan a line and whisk him away for a passionate week somewhere that actually had atmosphere, literally and figuratively.

She took another drag on the cigarette, pulling the

smoke deep into her lungs, despising herself for the weakness. Her addiction to the cancer sticks was her final flaw. She'd been addicted to stims at one point, long ago. Ethan had found her and hired her on the condition she kick the things. Rosemary felt sweat break out under her arms at the mere recollection of the detox he'd put her on. At least he hadn't demanded she give up the coffin nails. She'd done that on her own.

Well, sort of.

Smoke trickled out of her nose as she exhaled, looking thoughtfully at the hostages. This was not what was supposed to happen. What the hell was going on with Jake? What had that thing lurking in the temple chamber been, anyway? Protoss, yes . . . but something more. Something . . . *else*.

She thought of the dreams she'd had and suppressed a shudder, inhaling another puff of the calming nicotine.

R. M. had cultivated a reputation for getting the job done in the quietest, most efficient way possible. She'd eliminated more than a few team members in her day if she thought them too trigger-happy. Rosemary was not a big fan of the guns-blazing, testosterone-pumping, screaming-and-yelling takedown. Why waste the energy? And her attitude was one reason her name had been at the top of Valerian's list.

This expedition had been the fourth. The others had met with ignoble, humdrum failure, and Valerian, disappointed and disgusted, had sent them all slouching home with their tails between their legs. Jake had somehow figured out something the others hadn't. And that had really surprised her.

It wasn't that she thought Jake an unintelligent man. On the contrary, she'd have gone so far as to call him brilliant, and R. M. didn't use that term lightly. But he had a naïveté about him that would have been funny if it hadn't been so genuine.

She brought the thin white stick of death to her lips and inhaled again.

If only she'd gotten him to tell her what, exactly, he'd done to open that door. But the knowledge was locked inside his obviously messed-up brain, and R. M. wondered if anyone would ever get it now.

On the plus side, she knew Valerian had been pretty ticked off when three of three expeditions had failed so badly. The fact that the initial success had happened on her watch made him happy, and Rosemary knew a happy Valerian meant a happy Rosemary Dahl. Once the archeologists had been properly . . . debriefed, R. M. would get her money. Quite a lot of it. Maybe she'd actually take a break and have an honest-to-God vacation.

She thought of Ethan, of his jet black hair and coffee brown eyes, and felt a pleasant shiver of anticipation.

Her communications button crackled. She tilted her head to listen, tucking her chin in. Eddie, who had woken up after a brief stint of unconsciousness a while ago with the predicted headache, and whom she'd then brought in to sit with the others, was watching her. At her movement, he looked away. Rosemary didn't have to possess Jake's newfound ability to know what the young doctor was thinking— that with the motion, Rosemary looked demure and innocent. She knew she did. Rosemary Dahl was a professional, and professionals used every tool in their toolbox to get the job done.

"Dahl here."

"Dahl, this is Mason. We're going to be making landfall in about two hours. You'll need to get everyone suited up in order to get them on the dropship."

"Understood. See you in a bit, Mason."

Captain Robert Mason expressed no surprise, indeed offered no comment, about the sudden turnabout. He had been paid to do a job, just like Rosemary had, and questioning it was never a smart thing to do. As for the marines, most of them had been resoced, and an order was an order. The rest of them might raise an eyebrow, but there was nobody on that ship who'd hesitate for a nanosecond to do his or her job.

Rosemary took a final puff and ground out the cigarette on the table. She slid lithely off the table, shouldering the AGR-14 gauss rifle with an ease that belied her petite frame. She was little, but she was all practice and muscle.

"All right, everyone. We're going to put you into your suits so you can meet the dropship."

Darius let out an oath. It involved doing something to Rosemary that one normally associated with affection or at least desire, but Rosemary knew it certainly wasn't meant that way. She grinned. She liked it when they had a bit of spunk, even though it made her job harder.

"Oh, Darius," she said, her voice sweet as honey, "I'm afraid they're not going to let you do that. But since you piped up with such a lovely offer, you get to go first."

Darius clambered to his feet. Sebastien removed a knife from somewhere in the inner lining of his jacket, and for a moment a little gasp of fear rippled through the room. Sebastien calmly cut Darius's bindings, and the little ripple turned into a soft sigh of relief. Rosemary rolled her eyes. *We've got five gauss rifles trained on you. You think we're going to kill you with a knife?*

Aidan and Tom watched very, very carefully as Darius angrily got into the suit. Rainsinger might have been young and foolish enough to attempt an attack on her in the infirmary, but Darius had seen his share of years and had the common sense not to try anything. R. M. hoped they'd all be this smart. She didn't feel like wasting the energy to kill or subdue them.

One by one, the colonists got into their suits. Once they had done so, Sebastien retied their hands and had them sit. Suddenly Rosemary groaned inwardly.

Ah, shit. They'd left Patel unconscious in the infirmary along with Jake.

"Hey, guys, I'm going to go revive the doc and check on our star prisoner."

"Sure thing R. M.," said Kate, her rifle not moving a centimeter as she spoke.

"You know the rules," she said over her shoulder, grinning. "No killing unless absolutely necessary."

"We got it."

Being a former drug addict had its advantages. Rosemary knew exactly what she was looking for, even if she didn't know where it was kept. She opened the door cautiously, ready to defend herself if by some miracle Jake had gotten free or Chandra had woken up of her own accord.

Beautiful. Jake glared up at her, the metal bands still keeping his body well contained, and Patel's head lolled on her chest. A thin trickle of saliva ran down her chin, proof positive that the doctor was well and truly unconscious. R. M. nodded, pleased.

"Hey, Jake," Rosemary said nonchalantly as she swiveled the rifle to her back and began searching through the cabinets.

"I can't believe you're doing this to us." His voice was raw with pain. She shrugged, disinterested in his shock.

Ah, here it was. She took another syringe and began to fill it from the small bottle. It wasn't generally the smartest thing to do, and Valerian's . . . people . . . were going to have to wait until the drugs cleared Patel's system before they could do what they wanted to with her, but there'd be plenty of time for that during the trip.

"Oh God," breathed Jake. "Is that what's going to happen to us?"

His naïveté suddenly grated. "What did you think, Prof? They'd set you up with a nice comfortable suite, fine wine, and good food while you answered questions? You are an innocent, aren't you?"

She held up the bottle and carefully drew the correct amount into the syringe. Too much and Patel would be manic, not alert. To be on the safe side, Rosemary opened Patel's eyelids and examined the pupils. Yes, the doctor was most definitely out.

Jake had gone strangely quiet. R. M. ignored him. She tapped Patel's arm to get the vein to rise, and when it did so she injected the needle.

"You know what will happen . . . and you're still turning us over to them," Jake murmured softly.

Chandra stirred. It would take a few moments for her to come around, and she was still quite securely bound. Rosemary rose and turned to face Jake.

"I'd say I'm sorry, but you'd know I wouldn't mean it," she said bluntly. "This is my job. It's too bad for you, but hey, look at it this way—in the end, you'll be helping humanity."

He searched her eyes. "You know . . . I can almost understand why they need to do this to me. Something unique has happened to me, and they want to know about it. But the rest of my team—the protoss never even touched them! Why do they need to be dragged into it?"

Rosemary shrugged her small shoulders. "Hell if I

know, Jake," she said, suddenly tired. "Look. It's this simple. You're going to be put in the brig of the *Gray Tiger*. You will be in the tender loving hands of the marines, who will see to it that you reach your destination. Your mind's going to be probed, prodded, and sucked dry by people who, like me, are simply doing their jobs. They're going to haul everything out of you, from your crush on your first-grade teacher to anything and everything that alien uploaded into your brain. If there's anything left when they're done, and even if there isn't, you'll be killed."

Patel was awake now, staring at R. M. with a sick horror on her pretty, dark face.

"You're lying," Patel said, trying to sound brave and contemptuous and only succeeding in sounding terrified. "You're trying to frighten us."

Rosemary rolled her eyes. "You keep thinking that, Doc. Come on. Jake, I'll be back for you, don't you worry."

Jake Ramsey gazed at the petite, beautiful, fragile-seeming woman who was somehow capable of handing over fellow human beings to mental torture and certain death. She left, the door closing shut behind her.

We can stop her, came a thought that was not his own.

Oh God. He closed his eyes. Not only was he having visions, he was now hearing voices. An almost crippling fear surged through him at the realization. He wondered if he'd see the visions again.

Yes, you will. However, it does not have to be so distressing for you to behold them. You will have to trust me, Jacob Jefferson Ramsey. You shall become the master of what you see, not it of you. And I shall teach you how to control the thoughts which are not your own that bombard you. It was a seductive promise. Jake wanted badly to believe it.

Then do. Trust me, and you will see.

Who . . . who are you?

I am Zamara.

These things I'm seeing, these . . . visions . . . what are they?

They are not visions, Jacob. They are memories.

I'm reliving your memories then?

No, they are not mine. Not yet.

How can you have memories that aren't your own?

It is . . . complicated. But soon you will understand. We will work together on what you see, and why you are seeing it. We will work together so that you can choose what penetrates your thoughts, and what does not. You will require my assistance. Your brain . . . it is somewhat limited with regard to its ability to process telepathically.

The voice was cool, confident, slightly arrogant. Jake felt a twinge of annoyance and clung to it.

I've been told it's a pretty good mind, actually.

How can that be so? It is utterly lacking in any telepathic ability. I shall make it work, however. I must. Until such a time, you must not permit yourself to be taken prisoner.

In case you hadn't noticed, Zamara, I'm kind of restrained at the moment.

The thought was not couched in words, but Jake

got the distinct impression of Zamara dismissively waving a hand.

They will free you soon enough to transport you. I will not permit them, or indeed anyone, to stand in the way of what I must do. And that includes you, Jacob.

Jake had started to become more curious than frightened, deeply interested in what this protoss was saying. It was a strength and a failing, his curiosity. Though it had gotten him into trouble more than once, it had opened many doors for him as well . . . literally and figuratively. But now he suddenly realized that Zamara was attempting to take over his motor functions. He watched in horror as a hand lifted, began to tremble, the fingers moving slowly.

Four fingers . . . only one thumb. How very strange.

No!

The strength of his terror somehow silenced her, and his hand dropped. Jake was sweating when Rosemary returned within ten minutes, along with two of her goons. She gave him the decency of turning her back when Tom and Sebastien forced Jake into first his clothes and then the suit. She'd instructed them to go easy on him, but he felt fine. Terrific, in fact. If it hadn't been for the nausea-inducing sensation of three people's thoughts, all heightened with tension, slamming down onto his brain, plus the fact that he now had an alien presence in his head, he'd have felt great.

What could he do to stop this? What Zamara wanted to do to Rosemary and her team would destroy them, as surely and as thoroughly as the "debriefing" by the Ghosts would destroy Jake. Jake instinctively knew it. But while he certainly did not harbor any warm fuzzy feelings toward Rosemary, he knew one thing for sure—he did not want to stoop to her level.

Zamara had a cold detachedness about her that alarmed him. She had no love for humans, and she had a desperate goal which he suspected that, once she grew strong enough, she would stop at nothing to achieve.

Jake stood up in the suit and followed obediently, feeling the *other* inside him scratching busily at his mind, continuing to insinuate herself inside him. What would happen to him when she *did* grow strong enough?

Do not be afraid. You will not be gone. I need you. You will be . . . changed, that is true.

If I live long enough, he shot back to the entity inside his head that was separate and yet not separate. *You know what Rosemary thinks they are going to do to us.*

Yes. I will not permit that to happen. Although at some point they, too, must know. . . .

They walked over to the central building, where to Rosemary's surprise, the Marines were already waiting. Four of them stood outside the door, flanking it and at full attention. Jake assumed there were more inside.

These brains were different from those of the team. There was a fuzziness about their thoughts. It took a second for it to hit: He was sensing the resoc. Damn it. What did that process do to your brain, to cloud things up like—

A sudden realization slammed into him. Despite himself, despite his dislike of Rosemary, he opened his mouth to warn her. But it came too late.

R. M. walked up to the marines, grinning. "Hello, boys," she said. "You made good time getting here—"

The rifles came up. They were not trained on Jake Ramsey. They were trained on Rosemary and her team.

Jake closed his eyes, as if that gesture could somehow shield him from the raw shock and horror of Rosemary Dahl's thoughts as they slammed into his brain.

"What the hell is going on?" R. M. demanded.

"Orders," one of them said in a bored-sounding voice. "You're all to be interrogated."

CHAPTER 11

ROSEMARY PACED LIKE A CAGED TIGER IN THE confined space, clenching and unclenching her fists. How could she have been so stupid? The number one rule in her business was that you never trusted anyone. And there she'd gone, trusting Valerian, thinking that if she was a good little merc and delivered the merchandise as promised, she'd get a pat on the head and a treat like the obedient little *bitch* she supposed she was—

She kicked the wall and winced with pain. Another stupid move.

The *Gray Tiger* had had plenty of time to prepare to take them on. The cargo bay had been turned into a secured area, with each of them having his or her own, tiny cell. Prefab walls had easily been erected and were surprisingly secure. She'd investigated it quite thoroughly once the door had closed shut on her. Good old solid Confederacy know-how.

Rosemary heaved a deep sigh and slid down

against the wall, her head in her hands. She felt naked without her rifle, she realized.

She ran her fingers through her glossy black hair and wished she had a cigarette.

We will get out.

The voice inside his head was strangely calm. Jake marveled at it. He, frankly, saw no way out of this situation and didn't know how some alien mind could.

"You act like it's just a simple choice!" Jake exclaimed aloud, then bit his lip and looked toward the door.

It had been chance, pure and simple, that had assigned Marcus Wright to be his guard. Wright had told him so in that awful, raggedy voice. He had seemed to feel a bit sorry for Jake, but it was only in a detached manner, the way one feels sorry for victims of natural disasters that one catches on the news holos. *Oh, you've lost everything, too bad, I'm really sorry, it's time for lunch now.*

For a wild moment, as the giant cannibal gazed down at him with a hint of sorrow on his ugly face, Jake had thought that maybe Marcus could be persuaded to help him. But the rifle had not wavered and Wright had been resoced but good, and Jake supposed it didn't much matter if the guard who would put a slug through his head without a second thought felt sorry for him or not.

But now he had spoken aloud, sounding like he was talking to himself, which he guessed he was. Except he was quite definitely not alone inside his skull.

"What did they tell you about us, Marcus?" he asked in a louder voice, as much to keep the thoughts that were not his own at bay as to glean any useful information.

"They don't tell us very much, Jake," Marcus replied. "That's just how it is. We had orders to take you all into custody and deliver you for questioning."

Despite himself, Jake was surprised. "Really? They didn't tell you about—"

"Whoa, whoa!" Jake couldn't see the giant, but he could imagine him putting up a dinner plate–sized hand to ward off the words. "There's a reason they don't tell us things, Jake. No offense, but I sure don't want to join you wherever you're going."

He is our chance, came the cool, soft voice in Jake's brain.

What? Jake was careful not to speak aloud this time. *The guy's been resoced to the max. You can't reach him. He'd turn in his best friend without blinking an eye if he had orders to do so.*

And that, said the voice, *is exactly why he is our chance.*

Jake gave up. The way this thing thought was so alien to him that he couldn't follow its logic. And yet, even as that thought occurred to him, he knew it wasn't entirely right. They'd told him that after the attack, his brain was rewired. The alien—Zamara— had opened new areas in his brain that had lain dormant and reworked other areas. Chances were, his brain didn't really even look human anymore.

He buried his face in his hands. He recalled how

bereft and frustrated and ignored he had felt on Gelgaris. Now, he would have given anything to be on that backwater planet, to deal with the annoyances of shocking temperature fluctuations and insects and the hard dig. To be a nobody, a nothing. To be ignored, once again.

You must do this, the voice insisted. *You do not yet comprehend the full scope of the knowledge we carry. It will change . . . everything.*

Maybe for you and your people, Jake shot back, lacing the thought with resentment and venom. He was getting the hang of this, he realized; of forming words and instead of giving them weight and inflection with his vocal cords . . . almost coloring them with emotion. It was a creative process, the way speech was, but it was more like . . . like painting than singing. *Maybe for the protoss, whatever it is I don't know that I know is really important. But I'm just a human being, and all I want is my life back the way it was.*

That can never happen. The blunt words were softened with a wave of something that Jake supposed was compassion. *You have become entangled in something greater than your individual life. You will help . . . preserve knowledge that would otherwise be lost. And surely a part of you is intrigued by that. I know that you are curious, passionate in your thirst for knowledge of ancient civilizations and people. Once your brain has been fully and properly prepared, you will know things that no human has ever known. Things that most protoss do not know. Understand this, and be comforted.*

Jake supposed that one day, the tantalizing tidbits the alien was throwing out to him would be appealing. But right now he was hours away from psionic torture and execution, and he wouldn't be human if he didn't value the thought of waking up tomorrow more than he did the thought of rare and precious knowledge.

The thought cheered him. Maybe he *was* still human, after all.

Wright grunted slightly and shifted position, and Jake was again reminded that he was not alone.

The modifications are incomplete, Zamara lamented with a bit of concern. *But the sooner we act, the better.*

You sounded very human when you said that, Jake thought to the alien presence, and he sensed that she was offended.

Marcus Wright is a murderer and a cannibal, Zamara continued. *He has been neurally resocialized so that he may function productively in society. It is a simple process to perform, and even easier to undo.*

Jake's skin erupted in gooseflesh. *What do you mean?*

And then he suddenly knew.

"Oh, no," Jake muttered to himself, feeling sweat break out coldly on his skin.

Reach out to his mind with your thoughts.

No. I won't.

You would die rather than do so? Because such is your choice.

I'm not going to be part of this.

I will do this with your cooperation or not.

Oh God, oh God, you would, wouldn't you. . . .

That could possibly damage your brain, the protoss went on coolly. *I would regret being forced to do that.*

The cursed alien spoke the truth, Jake realized. She was sorry for him, but needed him; there was a strange affection for the human in her thoughts. This was a union of necessity, not choice, and even though what Zamara wanted to do sickened Jake to his very soul, he knew that the alien regretted it.

There is no other option, Zamara continued mercilessly. *I must work with you, and you are an imperfect tool. To try another way to take control of the vessel would be impossible, with your brain the way it is now. Marcus will do this task for us.*

Jake grasped his knees and clutched them to his chest. He knew that Zamara truly believed that the knowledge she bore was vital to the survival of her species and others. He was pretty sure Zamara had died to preserve that knowledge—and that she was also willing to kill to do so.

And she was willing to make Jake do something that went against everything he knew to be right. He buried his face in his hands, surprised and yet not shocked that his face was wet with tears he didn't remember weeping.

I can't do this. I won't do this. I don't care what's so important. This ship is crammed full of innocent people. I'm not letting Marcus loose on my friends. Wait until we get there. Maybe—maybe something will happen, we'll have another opportunity to escape.

I will not trade a certainty for a possibility, Jacob. I regret the pain this causes you. But there is a greater good which you do not yet understand.

And just that easily, Jake realized that Zamara had stepped to the fore.

Marcus Wright was hungry.

That was nothing new. He was almost always hungry. He was a big man, he had a big appetite, and the moments right after a meal, when he was sated and calm, were some of the happiest moments of his life.

Breakfast had been about three hours ago. Lunch wouldn't be for another hour. If he had not been on a specific security shift he would have ambled down to the galley and fixed himself a sandwich or two to tide him over, but he was stuck here until someone came with his lunch tray.

He wondered what they would have to eat. They'd had meat loaf yesterday, usually a sign of plenty of ground beef on hand. Maybe meatballs or—

—blood flew, spattering his face as he butchered the man as cleanly and precisely as if he were butchering a calf—

Marcus staggered. Where had that come from? Who in their right mind would do such a thing? And yet the image was so distinct, it was as if it had actually happened to him. Jeez, he needed something to eat. He was getting so hungry his mind was playing tricks on him.

—The hunger inside him would not be stopped, not until—

Marcus crumpled to his knees as the awful understanding washed over him.

These weren't random images. God . . . oh, God . . . These were *memories*. . . .

He vomited, closed his eyes, and pounded his temples with his huge hands as if he could physically shake out the thoughts, remove them from his head, but they were now suddenly blossoming like weeds.

"No, please, don't," he moaned, echoing the words of his victims, and knowing that there was no way he could continue to blot them out any longer.

Inside the cell, shaking and sick and begging Zamara to stop, to please, please stop, Jake watched helplessly as the entity within him steadily, carefully probed the madman's mind and found the memories. Zamara had been right. The memories and the perverted—no, no, *evil*; Jake had always been hesitant about bandying the word about but now he was fully cognizant that evil did exist and was right outside the room—desires that had caused Wright to create them had been sloppily covered up. It took very little to locate them, much as one might locate specific wires by their color, and to . . . pull them out.

Marcus screamed.

Jake Ramsey closed his eyes, wept, and hated Zamara for hijacking his brain like this, hated himself worse for not being able to prevent it, and watched as the protoss continued to unveil the horrors that those who had programmed Wright's resocialization thought they had buried forever.

And then as quickly as it had taken over Jake's brain, Zamara returned it to his control.

Marcus was silent for a long time. Jake was torn between fearing that the man had keeled over from a heart attack and praying that that was the case. Then Jake heard a slow scuffling movement outside. He got unsteadily to his feet and turned toward the door. He was sweating, and the sound of his own heartbeat thundered in his ears.

The door opened. Marcus Wright stood silhouetted in the doorway. Jake had just seen him an hour ago, but he was stunned all over again at just how gargantuan the man was. He was breathing heavily, and the reek of vomit made Jake's stomach roil. He swallowed hard.

"I don't know what you did," said Marcus in that rough voice that always before had had an incongruent sweetness to it but that now was dead and cold. "But I thank you, buddy. You made me remember who I am . . . what I've done. The resoc tried to kill that part of me. I'm going to give them bastards what's coming to them. Get your ass out of this brig right now before I change my mind. And then," he added heavily, "stay out of my way."

The angry, harsh sound of the alert startled Rosemary out of her reverie. She leaped to her feet with the litheness of a cat, her muscles tense and ready. What was going on?

Her guard, apparently, had the same question. She heard him talking into his comm, shouting to be heard over the wailing sound of the Klaxon.

"What's going on? We under attack?"

"Hell if I know."

"Not another damned drill."

"Could be, who knows."

The guard swore, the muttered curse unintelligible over the noise. Rosemary listened, every muscle tensed. This could be an opportunity. She crept up toward the door and pressed her ear against it. She heard the sound of booted feet striding purposefully.

Her guard said, "Hey, you know what the—"

A roar—bestial, furious, lifting the hairs at the back of Rosemary's neck. Then the rapid, unmistakable sound of rifle fire.

Rosemary dove for the farthest corner of the room, tucking her body up to present the smallest possible target against any stray gunfire. It seemed to go on forever, then there was silence—and the sound of booted feet retreating.

Rosemary uncurled and got to her feet. She moved quietly back toward the door, prepared to jump the guard if he entered. Sure enough, the door swung open. Rosemary sprang.

Halfway through her leap, she realized that this was no marine. It was Jake Ramsey.

What the hell?

Unable to halt herself in mid-motion, she turned her body so that she would hit the floor before he did. They collapsed in a heap, Jake sprawled atop Rosemary. His shirt and skin were damp and clammy and he was trembling. Rosemary scrambled out from under him, casting a quick glance through the doorway.

The guard was riddled with bullets. Blood oozed from beneath him in a scarlet puddle.

Her respect for Jake went up several notches.

"Good Job, Prof," she said grudgingly. "Now would you mind telling me what the hell is going on?" She got to her feet and held out a hand to help him up, realizing only then that he had no weapon. He reached up with both hands to pull himself to a standing position, and even so R. M. had to slip a steadying hand beneath his elbow.

"Oh, God," Jake moaned unhelpfully.

"Jake, what happened here? You didn't kill this guy—did you?"

He shook his head. He was very pale.

"No. But I did, in a way. Oh God."

Irritated, she gave him a quick shake before calmly stepping over to the marine's corpse and taking his blood-smeared weapon and spare ammunition. Practiced fingers quickly explored the body, seeing if there was anything else of value. Finding nothing, she rose and fastened the ammo belt around her waist. Even on the narrowest setting, it dropped to her hips and even threatened to slip off there. Not for the first time, Rosemary wished she weren't quite so tiny.

"Talk to me. What's going on?" she demanded,

sliding the clip into place and checking the weapon while simultaneously straining her ears for sound of pursuit.

"We're getting out of here," Jake said brokenly.

"I'm all for it. But that's a bit vague. Details?"

Jake turned bloodshot eyes to her. "She let him loose, Rosemary. And she used my brain to do it. She let him loose on the ship."

Gritting her teeth in frustration at his disorientation, Rosemary growled, "Who, Jake?"

"Marcus. She let him loose," he repeated.

She looked at him, not comprehending.

Jake licked cracked lips. "The alien in my head . . . Zamara . . . she undid the resoc. She removed the fake memories they planted in him. She let him remember who he was, what he'd done. She wanted me to do it but I couldn't, I just—but then she went ahead and did it without me."

Rosemary had done a lot in her day, had borne witness to even more. Yet at these words, her eyes widened slightly.

"My God," she breathed. "You . . . you can do that now?"

He nodded. "He's going after everyone else. He's going to kill them. I was told it was the only chance we had."

"Marcus said that?"

Jake shook his head. "No. Zamara. She told me that. She also told me to go find you. She said you'd get us out of here."

"Well . . . your protoss is a smart, uh, alien. And she's right, I can get us out of here. Come on."

He reached out to clamp a hand on her shoulder. "I didn't want to come find you, you know. After what you did to us. After you—" The other hand went to his temple. He was even paler than he had been a moment ago, if such a thing was possible, and he swayed as he spoke.

"We have to get the others," he rasped, barely audible over the constant wail that announced a murderer on the rampage. "Darius—Kendra—Teresa—"

His eyes rolled back in his head and he crumpled in a heap at Rosemary's feet. For a few seconds, she stared at him. Then she swore, sighed, and heaved the limp body that weighed almost twice as much as she did over her shoulder. She staggered, then got Jake settled appropriately.

"Sorry, Jake," she said, and she knew that if he had been awake and reading her mind, he would know that she meant it.

CHAPTER 12

JAKE RAN. HIS MIND WAS FILLED WITH HATRED, colored with a touch—just a touch—of fear. Beside him ran two other Shelak. Strong legs propelled them forward, powerful toes digging in the dirt to help them leap with each step. Sometimes they fell to all fours. He and his kin, Savassan, ran through deep grasses that caressed a nearly naked body covered with large oval spots of blood. Today, they called upon spirit of kal-taar, fast and lean and sleek and small, whose life depended on how swiftly he raced through the undergrowth. No predator, the kal-taar, but no other creature was faster. Jake saw the little beast in his mind's eye, felt its spirit flood through him just as its blood adorned him.

They were followed, like the kal-taar were. Followed by those who would slay them and use their blood for paint. And their lives, too, depended on how fast they ran now.

Jake swiveled his head over his hunched shoulder. He had no need to look to see his enemy, for their thoughts attacked him—their threats, their hunger for the kill. But he liked to see them. And so he did, brief glimpses of something dark gray amidst the bright green of the grasses. Something with glowing eyes, assaulting him with mental cries that were intended to freeze his blood but only enraged him.

It took all of Jake's self-control to not drop to all fours, wheel around, and rip out the throat of his pursuer. But that was not what he was supposed to do. This was an initiation for him. He needed to shield his true thoughts from his enemies. He could not permit himself to fall prey to his own bloodlust.

He faced forward again, leaping high over the huge trunk of a fallen tree. He landed in a crouching position and sprang forth with only the barest slowing. His pursuers cleared the trunk a heartbeat later. They were closing on them, and Jake felt panic, they were closing on them, would the others attack in time to—

"Temlaa! Control your thoughts!"

Savassan's rebuke was harsh and painful. Jake understood and was horrified at his slip. He had given everything away!

Behind him the pursuing Furinax skidded to a halt, gathered themselves, and turned to flee. But it was too late. Twenty Shelak dropped from the dark, looming jungle canopy onto the other protoss. Jake turned and joined his kin, leaping on the Furinax, using his sharp claws to tear open the bellies of their enemies. His skin knew the scent of fresh blood and moist earth, of flowers and decay. It was so good to kill, to feel the bloodlust surging through his veins.

Telkar, the leader of the Shelak, turned his glowing eyes on Jake. "Temlaa, you very nearly ruined everything!"

Jake shrank back. "I know. I will be better next time. I will be more disciplined."

"Temlaa's mistake did not come until we had already brought them close enough for the kill," Savassan said. "He did well for his first time."

Jake looked gratefully to the older protoss.

Telkar narrowed his eyes. "You will do better on your second time, Temlaa," he said, "or there will not be a third."

Jake wanted to leap and dance happily. He would be permitted to go on the hunt again! "Only the younglings spread their thoughts without care of who understands them," Telkar continued. "You must learn to control what you send . . . and filter what you receive."

Even with these words, Telkar stepped forward and pressed his hand to Jake's head. The blood of the slaughtered Furinax was warm and sticky. Jake squirmed with pride.

"This is the blood of those who would destroy us. Destroy what is left of the Ihan-rii. It is good that they are dead. Wear the mark of your battle proudly, until the time comes that you hunt again."

The sight of the body sprawled on the fertile ground, saturated now with the blood of the fallen enemy, moved Jake only to delight. If the bloodlust and pleasure that surged through him now was because of the Furinax's death, well, that was simply the nature of things. The nature of being protoss.

Beside him, Jake felt Savassan stir uneasily, his thoughts purple and dark with a tinge of regret.

Their leader looked at Savassan sternly. "The others do not understand us," he sent. "They destroy what they do not understand. We would be much further along in the fulfillment of our destiny if not for them."

Savassan lowered his head in a gesture of resignation. "I suppose you are right. And no matter what the cost, the things that the Ihan-rii have left for us to discover must be protected."

Jake turned his attention from the dead enemy to the glorious artifact that made this place so sacred, so inviolable, so in desperate need of the protection the Shelak tribe could provide it.

It had, he had been told, once been larger than this. Slammed deep into the earth by a force so powerful Jake could barely comprehend it, it had jutted skyward proudly. But centuries of weather and hate-filled attacks by the other, ignorant protoss tribes such as the Furinax had damaged it. Now it was only the broken stump of a slender, night black beam with strange things scratched upon it. When it was touched by reverent hands, the things inscribed upon it glowed and shimmered and a pleasing sound vibrated upon their skins.

But it was of the Great Teachers, the Makers, the Guardians, and that made it truly precious. That made it holy to the Shelak, and worth their very life's blood to defend. Except that it hadn't been their life's blood shed to feed the earth on this day; it had been that of their enemy.

And that was good.

He became aware of the scents first. Not the rich, multilayered smells of blossoming and decay and humus and blood, but a sterile, cold, dry, metallic odor. Jake opened his eyes and blinked, confused. He was not lying on the soft, slightly moist soil of his homeworld, but on a hard, artificial floor, the only bedding a single blanket tossed over him.

He had no idea where he was. He sat up cautiously, looking around. The words "escape pod" swam into his brain and he cringed and covered his head as the memory seared him:

"What the . . . ," Jake whispered.

"Well, good morning, Sleeping Beauty," came the voice of a human female.

Jake blinked, gasping for breath as the memory receded. He turned to see a petite woman sitting at the controls of the escape pod. She looked back at him, slightly concerned. The fall of her hair as she moved enraptured him.

"I was wondering when you were going to wake up. You've been out cold for twenty-one hours."

He blinked, dazed. *Out cold* . . . Without even thinking, he reached forward to the human's mind and plucked from it the information he needed.

As if he had unleashed a closetful of monsters, the memories—his own and R. M.'s—assaulted him and he again gasped and gripped his head.

The dying protoss—R. M.'s betrayal—undoing the resoc on Marcus Wright—blood everywhere—

"Darius? Kendra . . ." He cut short the litany of names as Rosemary's thoughts poured over him, not an attack this time, but like warm honey.

"Jake . . . listen. You and I were lucky as all hell to be able to escape *ourselves*. There was no way I could have gotten your team or even mine out. I had to leave them behind if we were to get out of there. We'd have all died if I'd gone back for anyone."

It was true, he realized, grief and horror welling up inside him as he stared at her cool blue eyes, soft now with a hint of compassion. He knew what she knew now:

Running down the corridor with the all but dead weight of Jake Ramsey on her narrow shoulders; stopping and hiding Jake while she coolly opened fire on people she had happily been in league with. Edging quietly past Marcus Wright, who had seized one of his former friends and was busily engaged in the act of physically ripping him to pieces. Tossing Jake inside the escape pod and diving for the controls while hell raged inside the ship. . . .

"Doesn't feel good to read minds, huh?" Rosemary asked, turning her eyes back to the console.

Jake shook his head. "It feels awful."

"Then don't do it."

"Believe me, I'm trying not to."

And indeed, he did not seem to be such an open target to random thoughts as he had been previously. But he did not need someone else's thoughts to feel sick and horrified and racked with grief.

"You don't suppose . . ." Jake's voice trailed off.

Rosemary chuckled without humor. "Hey, Prof . . . I don't need to be a mind reader to know what you're thinking. One way or another, your friends just aren't going to make it."

"Why even bother with me? Why didn't you just drop me and go?"

Rosemary sighed, her fingers moving efficiently over the console.

"Jake, you're one of a kind right now. That makes you useful and valuable. We're both wanted, so we have to trust each other. That does not come naturally to me, I admit, but once that marine trained his rifle on me, you and I became partners, willingly or not. We could be able to use what you know as a bargaining chip at some point."

He supposed he should try to read her thoughts again, see if she was planning to betray him a second time. What was the old saying—"Fool me once, shame on you; fool me twice, shame on me"? But he couldn't summon the energy. Jake's mind was racing with memories that he had had all his life, but had somehow been given a new color and vibrancy, like an old painting that has been painstakingly restored. Most memories were snatches of things, a word or two or an image; now, it was as if he was reliving it.

Darius, too busy on a dig to respond to Jake's inquiries about joining the team, glaring at him underneath the red Melkoran skies. "Who are you and what the hell do you want?" Jake could see the sweat glisten on his brow, hear the hum of flies. . . .

"Hi, I'm Kendra Massa," the girl said, sticking out her hand for a firm handshake, eyes bright and smiling. . . .

"Oh, God," said Jake.

A quick glance from Rosemary. "Tell me what's going on, Jake. Talk to me."

He shot her a furious glare. He didn't want to confide in her. He didn't even want to be in the same escape pod with her. Rosemary Dahl had handed his life over for money. He knew enough of her from her own thoughts to know that she was cold and selfish and calculating.

And yet . . . she was human. The being inside him—he could sense Zamara still within—was not

And so he spoke. "It's like . . . I'm reliving every memory of them I've ever had. Not just remembering—reliving, watching it happen all over again."

"Get something to eat. You need nourishment, and you're dehydrated for sure."

Quick, clipped advice, and he supposed it was what he needed. He certainly did not need more emotions pouring over him like cascading waterfalls. Jake stumbled to his feet and helped himself to rations. He drank the tepid water and choked down the dried . . . whatever it was.

You can block others' thoughts if you choose, came Zamara's voice. *Temlaa learned how, and so can you, with my help. Your brain is still adjusting. You will soon comprehend how to do this.*

There was a slight hesitation, then she continued. *We protoss follow a doctrine we call the Khala, which asks of us to unite all our thoughts and emotions, so that we are not many, but one. But even among our own people, there are those who wish to remain apart. We have called them the Dark Templar in many ages past, but recently we have learned they may not be quite so dark after all. For you, unused as you are to dancing with another's inmost being,*

*such might be the safest path. I remember this. . . . You will
as well.*

Jake shuddered. He still hadn't gotten used to this,
and wondered if he ever would. It was probably his
imagination, but he thought he could . . . feel . . . the
alien presence opening parts of his brain, merging her
memories with his own. The dream which he was
now certain was a memory had placed Jake at the
center of the action. He was a protoss, someone
named "Temlaa," but he was himself as well.

He looked down at his hands. They looked completely right to him—smooth and pink, with four fingers and a thumb. But before, when they were purple
and long and had four digits, they had looked completely right to him as well. . . .

"You said you undid the resoc on Marcus."
Rosemary's voice startled him out of his reverie. "How
did you do it? From my understanding of it, the doctors do a damn good job brain-panning."

Jake realized he was still sitting on the floor.
Darius's glowering face swam into his mind, and his
breath caught. He forced the image away and moved
forward along the small cabin to sit in the copilot's
chair next to R. M. He gazed out at the sky, taking an
odd comfort in the vastness and impartiality of the
stars. Things were too intimate for him right now, and
their disinterest calmed him.

"Well?" Rosemary pressed a button and some
information flashed on the screen. Her blue eyes
scanned it quickly.

It was a good question. How *had* he done it? The answer came easily, information that had been held in a brain that was not his own.

"A criminal's violent memories are potent. They're—really emotionally charged. The resoc finds those memories and buries them, then overlays new, false memories."

Rosemary chuckled huskily. "Yep, you're a professor all right. Cut out the 'As you know, Johnson' crap and cut to the chase. How'd you do it?"

He felt a twinge of annoyance and clung to it like a drowning man. It was his own feeling, from his own memories and past and personality, and damn it, it felt really good.

"You have to understand how resoc works if you want to know what I did," he replied irritably.

She smothered a smile. "Well then, Professor, pray enlighten me."

He waved a hand, suddenly weary again. "You know how it works. What Zamara did—not sure how yet—was to find those memories and bring them to the forefront. She made Marcus realize what they had done to him. That everything he believed was a lie. And with the return of the memories, of the knowledge of what he had done, came the violence and the same desires he'd felt while . . ."

He tasted bile.

"While killing, dismembering, and eating people," Rosemary said without skipping a beat. She nodded. "Makes sense."

Jake stared at the vastness of space yawning before him. He didn't want to say more, but he felt he had to. Bracing himself, he reached out and touched R. M.'s mind. He didn't go deep; he didn't want to go deep. He just wanted to know if, really, he could trust her. He sensed no deception from her, no blocking; no mustache-twirling, hand-rubbing villainy. Just curiosity, a slight contempt for his manner of speaking and word choice, and below that a simmering cauldron of fear, fury, and determination.

Jake winced at the passion of her hatred.

She turned to look at him. "You okay?"

Obviously, she hadn't felt him probe her thoughts. That was good. He nodded.

"Yeah, I'm as okay as I can be, I guess. Anyway—it was like untying knots. She was able to go into Wright's mind and find those . . . those dark things and free them. And . . . she was able to do something more."

He paused, wondering if he would ever shed the guilt about what his brain had been forced to do, wondering if the protoss's knowledge, the knowledge she claimed Jake now possessed, really had been worth unleashing a madman on the crew of the *Gray Tiger.*

"You know how it is when you remember things? Most of the time it's kind of dim and imperfect. You remember it, but it's very . . . shadowy and lacks the punch it had when it happened."

"Yes," R. M. said. "I know. You can remember an

incident and feel happy or sad or whatever, but it's very distant."

"Well," Jake said, "Zamara knows how to make memories feel like they're actually happening again."

She turned to him, eyes wide. "Wow," she said.

He nodded.

"So, when she uncovered Marcus's memories, they weren't just memories," she said slowly.

"No," Jake said, hunched and miserable.

They were silent. Nothing more needed to be said. They both understood the significance of what had been done. The silence stretched between them for a long, long time.

"Well," R. M. said at last, her voice shattering the still air between them. "Don't feel too bad about it. Those people were taking us to have our minds raped. And after that, we'd have been killed. You saved us, Jake."

"Tell that to Darius and Kendra," Jake said.

Rosemary shrugged her slender shoulders. "You can wallow in guilt all you want, but at least you're alive to do the wallowing."

Jake looked at the console. "Any sign of pursuit?" he asked, trying to distract himself.

"None," R. M. said. "I kept a good eye on it the first few hours, believe me, and I've monitored all communications. Last I saw of the *Gray Tiger* it was dead in space. Before we left I was able to mess with the ship's systems enough so they'll have no idea where our pod might have been heading. If I'd had a little more time, I could have entered a fake flight path, but I was trying to get out as fast as I could. Even so, I bought us a few hours."

She tossed the information out calmly, and he supposed that she did feel calm about it. Three words she said made him soul-sick, though: *dead in space*.

"You don't think anyone . . . I mean, he's only one man."

Rosemary turned and looked at him searchingly. "Jake," she said quietly, almost gently, "you—okay, not you, Zamara—set an insane criminal of the worst variety loose on the people who'd done this horrible thing to him. What did you think would happen?"

Jake buried his face in his hands.

Rosemary sighed. "It's done. Let it go. We need to concentrate on staying alive."

"And I bet you've got a plan," he said, bitterly. He was suddenly very angry at Rosemary, angry at her for not feeling what he was feeling, for not sharing the horror he felt at what he had done.

"I do," she said, not reacting to his resentment. "I've got an old friend who might be able to help us for a bit. Give us a place to hide and think for a few days, anyway."

Jake almost fell out of his chair. "What? We've got to have prices on our heads—"

Rosemary held up a calming hand. "Relax, Jake. This guy and I go way back. We've been through a lot together. I know I can trust him. He may be the only person in the galaxy I trust, but I do."

Jake ran his fingers through his hair and realized it was stiff with sweat. He felt filthy. He wished the escape pod had a shower. He sighed.

"R. M., you know a lot more about this kind of cloak-and-dagger world than I do. I'm just an archeologist with an alien intelligence in his head."

She laughed. He didn't think he'd ever heard a real laugh from her, and certainly didn't expect to hear such a cheerful sound now.

"I had no idea you had such a sense of humor, Jake. It's good to know."

Jake Ramsey gave her a forced smile. He thought it would be best if he kept to himself the fact that he hadn't been trying to be funny.

CHAPTER 13

"WHAT DO YOU MEAN WE CAN'T RAISE THEM?"

Valerian's voice was low and carefully controlled. His father had taught him this. *There will be times when you'll want more than anything to shout at people, and to follow that up with a good throttling. Resist the impulse, son,* Arcturus had said. *If you scream at them, all they'll hear is the volume. And if you throttle them, why,* and he had laughed and taken a sip of port, *it makes it hard for them to talk.*

So now, when Valerian wanted very badly indeed to shout at Whittier and then throttle him—or perhaps execute both maneuvers simultaneously—he curbed the impulse and kept his voice and manner calm. Such was not the way of a true warrior, nor a future emperor. He knew from the way the color drained from Whittier's face, however, that he hadn't managed to control the fury in his eyes. He would have to work on that.

"Simply what I said, sir. According to our charts,

they haven't moved from their position in several hours. And no one is responding to our queries."

Valerian breathed deeply. A vein in his temple was throbbing and he put a manicured hand up to physically calm the agitated vessel. He inhaled the scents that he loved: the smell of leather and polished wood, the spicy aroma of pipe tobacco. It calmed him. A little.

"I see." His voice was composed now, and he lowered his hand. "Well, it sounds like something has happened. Was there any evidence of an attack?"

Relieved to see his employer calming, Whittier turned back to the screen. His long, thin fingers flew as he called up image after image.

"Negative, sir. There is no debris in the area, no trace of enemy vessels. If the protoss had hit, we'd be seeing energy residue; if it was the zerg . . . well, sir, you know as well as I we'd be seeing floating debris and nothing else."

He knew his aide was right. The *Gray Tiger* had not been attacked.

Not from the outside, anyway.

"Call up the bios of Ramsey's team again," he said. Whittier wisely did not remind Valerian that this was the fifth time he had asked his assistant to do so, and simply obeyed the command. Valerian's jaw tightened as his gray eyes flickered over the information. But this time, he was reading the little reports with an eye toward who in Ramsey's team might have tried to instigate an escape.

It was a collection of brilliant, but not criminal, minds. None of them should have been able to stage any kind of escape or even disruption sufficient to stop a battle cruiser dead in space. What, then, had happened?

Valerian got his answer twenty-seven hours later.

Hector Santiago, the fleet admiral with whom he spoke, looked shaken, even for a hardened military man.

"Sir, we have boarded and secured the *Gray Tiger*," Santiago said. "I regret to report that all aboard are dead."

"What?" Valerian couldn't help himself. This time, he shouted.

"All aboard are dead," Santiago repeated. "We are investigating now. It appears that one of the marines opened fire on his own shipmates. His name was Marcus Wright."

"How is that possible? The resocialization on these people is quite thorough. He shouldn't have been physically able to turn a weapon on any of them—at least not without an order."

"I'm aware of that, sir," Santiago replied. "However, our initial information does show this to be the case."

All right, so somehow, some way, the resoc had spontaneously unraveled. Even so . . . "One marine couldn't possibly kill everyone on board."

"By gunfire alone, certainly not. The others would have neutralized the threat before then. So far we have located only nine who were shot to death. The rest died when Wright sabotaged the vessel's life support systems. He also destroyed their communications systems as well, so they couldn't send out a distress call."

Charles Whittier was looking like a frightened rabbit as the tale unfolded, and even Valerian was a bit rattled. He did not give a tinker's damn about the Marines, or the crew, or any of the archeologists except one. To have lost Ramsey—from everything Rosemary had told him, Jake Ramsey had had a unique experience. Mentally bonding with a protoss. The things he could have revealed to them. . . .

The discovery of wonders.

Valerian sighed, even more bitterly disappointed than he had expected to be. Ramsey's unique experience aside, now he would have to assemble another team to recover the protoss vessel. And he would never know exactly what the hell Ramsey had done to get inside that damned chamber. Why, why had he lost Ramsey?

"Sir," Santiago said, interrupting Valerian's angry reverie, "we, uh—I don't know if you want to see this or not, but we have a prerecorded message from Wright himself."

"Of course I want to see it!" Valerian snapped. "Put it through immediately."

Santiago hesitated. "Are you familiar with the crimes that necessitated the resocialization of this particular individual, sir?"

"No. Does it matter?"

"Well . . . It's a little . . ."

"Play the message, Admiral," Valerian demanded in an icy voice.

Santiago inclined his head. "Yes, sir," he replied. He reached forward, then his tanned face was replaced by one that was bloody and grinning. Whittier drew back with a gasp, and even Valerian's eyes widened slightly.

"Well, hello there, whoever gets this," Marcus Wright said in a gravelly voice. He was grinning fiercely. There was blood on his uniform and, oddly, around his mouth, but he did not appear to have been injured.

"Let me save you a little time here. If you're watching this, then I assure you, you won't need any medics. We'll all be dead here by then. I've blasted the brains out of nine of my compadres thus far, and now the rest of them're trying to hunt me down and shoot me like a rabid dog. I've blown the hell out of the life support systems as well as external communications. It'll all be over in about three hours. You've got your precious Jake Ramsey to thank for this whole thing."

He grinned, and Valerian found himself staring as if hypnotized at the blood around the man's mouth. Then the meaning of Wright's words struck him. Ramsey? What did the rather gentle archeologist have to do with this madman's rampage?

Wright leaned in closer to the camera. "He undid it," he whispered gleefully, as if he had heard Valerian's unasked question. "Undid the resoc. Made me remember who and what I was. Made me remember the joy of what I did. And made me remember how damn bad it hurt when you boys played with my brain to make me all docile-like."

Whittier gasped. Valerian was shocked and horrified and excited and shattered all at the same time. Ramsey had done this? Then what had happened to his brain had to be even more profound than Valerian had hoped. And now, Ramsey was dead, frozen to death in the coldness of space along with the rest of his team and the crew of the *Gray Tiger*.

Damn you, Wright, Valerian thought fiercely, then smiled coldly to himself. If there was a God, as some still believed, then certainly, given what Wright had likely done in the past, the hulking bastard was indeed damned.

The thought wasn't much comfort.

"So now I'm getting back at you," Wright continued. "All the other boys and girls in the marines—they don't understand like I do, they don't yet realize that it's better to be dead and who you are than walking around with everything that made you *you* buried and smothered with fake chocolate-coated memories. That ain't living. They're better off dead. As for the rest, they don't mean nothing to me. You want these people, these archeologists? Then I want nothing more than to see to it that you never get them. They'll be frozen stiffs by the time you get here."

Wright leaned into the camera. "I'll see you in Hell." He sat back, placed the gauss rifle beneath his chin, and pulled the trigger.

Whittier whimpered and averted his gaze. A muscle twitched near Valerian's eye. A heartbeat later the gory scene was replaced by Santiago's deadly serious face.

"Well," Valerian said calmly, "at least now we know what happened. Tell your crew that I don't really care about anyone else, but I want the body of Professor Jacob Ramsey recovered and put into stasis as soon as possible. We'll need to perform an autopsy on him."

And see if in death he's left us any clues at all, Valerian thought with a wave of deep regret. *There might be some changes in his brain that we could learn from. Though we would have so very much more if he were alive. Ah, Jake. You and I were kindred spirits. If only I could listen to you tell me what you found over a glass of port. That's how I wanted this to be.*

Santiago nodded. He was handed a report, and his eyes played over it quickly. His black brows rose slightly as myriad emotions darted over his face.

"Sir . . . ," he began. "I've just been informed that there are two of the archeological team unaccounted for."

"What?" demanded Valerian. "What are you saying?"

"All the gunfire casualties were marines. The archeological teams remained in their cells and died there. But—"

"Wait, what . . . cells? What was the team doing in cells? At least one of them was badly injured and should have been in sick bay!"

"Sir," Whittier managed, "the marines do not have a reputation for gentleness and social manners. They might have decided to temporarily put them in cells to keep them from panicking. A foolish decision, but quite likely."

"I suppose that's possible," Valerian said, frowning. "Now we'll never know. Continue, Santiago."

"As I was saying, two cells had been opened. We also have a record of an escape pod being launched prior to Marcus's sabotage."

Hope surged in Valerian's breast. Could it be . . . He leaned forward, his hands on the desk, as if Santiago were actually physically present.

"Admiral Santiago," he said calmly, smiling the smile that always charmed his audiences . . . the same smile his father used as a weapon in his arsenal. "If you can tell me truthfully that one of the two missing prisoners is Jacob Ramsey, you will please me very much."

Clearly Santiago hadn't known how Valerian would react, and the man's features brightened with pleasure.

"Then, sir, I have very good news. One of the two cells that were opened was Ramsey's."

He was alive! All they had to do was track the escape pod. A wave of elation washed through Valerian, and he had to force it down. Suddenly curious, he asked Santiago, "You said two cells had been opened. Who was in the second one?"

Santiago glanced at the report. "Dahl, R. M."

Ah, he should have expected that. Rosemary was a fighter. Her porcelain skin, black, silky hair and slight, petite frame belied the fact that she had nerves of paristeel. In a way, he was glad that she had survived; he liked the feisty little thing. But she was an extremely shrewd woman, and likely she was highly suspicious of him now. Who knew what that monster had said as he went on his rampage? After being shoved into cells, probably with no explanation, R. M. may well have thought that Valerian had turned on her. If she wanted to keep Jake lost and out of Valerian's clutches, there was a good bet that the wayward professor whose brain had been so profoundly manipulated would be a very difficult quarry to hunt.

"I see" was all he said. He straightened and sighed. "I'm going to make a little bet with you, Admiral. I'm going to bet that you won't be able to track them."

Santiago smiled, a touch smugly, Valerian thought. He obviously had every confidence in the technology at his disposal. *You don't know my little Rosemary.*

Even though it meant that, at least for the moment, the quarry had lost the hunters, Valerian was a little pleased to see the smile ebb from Santiago's face. The man took another look at the report he had been handed and laughed shakily.

"Well, sir, I won't take that bet," Santiago said. There was a hint of nervousness in his demeanor. "The systems have been completely scrambled. Whoever did this knew what he was doing."

"*She,*" Valerian corrected. "Rosemary Dahl is intelligent and dangerous. I'd have been much happier had our little professor stumbled into the escape pod on his own. With Dahl along for the ride, he will prove to be difficult to find. And I imagine that too much time has now passed for us to pick up on energy trails?"

Santiago was definitely looking a bit worse for wear as he nodded. "Correct, sir. I will have my best people on this. The prisoners only have so much food and life support on an escape pod. They'll be forced to make landing soon. We'll investigate all possible planets they—"

"Negative, Admiral," Valerian interrupted smoothly. "Your best people won't be good enough. I will set *my* best people on this. In the meantime, you are to destroy the *Gray Tiger* and purge all records of this particular assignment. Is that clear?"

Santiago's jaw clenched but he snapped a smart salute. "Clear as crystal, sir."

"Excellent. I'm pleased to hear it. Thank you, Admiral." Smiling, Valerian nodded to Whittier, who pushed a button. Santiago's face was replaced by the Dominion insignia.

Valerian sighed. Bad news indeed, that Ramsey had fled, especially with Dahl to shepherd him. Good news, that he was still alive. They would be slippery fish, but in the end, they would not escape Valerian's net.

CHAPTER 14

ROSEMARY GLANCED OVER HER SHOULDER AT Jake. He was asleep, his breathing regular and deep, punctuated occasionally by a soft snore. He seemed to be sleeping an awful lot and looked tired even when he was awake. But, then again, if an alien intelligence was uploading centuries' worth of memories into her brain while she slept, Rosemary supposed she would be pretty tired too.

She had not told Jake just how much jeopardy they were in. He was not used to this kind of life, as she was, and with all that was going on with him he was liable to panic. She had told him just enough, and frankly, that mind-reading trick of his had extracted more than she'd wanted him to know. Fortunately he seemed to be getting some level of control over it and found it as upsetting to read her mind as she did to have it read. And, also fortunately, she hadn't been hiding anything when he *had* read her mind.

Thank God.

Bad enough that he'd known what she was up to and converted what could have been an easy turnover into a hostage situation. But, then again, it had been those strange powers that neither of them yet fully understood that had gotten them off the ship.

Undoing the resoc of one of the most dangerous killers it had ever been Rosemary's misfortune to run across—she wondered if Jake had told the truth when he said the alien did it without his permission.

Rosemary shook her head to clear her thoughts. Whether it was Jake or the protoss intelligence in his head that had done anything didn't really matter. All that mattered was that there *was* this alien intelligence in his head, and that it could be very lucrative indeed.

She had sent an encoded message to Ethan, the one person in this universe she thought would shelter them and aid them without turning them in for the no-doubt-staggering reward. Personally, Rosemary didn't give a rat's ass about Jake Ramsey. She did, however, care passionately about her own life. And while it might not always be the case, right now, her life hinged on his.

When the console beeped, she started and cursed, so wrapped up in her thoughts that even that soft noise took her by surprise. She examined the signal, then her body relaxed and her lips curved into a smile.

She pressed a few keys, and Ethan's darkly handsome face appeared on the monitor.

"Hey there, Trouble," he said in his silky voice.

Rosemary's smile widened. That was his nickname for her; they always seemed to find trouble together. "I hadn't expected to hear from you until you finished that cushy assignment you told me about—if then."

Their relationship was unique in Rosemary's experience. They had fought together, side by side, for seven years. They'd begun as employer and employee and soon graduated to equal partners. There was no one else she'd trust to have her back, and she'd saved his life more than once. The trust carried over into their personal lives, and more than once, a day that had begun with assassination and violence ended with an almost equally violent bout of coupling in bed. Those had been good days. Sweet days.

Then Ethan announced that he was taking his earnings, investing, and retiring. He'd invited Rosemary along, but she had declined. She was happy where she was. They had parted easily, comfortably, with a long, passionate kiss and a wink. She saw him infrequently after that, but when they were together, it was as if no time had passed. Their bodies remembered each other's touch, and their minds, so much alike, relished the chance to catch up with one another's exploits and adventures. It was the perfect relationship for both of them. Did he have other lovers when he wasn't with her? Probably, and she didn't give a rat's ass about that, either. She opted not to have any other relationships, but that was her decision, based on her needs and wants.

"My sources had heard a little something about this

before I even got your message, and damned if I didn't think, *I wonder if Trouble isn't involved in this."*

He grinned, and even though it was a prerecorded message, she grinned right back.

"I know you couldn't tell me the full story, but this might be your best one yet. I look forward to hearing it over a bottle of wine. I'd say take care of your cargo, but I know you always do. According to our calculations, the location of our first date isn't too far out of range for you. Come to the main watering hole and someone you recognize will be there to assist you. I look forward to our meeting."

Rosemary did too. In addition to seeing Ethan, she was looking forward to that bottle of wine. It would be better than anything she'd had in a long time, she suspected, for Ethan's "business" involved dealing on the black market. He'd probably have an honest-to-God quality cigar waiting for her too, even though he'd hassle her for lapsing back into her old habits.

Briefly she wished he'd have something harder for her, then shook that thought away. She'd kicked that addiction, and Ethan had been the one to help her do it. It took far more than it had ever given her in return, and Rosemary did not like to be bound to anyone or anything.

The "location" he referred to was a dangerous town on a dangerous planet. The planet had the dreadfully boring official designation of D-3974 and the more colorful and unofficial one of Dead Man's Rock. The main watering hole was a sewer of a town called

Paradise, the name not describing how pleasant a place it was, but rather where one was likely to be sent if one made a wrong move there. The Dominion knew about it and left it alone; it was far too distant and difficult to police.

She rose, stepped over Jake's slightly snoring body, and examined what was left of their rations. Not a whole hell of a lot, and they'd been going easy on them the last few days.

Rosemary's thought had been to fly in an erratic pattern, so that they could not be traced. It was a smart tactic and so far had worked. But she could no longer waste either the fuel or the time in any maneuvers other than getting to their destination.

Blood. Fury. Hatred, of himself, of the others, of the Ihan-rii . . . *No, no we love them, we cannot hate them for leaving us, we are flawed, we are flawed—*

Jacob?

Make it stop! Please, make it stop. . . .

In his sleep, feebly, Jake reached to claw ineffectually at his head. His eyes darted back and forth rapidly beneath his closed lids.

To halt it altogether would defeat my entire purpose. But I can help you to manage it. Understand it. See and feel and hear it without fear.

I want it to stop! I didn't ask for this! I want it gone. You've already used it to kill dozens of people. Why should I trust you?

Because you have no other choice. You are correct, you

*cannot manage these memories on your own. I can help you.
If you do not permit me to help you . . . you will go mad and
all my efforts . . . all these memories would be lost. And the
deaths of your friends would mean nothing at all.*

It was the last comment that got him.

. . . All right.

In his dream, he saw Zamara as he had seen her
before she reached out to him. To his eyes, she was
not beautiful, but she was graceful and strong. She
reached out a hand—two fingers, two thumbs—and
he took it. Again he remembered the spiral of light,
the Golden Mean ratio. He sensed warmth and affection from her.

*Soon you will understand that, too. And why I chose
it . . . and what made you unique. Alone of all those who
could have found the temple, and understood the code, it was
you, Jacob Jefferson Ramsey. Take my hand. We will walk
calmly through this, not race with fear and ignorance.*

Dreaming, calmer than he had been since this
whole ordeal began, he took her hand.

*Jake bore the body of the slain enemy this time as he and
Savassan made their way to the lair of the omhara. The sun
was setting and the jungle was coming to true life. Sounds
reverberated along his skin, scents washed over and through
him as Jake moved carefully, holding the dead protoss in his
arms like a child. Only now was the Akilae worth treating
gently, because only now was it of any good purpose to the
Shelak.*

Now, the Akilae was an offering.

• • •

"I'm here too . . . but I can't control what happens in the body," Jake said to Zamara. He was fully in this place now, his essence inside Temlaa's body as if he were in a vehicle that was on autopilot. He looked down with Temlaa's eyes at the dead body he carried, and felt sick. "Are these . . . is he really a protoss? He's nothing like what I've seen on the holovids." He recalled the images of the gleaming, precise, controlled warriors in their protective armor. Even the ruined vessel of Zamara's that he'd glimpsed had grace and calm to it. But these things running around, feral and deadly, painted and covered with bones and feathers . . .

Zamara, present inside Jake's body and brain as he was present inside Temlaa's, brushed away his thoughts. "These are our origins," she said. "This is where we came from. It is imperative that you must grasp what we were in order to understand how we became what we are."

"Can't you just tell me?"

"It is not about telling. It is not even about showing. It is about . . . *being*."

Jake's footsteps slowed as they approached the omhara's lair. He turned to Savassan, his eyes wide, and Savassan sent a message of reassurance. Not for the first time, Jake thought about the ways other creatures obtained sustenance. For the protoss it was easy—the White Circle of night and the Golden Orb of day showed their favor to the protoss and nourished them. Their light, and that of their children, the smaller glittering sky-gems that appeared at night, was all the protoss needed to flourish.

Other beings killed for food. Sometimes, Jake envied them. How good it would be to take the flesh of a fallen foe and bring it inside the body. What greater mastery could be shown over one's enemies than eating them?

The omhara in its lair growled. Jake's thoughts focused instantly.

"Be easy," Savassan sent. "It will scent your fear. Leave the offering and your thanks to it and come away."

Nervous, Jake reached out with his thoughts and touched those of the omhara. It was primal, base, simple, but very powerful, and very much aware of him. Jake could hear its breathing, see its three eyes glittering in the cave's darkness.

"Omhara, great one, sleek of form and sharp of tooth, we bring you this one we have slain. May its flesh nourish you and—"

A soft fall of hoof on the earth. It was coming.

"Oh, jeez," Jake murmured in his sleep, suddenly himself again.

"Savassan's advice holds for you as well," Zamara said. "Be easy, Jacob. Nothing you see here can hurt you, nor can you change what is unfolding. Breathe into it. Hold on to who you are."

" . . . and may you bestow your blessings upon us." Jake finished quickly and backed away. He sensed the thing's thoughts—curious, focused, intense. Now it scented the food, and its thoughts were only of hunger and feeding.

He caught the barest glimpse of it in the twilight shadows as he and Savassan hastened back to a safe distance.

"You did well," Savassan said. "I am glad I did not have to attack her. She carries young."

"She does?"

Savassan laughed, half closing his eyes and tilting his head in a way that conveyed gentle, affectionate humor among the protoss. "You have a ways to go yet in reading the minds of things different from yourself."

"I suppose I do. But it will come," Jake said with a touch of arrogance. "I am Shelak. We are the chosen ones of the Ihan-rii. The ones they selected above all others on Aiur to shape and mold and protect."

"We were chosen, but we were abandoned," Savassan reminded him. "And it is that abandonment that constantly reminds me that we must temper our arrogance. Only when we learn about the Ihan-rii's reasons for first selecting us and then being displeased will we be able to properly judge."

Jake thought the sentiment Savassan had just expressed was the reason he confused so many. He immediately wished the thought back. Savassan replied in Jake's mind, "Of course, of course. And yet, they still let me poke and pry and question."

"There are few more respected in the Shelak than you," Jake replied, and it was the truth. Savassan accepted the comment as the fact it was.

"I sometimes wonder if the poking and the prying is exactly why I am respected, even though it puzzles most."

Jake was embarrassed, and shielded his thoughts. Savassan changed the subject.

"I like this time of day," Savassan sent to the younger protoss. The air was thick and heavy with mist. The earth was wet beneath their bare feet as they loped back toward their home. *"It is a between time . . . a powerful time. No longer truly day, yet not yet night. The artifacts are like this too. They are between things. They are physical, solid, real . . . and yet more than that."*

A thrill of excitement rushed through Jake. He loved it when Savassan spoke of the artifacts. No one knew more about the mysterious relics than Savassan. Jake knew that Savassan understood how badly the younger protoss hungered for knowledge. He wanted to work with Savassan, become a High Keeper of the history, imperfect and fractured as it was.

"Please . . . tell me more. . . ."

Savassan turned to look at him, his huge eyes unblinking as his thoughts probed Jake's.

"Yes . . . yes, I think you are ready for more. I have a theory, about us, about the artifacts. I think . . . I think we, too, we protoss, are 'between.' We are not what we were, we are not what we are to become. And yet both of these things are in us. The relics, the artifacts . . . I think they have a story to tell us."

"But—they are not living things. They have no thoughts. They don't even have mouths like the lesser things to communicate with. How could they possibly tell us things?"

Savassan again laughed. *"Ah, Temlaa, like so many of our people, you are literal."*

Jake ducked his head in shame. Savassan placed a friendly hand on his shoulder. *"There is nothing wrong with that. But I think you can grasp more than what has hitherto been understood by our people. I think these artifacts hold knowledge inside them somehow."*

They had reached the place where they had hidden their weapons while attending to the omhara, and Savassan picked up his spear. Jake followed, curiosity swelling inside him. Savassan was keeping his mind carefully blank except for one thing: *"I want you to see this without any help from me, young Temlaa."*

Jake was barely breathing as he followed Savassan to a patch of damp earth. The light was fading, but protoss eyes were keen and Jake was so focused that everything seemed sharp and almost painfully clear.

Savassan bent and smoothed out the patch of earth, clearing it of pebbles and grasses. He glanced up at Jake and then back down at the earth. Grasping his spear, he began to cut into the soil.

Shapes appeared, lines following the spear's point. Jake frowned as he watched. A circle, with two smaller circles in it. Two lines running down from the circle, meeting with a third line at the bottom. Two lines from the bottom of that form, two lines from near the first circle running horizontally, another line running vertically.

Jake's heart raced as Savassan turned to him, his thoughts still carefully shielded. What was this supposed to mean? Clearly Savassan wanted him to infer something from this—this strange collection of lines scratched into the earth. But what? He began to panic. This was a test, he knew it, and if he failed, perhaps Savassan would not deem him worthy of further enlightenment. And Jake desperately wanted more.

"Look at me, Temlaa," Savassan said in Jake's mind. Jake lifted his eyes from the marks in the earth and gazed at the older protoss. Savassan stood straight, his feet firmly planted in the soil. As Jake watched, Savassan lifted his arms and held his spear out. "Now look at the marks in the soil. See."

Frustration battered Jake like one of the torrential down-pours that sometimes drenched the land. What was he sup-posed to see?

He tore his eyes from the rigidly standing elder to the marks Savassan had made.

His eyes widened.

Savassan, standing straight . . . his head a circle, with two circles in it. His legs two vertical lines, his arms two hor-izontal lines, his spear another vertical one. Jake trembled and knelt, reaching to gently touch the scratches in the sand with a knobby hand as if to imprint them on his mind.

"It's you," he thought. "Savassan . . . you have put your-self on the soil!"

"I knew you would understand!" The thought was as loud in Jake's mind as the roar of the omhara in the night. Savassan clapped a hand on the younger protoss's shoulder and squeezed, further conveying his approval.

"You can put an . . . an image, a representation of any-thing in the soil. Look." As excited by Jake's ability to see as Jake himself was, Savassan made more lines in the dirt. "This is a tree," he said, busily scratching lines. Now that Jake grasped the concept, it was as if a covering had been lifted from his eyes. Jake immediately saw the tree in what would have appeared as meaningless marks but a few

moments earlier. "And this is the sun . . . and this is the pond."

"Yes . . . yes, Savassan, I see them, I see them all!"

"Do you remember what I said earlier? That I believed the Ihan-rii *relics had a story to tell us?"*

"Yes, and I said that the relics had no thought, not even mouths to speak with. I—I was foolish to say that."

"Not at all. This is something that our people have never grasped before—that communication does not require thoughts being understood, or even sounds. But images. Something that can be put in one place, and then understood by someone else who would stumble upon it even when the one who placed it there is nowhere nearby. Captured thoughts, as it were. Captured sounds and meanings. This is how I believe the Ihan-rii *will tell us their stories."*

Jake sat back hard, physically shaken by the revelation. Now he vividly recalled the images of all the artifacts he had seen. There were strange designs carved on them, just as Savassan had made these marks in the moist soil. Sometimes they glimmered into dancing life when touched in a certain way. But the marks on the artifacts would not be washed away with rain or obliterated by footprints. Etched in, they would linger, perhaps forever. When they went on hunting parties to attack other tribes, the protoss often adorned themselves with items such as feathers, strings of bone, or bright colors from berries or blood. But these markings meant nothing. The other protoss had not made the jump.

Savassan, somehow managing to read Jake's thoughts despite their incoherency, nodded.

"They have not. But once I have been able to prove that my idea is correct, they will."

Again Jake looked down at the captured thoughts on the ground. *"They are complicated, though."*

"They don't have to be. Look. If you know that this is me," Savassan said, pointing to the first image he had drawn, *"then this could also be me."* He made three lines: one vertical, which Jake now understood to be a simplistic rendering of his torso; one horizontal—Savassan's arms; and another vertical one to represent his spear.

"And this could be the tree . . . and this the sun." Savassan continued busily scratching. Each of the symbols now was much simpler, much faster to write. And Jake understood each one of them.

The sun moved slowly across the sky as the two Shelak bent their heads together, creating things that almost magically went from meaningless lines in the dirt to potent thoughts. At last there was too little light to see.

"It is time to return," said Savassan. *"We must say nothing of this until we have perfected it. Until we have been able to confirm that indeed, the legacy of the Ihan-rii is chiseled into their relics."* He hesitated. *"Temlaa. You have more than proved your worth. I could use an extra pair of eyes and hands in my work. I would like to take you on as my apprentice. What do you say?"*

Jake shielded his thoughts and turned toward the earth. With his finger, he traced lines in the soil. He drew himself, leaping up, arms flung out, with the sun above him.

He drew himself happy.

• • •

Still asleep, still drifting, Jake realized he felt . . . good. "It wasn't so bad this time," he said. He was still having trouble reconciling the elegant, gleaming warriors of the present with these violent, almost brutal beings of the far distant past. But he could understand Temlaa.

"You never told me how it is that you have memories that aren't your own," he said. "Is it this way with all protoss?"

"Not all; in fact only a very, very few," Zamara answered. "But that is not important now. Can you handle more?"

Jake considered. The fear had receded. He still wanted his old life back. He still despised the woman he was forced to travel with—

"Why did you want to bring her anyway?"

"I have my reasons, and those, too, are unimportant at this moment. You have not answered my question."

Jake thought it rather unfair that he was expected to answer her questions whereas she felt perfectly fine being mysterious and cryptic when it came to his. Laughter, warm and calming and purer than any he had ever known before, washed over and through him as she read his thoughts. He felt calm and comforted, and a step—a single, tiny step—closer to understanding this seemingly unfathomable being.

"Yes," he said. "I am . . . curious now."

"That is another trait that brought you to me."

"Another? What was the first?"

"That is also—"

"Unimportant," Jake sighed.

The Ara descended without warning.

And they had come in force, falling upon the unsuspecting Shelak and setting fire to their dwellings of piled trees and leaves and skins, with shattering results.

Jake's head whipped up as the mental cries assaulted him.

Telkar sent his orders in thoughts more primal than words, and his tribe leaped to obey him. His eyes stinging from the smoke, Jake seized his shikma and fell in with the rest. He leaped over spasming, bleeding bodies of males and females and young, fell raging upon the Ara and cut and stabbed and sliced and tore, the warm blood marking him.

He was startled to sense Savassan crying out. "The relics! They have not come for us, they have come for them!"

Jake's inattention cost him. An Ara female, wielding a hooked sal'bak, lunged for him, barely missing his stomach. He leaped back quickly, ducked to the side, and came at her with the shikma. He sliced her open neatly, then sprang over her still-clawing form to race to the aid of his friend.

A horrific sight met his eyes. The maddened Ara had brought tools to destroy not just the Shelak, but the precious things they guarded. One had taken damage, its smooth black surface crunched in by a stone tied to a stick. Another had been partially uprooted, as if several Ara had tried to knock it over. Even as Jake raced to aid his friend, more Ara swarmed out of nowhere. Savassan had been right. The attack on the village had been a distraction. This was the true target.

Jake sent out a mental scream and fell upon his foes. So enraged was he by this blasphemy, this violation, that he barely felt the injuries they inflicted upon him. It was only when he dropped his weapon and stared stupidly at his bleeding arm that he realized what had happened.

The Ara closed in for the kill. There was a blur of motion and Savassan was there, knocking Jake back to safety, falling upon the enemies of the relics with a fury Jake seldom saw in him. Inspired, he stumbled to his feet and continued to fight.

Finally the mental cries were silent. The fires burned for a long time, but they were at last extinguished. The wounded were attended to, the slain Ara thrown scornfully in piles to be taken to the omhara, the murdered Shelak to be ritually bathed, dressed for burial, and laid tenderly in the earth.

The next day Jake limped back toward the relics. He ran a hand along the smooth surface, wincing as his fingers touched the wound the Ara had made in the surface of one of the large black pillars. He bowed his head and grieved, his body shaking, his skin becoming mottled with his pain.

Savassan and Telkar had shielded their thoughts, so he became aware of their presence only when he saw them walking up toward the relics. Telkar did not look happy, but Savassan appeared completely at peace. Jake calmed himself and moved toward them hesitantly.

Both Shelak heads came up and gazed intently at Jake. He looked from one to the other, his thoughts no doubt loud.

"Temlaa," sent Savassan, "We must move the relics. The Ara know where they are now. And . . . I am leaving the Shelak tribe."

Jake stared at Savassan in horror. "No! We need you!"

"Exactly what I tried to tell him," sent Telkar. "Perhaps he will listen to you, Temlaa. He does not listen to me."

Shaking his head, Telkar stalked off. Jake turned to Savassan, thinking questions.

"Temlaa . . . you know the value of the work we have been doing," said Savassan. "You more than anyone else in the tribe understands that."

"Yes, of course," Jake thought back. "It is wise to move the relics, though it will be difficult. But why are you leaving us?"

"The thoughts . . . I need to have my thoughts clear. I cannot sit with the artifacts and try to be open to anything they may inspire with a dozen thoughts of bloodshed and hatred and violence in my head."

"But . . . we must defend ourselves! We must defend the artifacts from those who would destroy them! Always this has been the way of the Shelak!"

Savassan closed his eyes and looked pained. "Yes, it has. And I agree. The Shelak must fight, they must defend what the Ihan-rii have left behind. But . . . that is no longer my task. Not now that I have discovered that there is another one before me. I do not say greater, because what the tribe does makes what I need to do possible. My task is not to defend them, but to understand them."

Jake continued to stare. "Wherever we move the relics . . . that will be your new home. But . . . what about me?" Savassan looked at him, his eyes kind. He reached and placed a hand on the youth's shoulder.

"You, dear Temlaa, have a very important decision to

make. You need to decide if you will come with me or remain here. You must choose which path you will walk— that of a student of the Ihan-rii artifacts, or one who fights to protect them."

Jake looked at his mentor helplessly, then back over the camp. He saw his tribe mates moving purposefully, their purple, smooth-skinned bodies long and lean and strong. They were repairing weapons, adorning the dead, speaking of war tactics, and they looked right and well suited to the lives they led.

He dragged his gaze back to Savassan, then to the relics. They had found eight of them, had brought them all here to this place. Some were black, their surfaces smooth. Some were the colors of twilight, and seemed to glow at certain times of the day when the light caught them just right. Some rippled and turned in on themselves, others were bold and jagged. Some were small, mere fragments; some were flat tablets, others spheres. He thought of the beautiful black spire that had been so badly harmed by the angry Ara, of the strange inscriptions it bore, of the revelation that had thundered through his body when Savassan had made his marks in the soft, wet earth. And he knew his decision had been made already.

"I will come with you," he said. "The relics call to me. The mystery, the questions they pose—they burn in my heart. I have to know the answers to them."

Savassan half closed his large, lambent eyes and tilted his head in a smile. "Then gather your things, my young apprentice. Come and we will plumb the mysteries of the Ihan-rii together. Surely not even the secrets of the relics can *hide for long when faced with such a passion for knowing."*

As Savassan thought the words, a shudder went through Jake. And he knew somehow that his life was about to change in ways he could not possibly imagine.

Jake opened his eyes.

Zamara had subsided back to . . . wherever it was she went deep inside his brain when she was not actively present. Temlaa and Savassan. Who were these people? He felt a kinship with him that lingered even when he was awake, even when he was not seeing and feeling things through Temlaa. These two were primitive archeologists. Defenders and protectors of relics. Savassan understood that inanimate objects had a story to tell, and he and to a lesser extent Temlaa had made some amazing leaps. His own heart had soared to watch the two protoss work their way through such complex ideas as symbolism and, hell, even writing. Was this why Zamara felt he needed to "be" in Temlaa's body?

He was sorry he couldn't sleep any more. He wanted to see what their next discovery was. They were two voices of reason, of hope, in a world that was fueled by death and violence.

"How you doing, Jake?"

Jake started at Rosemary's voice. She had turned and was grinning at him. Jake realized that just as Temlaa and Savassan had been forced to leave behind everything they knew, so had he and Rosemary. They had only each other now. He'd rather have Savassan as a traveling companion. Despite Zamara's reassurance that Rosemary was a necessary evil, he resented the fact that the protoss had thrown them together. Nevertheless, the pleasure and tingling sense of excitement and discovery he had vicariously experienced, along with being very rested, make Jake feel a bit mischievous.

Rosemary had asked how he was doing.

Then gather your things, my young apprentice.

Jake looked at the tray of half-eaten MREs, at the pile of congealed goop which was no doubt intended to represent mashed potatoes. Jake poked two holes in the white substance and drew a semicircle underneath it.

Rosemary's blue gaze fell to the drawing, and she cracked a grin at a symbol not quite as ancient as those the protoss had created, but old and recognizable nonetheless—a smiley face.

CHAPTER 15

HE SAT BESIDE ROSEMARY, STARING OUT AT THE stars as she spoke. "Space is a big place, Jake. Even when you're the son of an emperor. We were at the highest risk right at the outset." She leaned forward and touched the console, and he watched absently as another star map was called up. It looked to his eyes exactly the same as the last several she'd scrutinized.

"I feel fairly confident we've lost them, but I'm not going to get too comfortable. A few more days and we'll be with Ethan. Then," and a smile curved those Cupid's bow lips, "then I'll . . . relax."

"Tell me a little bit more about this place we're going to."

"Dead Man's Rock? Not much to tell. Good place to hide out if you have to. Great place to do shady business, if that's what you're looking for. Dominion knows about it, but they never go there."

"They might go there this time," he said. "I'm not a petty criminal."

"Ethan's people will be there before us," she said. "They'll contact us if there's any chance of that."

"You're very certain about Ethan," he said. It was a statement, not a question. He'd read her thoughts on the man. They were mostly rather base and physical, but through all that shone an absolute, almost pure trust he hadn't thought Rosemary Dahl capable of.

"I am. He's good at what he does, and he won't let us down."

"I hope you're right."

She smiled at him. "Come on, Jake. Back on Nemaka I let you do your job, didn't I? Now let me do mine."

Suddenly he was angry at her all over again. She'd done her job back on Nemaka, too. Her smile faded slightly as she saw his brows draw together in a frown.

"Why the hell should I trust you? What's to stop you from turning me over to Ethan when we get to this . . . this Paradise? You tricked me but good before."

"You couldn't read minds then. We're on the same side now, Jake. I wouldn't sell you out for a billion credits at this point."

He scanned her thoughts quickly and saw she spoke the truth. Rosemary Dahl liked to keep things impersonal and businesslike, but if someone stabbed her in the back, it got very personal very quickly. She'd trusted Valerian and he'd turned on her—or at least his people had, which was the same thing. He could trust her with his safety, if only for the hatred she now bore toward the Heir Apparent and what he represented.

"I don't like you," he said bluntly.

She shrugged. "No one said you had to."

It was true. Not even Zamara had said he needed to like Rosemary. He just needed to work with her.

At Savassan's suggestion, the Shelak decided not to put the relics out in the open any longer. It was too dangerous. They were too vulnerable to attack that way.

"This is the way it has always been done, since the Day of Darkness when the Wanderers from Afar departed and left us to guard what remained," Telkar had protested.

Savassan's gaze was steady. "The way it has always been done no longer serves the relics. You are a good leader, Telkar. You will put the interests of preserving these holy things above tradition. The cave can be better guarded in case of an attack."

There was no denying the logic, and Telkar agreed. It would take a long time to move such large, heavy objects. But no one believed the project would fail. While the move was under way, Savassan decided he and Jake would embark on a search for more relics.

"It seems wrong, to leave the precious things behind," Jake sent.

"Sometimes you must leave something for a time in order to return to it better able to appreciate it, Temlaa," Savassan said.

They traveled many leagues from their home, going farther in three days than Jake had ever been in his life. Savassan had taken the concept of capturing information, as *the pair had taken to calling it, even further. They had packed lightly, but each one had taken a tanned omhara hide upon which to sleep, along with weapons with which to defend themselves if they were ever set upon by another tribe. Savassan had also taken a third hide. Jake wondered why, and Savassan had said only, "You will see." That first night, Savassan had made a fire. Jake had been puzzled; the need for a fire for warmth was rare.*

"Why are you lighting a fire?" he had asked. "It is not cold tonight."

Savassan had turned to him, half closing his eyes and tilting his head just so in the gesture that indicated amusement. "You will see," he said, repeating his earlier cryptic comment, and shielded his thoughts so completely Jake could not catch even a hint of them.

Savassan had reached for one of the sticks that had lain in the fire, its end burned quite black. He examined the charred wood and nodded to himself.

"Bring out one of the sleeping hides," he told Jake, and the younger protoss, utterly confused, nonetheless scurried to obey. He returned and started to spread it out on the grass, but Savassan interrupted him.

"No, no, Temlaa, put it fur side down," he instructed. Jake glanced at him, confused, but did as he was instructed and sat to the side, watching.

The moon was full, and between its glow and the orange light from the fire, it was easy to see. Savassan rose and went to the pale, stiff surface of the tanned hide. He glanced at Jake.

"You have impressed me more than once before, Temlaa. Can you do so again?"

Jake looked at the stick, looked at the hide. His mind reeled as comprehension dawned on him.

Savassan had scratched things in the earth with a spear point, but they had been vulnerable. A brush of a hand or foot, a rainfall, and the symbols would be lost. The blackened stick would leave a mark on the light color of the sleeping hide. The hide could be rolled up, protected from the elements, taken from place to place. He saw Savassan nod in excited approval as he thought this.

"I knew it. You are a gift from the Ihan-rii. I wonder if you are one of them in disguise."

Jake was embarrassed and flattered at the same time. He did not know what to say.

"But I require another leap from you. I am not going to draw the symbols we know already. I am going to put down what we have seen, where we have been. I am going to mark our journey."

"How?"

"We have ventured high above the canopy of the jungle before." Savassan started to draw on the hide with the blackened stick. "We can see for long distances when we are above the earth. Think what it would be like to be a bird, to fly above it all. What would the ground look like?"

Jake's gaze was fastened on the stick. An intersection of two lines appeared.

"This might be our encampment. And this," Savassan continued, "would be our cave, where we hide the relics. And this would be where we sleep tonight." He looked up at Jake, who stared, dumbfounded. "Do you see?"

Jake nodded. They could now track where they had gone.

If they discovered anything of import, they could mark it down on this hide. Then if they needed help, they could return to the Shelak encampment for aid in transporting anything of note to the cave. Even more important, if anything should happen to either of them, they would have this information marked down permanently. Others could follow in their footsteps.

Each day that they traveled, Savassan and later Jake himself would carefully draw their campsite, trying to estimate proper distances and making certain markings that would clearly identify each site. One time, it was a cave that made an area distinct; another time a waterfall, or two trees whose trunks entwined.

Only once did they come across a small party of Ara. Their scent floated to Jake's nostrils, and he tensed. Bloodlust surged through him, primal and all but impossible to deny. He prepared himself to attack, his spear at the ready, but Savassan's strong hand closed on his arm and yanked him back.

Jake whirled on his mentor. "They are Ara! They hate the artifacts! They were the ones who destroyed the—"

"I know this!" Savassan sent back. "But they outnumber us two to one, and we are encumbered with the hides. Preserving this information is more important than killing a few in an attack before we ourselves are slain. Besides—they are protoss. Like we are."

Jake stared at him. What was Savassan saying? That the Shelak should . . . should embrace the Ara, the Akilae, the Furinax, the Sargas as brothers? Share with them the knowledge that the Shelak had spilled so much of their own blood over in an attempt to protect?

His thoughts were not formed well, but Savassan understood him nonetheless.

"Eventually, what we learn must be shared with all protoss. It was never meant just for the Shelak. The Ihan-rii chose us as a race; they made no distinction among tribes. One day, we must emulate them."

The bloodlust had been cooled by the shock of Savassan's words. The party of blood-painted, decorated Ara warriors had moved on, never knowing that two of the hated Shelak were but a short distance away from them. The wind had favored Savassan and Jake this day. Jake looked after them, and back at Savassan.

"When were you planning on telling me this?"

"When I deemed you ready, Temlaa."

Jake turned to watch the warriors disappearing in the distance. "I think the Ara forced your hand."

"Perhaps. Perhaps not. That will depend on your reaction to what I have said."

Jake again turned to regard Savassan. His vision of the elder was different now. It was not filtered through a youngling's worshipful, ignorant gaze. He had spent many weeks traveling with Savassan, and had gotten to know and understand him. He had learned much from the older protoss, and while he knew he had much yet to learn, he was feeling more like an equal, a companion, than a student of a teacher.

He knew that if Savassan had uttered such a thing in front of the rest of the tribe, they would have deemed him a traitor. They might have leaped upon him and torn him to bits with their bare hands, or hamstrung him and left him exposed, bleeding and unable to walk, for the omhara to dispatch.

Or even the Ara.

But Jake found that after his initial shock had worn off, he understood what Savassan was trying to say. True, he could not conceive of anything he hated more than the other protoss tribes. The Shelak were the protectors of the Ihan-rii artifacts. But what if the stones, and tools, and other strange items they could not even understand were not the only legacy that the Ihan-rii had left the protoss on that dark day when they had ascended into their ships and left Aiur behind forever?

What if the legacy had been the protoss themselves? How could attacking each other be the answer then?

"I knew I had chosen wisely," came Savassan's thought in his mind. "But even I, I who saw your potential, Temlaa—even I could not have anticipated how well you would grasp this. The capturing of ideas that we have created—once this knowledge is shared, then we will be able to communicate with other protoss a long distance away, as well as with our own tribe. Once we have somehow deciphered what the Ihan-rii were saying on their artifacts—that, too, must be shared with other tribes. Proud as I am to have been born into the Shelak tribe, I am not so arrogant as to think that we are the only ones who think this way. We are fortunate in that we were born into a tribe that encourages such things. Can you imagine if you had been born into the Akilae or the Ara? Where you would be killed for simply wondering if perhaps the Ihan-rii cared for us even though they left? Or perhaps told by your elders that the Great Teachers were evil?"

It was all almost too much for Jake to handle. Savassan

sat beside him, and together they stared into the twilight. He wondered if Savassan was right, if somewhere out there was a protoss of the Akilae tribe who looked up into the purple dusk and wondered about the Wanderers from Afar.

"How?" was all he asked.

Savassan understood. "We trust that we are on the right track," he replied. "We trust that bit by bit, little by little, we are on our way to uncovering what it was the Ihan-rii intended for us. They left us, Temlaa. Because we were flawed, somehow. They left us behind. But they left other things behind, too, with the artifacts that we cherish so deeply. Maybe we can use what they left behind to move further along the path they originally intended for us to travel. Once we understand what they wanted, I believe with all my heart that the other protoss will listen. Others hunger for what we are going to discover, Temlaa. They just don't understand what it is they yearn for. But once we find it—I know we will no longer be alone."

It was both a frightening and a reassuring thought. While it was seductive to think that only the Shelak would uncover the ancient lost secrets, and would then keep them all to themselves, at Savassan's words Jake found he wanted to share the information. He tried to imagine a dozen . . . a hundred protoss, of every color and tribe, sitting in harmony and agreement.

He found he couldn't.

"Savassan. . . ."

"Give it time, Temlaa," Savassan said gently in Jake's mind. "The healing will not happen in a day. It may not even happen in our lifetimes."

"But . . . you do believe it will happen?"

"Yes," Savassan *sent firmly. "With every fiber of my being, I believe this."*

Jacob Jefferson Ramsey awoke with tears in his eyes, wishing he could reach back through time to Temlaa and Savassan, whoever they were, and tell them what he knew.

Tell them . . . that Savassan had been right.

CHAPTER 16

THUNDER BOOMED. WIND RUSTLED THE BRANCHES, and whispers and creaks and groaning sounds arose. A crash of lightning illuminated the darkness of the world beneath the canopy of thickly entwined trees, throwing it into stark relief. Jake's eyes narrowed against the brightness, then struggled to readjust. His mind was wide open to the thoughts of the creatures around him. Although he knew that if any hostile protoss were also seeking refuge here, he would likely not sense them. He clutched the precious hide closer, folding it close to his body, shivering as his purple skin was drenched even here under the canopy. Jake and Savassan were more grateful than ever for their map of—

Jake blinked, for one wild second still in the dream, in the memories, and yet simultaneously fully cognizant of his identity outside of the Shelak protoss known as Temlaa. Temlaa didn't know that word, but Jake did.

"Yes," said Zamara. He could almost imagine her sitting beside him now. "You are starting to integrate the memories. You are bringing Jake to Temlaa, bringing your own theories and concepts and understanding."

"Can . . . can I help them?"

"No. These are things that have already happened, long, long ago, when we were a young race. You cannot alter anything you see here. Bring yourself fully to this experience, Jacob, but do not try to shut out Temlaa, either. Only when you feel as he feels and yet know what Jacob Jefferson Ramsey knows will you have grasped the subtleties of becoming a Preserver."

"A Preserver?"

But she was silent now, and he continued to experience the unfolding. The two protoss had grasped the concept of writing, of maps, of—

—their travels, for they had drawn the locations of caves and other areas where they could place the hides while they went exploring. They had been setting out to investigate a new one, but rain had caught them unawares and they had ducked into the first shelter they had found. But now, Savassan read Jake's thoughts and sent, "We should get to that cave." He pointed to a dark smudge against the foothills. Jake nodded agreement, folded the skin as tightly as he could against his body, and together they raced for the entrance.

"Cave" was hardly the proper word for it. It was really just a slight opening in an embankment, and as they headed toward it Jake wondered if it would offer any more protection than the canopy. They reached it and slipped inside, shivering. Jake risked a look down at the skin.

"It seems to be all right," he sent, but Savassan's thoughts struck him like a blow from a shikma and he whirled.

There was little light, but a single shaft of rain-dimmed sunlight from the entrance knifed through the darkness and struck something that glittered.

Slowly, they moved forward, squeezing through the narrow aperture between the walls of rock and earth, Jake still careful to protect the skin and the writing it bore. Then completely unexpectedly, the passageway opened up into a cavern. The two protoss stared.

Dozens of stones, translucent as water but radiating muted light in shades of green and purple and blue, illuminated the cavern. They were enormous, as tall as any relic left by the Ihan-rii that Jake had ever seen. At the bottom of each pillar of these shafts of light given solid form, like younglings sitting at the feet of their elders, were dozens, perhaps hundreds of smaller ones. Each was beautiful, perfect. Some were tiny, barely the size of Jake's hand, others the size of spears. Beneath his feet, the earth felt slightly warm.

"This cavern . . . it's like the inside of the temple!"

"Indeed," Zamara said in Jake's mind. "Indeed . . . it is quite similar."

"Is this why you wanted me to see Temlaa's memories?"

"It is one reason among many."

"But there's no humming."

"No humming. At least . . . not yet."

Jake recalled Rosemary's dismissive comment: *A*

bunch of pretty standing stones . . . he wanted a big payoff for a room that was so difficult to enter.

If only Valerian knew what kind of payoff there really *had* been inside the chamber.

"I have never seen anything so beautiful. They look like . . . like shafts of light, or spears."

Savassan nodded. "I have lived long, and even I have not seen anything like this." He gazed at the crystals, then slowly, as if drawn, stepped forward and placed his hand on the smooth surface of one of the largest crystals, as he had so often done with the Ihan-rii relics.

His back arched suddenly. Every muscle in his body went rigid. Jake uttered a mental cry of alarm and tackled his mentor, clutching him around the midsection, pulling him away from the beautiful but clearly dangerous objects. He stumbled on the uneven cave floor, and they both fell hard.

"Savassan! Savassan, are you all right?"

Savassan did not reply at once. Jake reached to touch his mind and for a second encountered nothing. Panic flooded him. "Savassan!"

Savassan blinked his eyes and touched Jake's mind immediately, reassuring the frightened youth.

"I am all right. Better than all right. I—Temlaa, the crystals—I touched them and—it was as if suddenly all kinds of thoughts . . . no, not thoughts—feelings—were flowing through me. And there was . . . something about it. . . ."

He shook his head, unable even to think the words. "This will change everything, Temlaa. Everything. This is what we have been hoping to find." Savassan got to his feet, seemingly unharmed.

"Go ahead, Temlaa. Touch the crystal. It will feel overwhelming at first, but it will not hurt you. Feel what I felt . . . know what I now know. You have earned this moment. Take it."

On legs that trembled only a little, Jake walked the few steps to the jumble of glowing stones at the foot of the monolithic crystals that filled the cave, this cave they had almost missed, this simple gash in the side of a hill, so deceptively nondescript to hide such treasures. He extended a hand that shook, and gently laid it on the cool, smooth surface.

It snaked into his mind, coolly and subtly at first, weaving itself in and around his thoughts. The intensity increased, and Jake felt his body tense—

Lying asleep on the floor, wrapped in blankets, Jake tensed.

"Be easy," Zamara soothed, as she had before. "Open your thoughts. Trust me. You are simply taking another step into this world."

He was learning to trust her. But then again . . . he had no other choice.

—as thoughts that were so far beyond thoughts settled into his very bones. It was more than thought, it was feeling, it was sensation, emotion, and without knowing fully what he was doing Jake had turned to Savassan and touched his mind even as one hand still grasped the crystal.

"I—I can feel your thoughts, master," he sent. Joy and

awe flooded him, and he felt it wash into Savassan's consciousness like a wave surging up onto a beach. And like the tide receding he felt the thoughts and feelings return to him, followed this time by Savassan's emotions of shock and delight and a deep, deep sense of gratitude for the opportunity to harness this gift.

Then suddenly it was too much and Jake released the crystal. At once the feelings that were not his own subsided and the only thing that brushed his mind were thoughts.

He stumbled, dizzy, and Savassan caught him and supported him.

"I felt your emotions," Savassan said. Jake inhaled rapidly through his nostrils, trying to recover. "Not just your thoughts, Temlaa. Your feelings. And you felt mine, I know you did."

"Yes," Jake managed. It felt so . . . distant to be speaking only with words in Savassan's mind. He had thought they understood each other, were friends as well as colleagues, but now that they had been able to exchange not only information but feelings in their minds Jake realized how separate the protoss were from one another. He clumsily formed the thought. Savassan nodded.

"How terribly isolated we have become! And . . . how strangely familiar it felt. Not to me personally, but . . ."

"As if it is a memory deeper than your own memory. As if it is in our blood somehow."

The words sounded so bizarre. How could he possibly convince those who did not feel such things with so foolish an argument?

"We will not have to," Savassan responded. "This is what

we have sought, Temlaa. I think they are from the Ihan-rii, *or connected with them somehow. I believe that with these crystals we can decipher the communications written on the artifacts. They will teach us things we can only imagine . . . things we cannot even imagine. Temlaa—we do not know how much we do not know."*

Savassan went again to the crystals, although he did not touch them this time. "Help me gather a few now. We will return with the rest of the Shelak for more. We will work with these. We can begin to unlock the secrets of the Wanderers from Afar. We will learn their knowledge, learn what they wanted for us . . . and become everything we were meant to be."

"Jake?"

The voice belonged to a female, but not Zamara. It was a voice in his ears, not his mind, and Jake slowly opened his eyes.

Rosemary was looking down at him with concern. She held something in her hand from which steam wafted. "You've been asleep for a long time. I was starting to get worried."

Still somewhat sleepily, as if he had been doing it all his life, as if he were Temlaa or Zamara and not Jacob Jefferson Ramsey, he touched her mind without really considering what he was doing. To his surprise, she had spoken the truth. She had been worried for him. The shock of the revelation woke him up more fully and quickly, and embarrassed that he was snooping, he retreated from her thoughts.

"Thanks," he said, sitting up. He sniffed, and his stomach growled. "That for me?" he asked, indicating the reheated MRE she held.

"Compliments of the Dominion—only the finest cuisine," Rosemary replied, grinning and handing it to Jake. She retrieved another for herself and sat down on the floor cross-legged. Peeling back the cover, she sniffed and then sighed as the same muddled, indecipherable food-scent wafted up.

"Stupid of me, but each time I keep hoping. Care to tell me what you were dreaming about? It looked pretty intense."

He frowned and jabbed at the food with a fork. "Why should I share anything with you?" Every time he thought about what she'd done to him and his friends, he got angry with her all over again. What really bothered him, though, was that sometimes, he forgot to remember. Sometimes, he started thinking of Rosemary Dahl, killer for hire, as a human being.

She sighed and shrugged. "Maybe because other than the alien in your brain, I'm the only one around to talk to."

"Maybe she's better company."

"Jeez, forget I said anything," she said, getting to her feet. He scowled at her. But there was something in her tone. . . .

Before he realized what he was doing he was in her thoughts again. And for the second time in almost as many minutes, she surprised him. R. M. really had been curious. She wanted to know. She was interested in what was going on with him. Part of it was boredom—he sensed that—but part of it was true interest. He brushed something else as well, a craving for something, an . . . addiction? Cigarettes. And maybe something harder.

He pulled back out of her thoughts at once. *I have no right to take the moral high ground*, he thought. *Eavesdropping like that.*

"Zamara . . . the protoss who initially made the contact with me . . . she's been helping me to adjust to everything."

Rosemary raised an eyebrow. "I see." She made no move to sit back down.

"She's . . . some kind of memory-keeper. And she's taken me back to the origins of the protoss. They were horribly primitive, Rosemary. Really violent and . . . kinda scary."

"Protoss? Those poised and shiny things?" Rosemary was now obviously intrigued, and resumed her seat.

He nodded and kept eating. "Shocked the hell out of me. But . . . I've been following two in particular. I've watched them figure out writing, and maps. And now they've found these crystals. Big, beautiful, glowing things. Ring a bell?"

She laughed. "You're kidding me. The same type of crystals as in the cavern?"

"Yep. But there's something special about them if you're a protoss, apparently. Savassan—the older protoss—touched one, and it helped him understand his protégé better."

Her brow furrowed. "That's what made them able to read minds? Those crystals?"

"No, no, they could already do that. But the crystals helped them sense each other's emotions. It's kind of like . . ." Jake floundered. In the dream, when he was experiencing it, it was so clear. Crystal clear, to make a dreadful pun. Now that he understood how to read thoughts as the protoss did, at least somewhat, he was finding human speech clumsy and ineffective.

"It's like reading song lyrics," he said. "You can read the lyrics as a poem, and get the basic information. But when you add a melody to it, and a voice, it becomes something different entirely."

Rosemary paused, a forkful of something gray halfway to her mouth, and grinned.

"Damn, Jake, you're turning into a poet."

He blushed. "Well . . . the protoss are a poetic people."

She raised an eyebrow skeptically. "I'm afraid I don't look at them and think 'poetry.'"

He said, very seriously, "That's because you haven't been one."

CHAPTER 17

HATE AND DISGUST FUELED HIM.

Jake felt it surging through his body, pumping with his blood, filling him to overflowing. It was pure, it was sweet, and he reveled in it.

His tribe did not know where the Shelak hid the abominations, but that was all right. The Furinax would concentrate on eliminating the Shelak, and—

"Whoa, whoa, I'm Shelak! I'm Temlaa!"

"You are Jacob Jefferson Ramsey," Zamara replied with maddening calm. "You are not Temlaa. You were only reliving his memories."

"Who's this guy? He's trying to hurt the Shelak."

"Of course he is. You need to understand him as well as Temlaa. You need to know him to the bone if you are to be a proper caretaker of these memories. I bear the memories of every protoss who has ever lived, Jacob. Soon, so will you. Be silent, and learn."

• • •

—leave the offending relics of the Great Betrayers behind to succumb to weather and time. Let the jungles reclaim them. Let . . .

Jake hunched his shoulders and shivered. His skin became mottled with his grief. Even now, even so long after the Great Betrayers departed, the wound was raw among the Furinax. Why? Why had they gone? Why did the Shelak persist in honoring them? The Furinax had tried to tell them. They had tried to tell the Shelak that the Great Betrayers were not worth honoring. And there were rumors that the Wanderers from Afar did not mean the protoss well, though the details had eroded with time the way stone did. Jake loved the Great Betrayers—he hated them—he raged and whimpered. Whatever was the truth, he knew one thing: The Shelak were foolish in their blind adulation.

Jake clenched his fists as his skin picked up the scent of two Shelak who had wandered too far from the safety of the village. He closed his thoughts off from them, and began to stalk.

"I don't want to see this. I don't want to *be* this."

"Yet you were Temlaa, and with his hands, you slew the Furinax."

"That was different."

"No," and Zamara's mental voice was adamant. "No. There is no difference. Veskaar's feelings of fear and hatred are no worse and no better than Temlaa's. A Shelak is no different from a Furinax. You must grasp this!"

• • •

"Yo, Sleeping Beauty, your mush is getting cold."

Jake bolted upright, relieved.

You cannot avoid this.

I can for now.

Zamara grudgingly subsided. Jake gratefully took the reheated MRE and peeled back a corner.

"We're a couple of days out. Soon we'll be having hot baths and eating real food," R. M. said.

"Sounds like . . . paradise," Jake quipped.

"Not quite," she said, grinning at the joke. "So, one thing I've been meaning to ask you. How did you figure out how to break into that damn chamber? I bet you shocked the hell out of Val when he got my message about that."

"Pleased, yes, but shocked?"

She looked at him, and if he wasn't indulging in wishful thinking, he thought there was a hint of compassion in her eyes. "Jake . . . you know you weren't the first. You were actually kind of . . . the bottom of the barrel as far as Valerian was concerned. He'd tried all the top people first. You were a desperate, against-all-odds, last-ditch effort. He'd tried everything reasonable, so he brought in someone who wasn't."

Her voice was kinder than he'd ever heard it before, and he tried to hide his surprise, embarrassment, and disappointment. "Really? Well, I am a crackpot, you know."

She looked at him for a long moment. "Right," she said. "So, Professor Crackpot, how did you manage to do something the quote-unquote real scientists couldn't?" She flopped over on her back, tearing open a packet of something dried and pouring it into her mouth. Her hair spread out in a blue-black halo beneath her head. She looked up at him, her blue eyes curious.

Jake's breath caught. He focused on the question.

"I realized I was trying too hard to think like a protoss. Which was foolish, because no one knows what a protoss thinks like." He quickly amended, "Well, no one did then. I guess I do now, at least a little. So I was wandering around that night, and I looked at some of the fossils near the temple. And I realized I had to think on a grander scale. I had to think universally. And looking at the fossils, I was reminded of the Golden Mean."

"What the hell's a Golden Mean?"

"It's a mathematic ratio found over and over again in nature and in art and music. One to one point six. It's called phi."

"Fee?"

"P-h-i," he spelled out, sketching the symbol for it in his cold mashed potato-like substance.

Rosemary tilted her head and looked at it upside down. "Ah, okay." She shrugged and poured some more dried crunchy things into her mouth.

"I realized the rectangle was drawn in that ratio, so I calculated where it would start. It's called a Fibonacci spiral. I put my hand on it and then moved it in a spiral. And poof . . . open sesame."

Rosemary looked thoughtful. The combination of

the expression and the upside-down position made her look very young, and very appealing. The idea popped into Jake's mind to simply lean forward and kiss her while she was lying on the floor looking so . . . well . . . kissable. But he dismissed it at once. For one thing, he still didn't like her, no matter how attractive she looked. For another, she'd break his nose before he got within three inches of her.

He distracted himself by peeling off the covering on the so-called dessert section of the MRE. And gasped.

Rosemary flipped over quickly, following his gaze.

"Oh, my God, my God," she said, moaning a little in a way that made Jake's heart speed up. "Peach cobbler . . ."

Only one in about six hundred MREs had this dessert. Jake knew it was rare and precious. If he'd uncovered this while on the *Gray Tiger*, he'd have had offers of cigarettes and other bribes raining down upon him. It was the one thing that actually tasted *good* in an MRE.

He looked up at Rosemary, and found her blue eyes fixed on his.

Jake sighed, swallowing the moisture that had suddenly flooded his mouth. He shoved it toward her. "You take it."

She almost did, then hesitated. Her smooth white brow furrowed. "Nah. You're the one who has to deal with these crazy dreams. You should have it."

"We're in this together," Jake said. "We'll share it."

He deliberately did not read her thoughts, and so

when he saw the varied expressions that suddenly flitted about her face, he was not able to ascertain their meaning.

Together, they dipped their forks into the peach cobbler and tasted ecstasy.

Jake fell asleep after eating.

He dreamed.

He was Veskaar, and he ripped apart two of Temlaa's family, and splashed their blood on his face, and tasted the Furinax's joy.

"This . . . this has got to stop," Jake said to Zamara. His stomach churned, and he felt physically and mentally sick.

"It will," Zamara said. "But not yet."

Savassan and Jake proceeded to experiment with the crystals. They were cautious at first, as Savassan was worried that the beautiful objects might pose a danger.

"You think they are weapons?" asked Jake

"I think they could be used to cause harm. A staff can help you walk across difficult terrain. It can also bash in an enemy's head."

"It is well we were the ones to find them," Jake said. "If any other tribe had found them, they would indeed only have used them as weapons. We will try to learn from them."

"The question is . . . learn what? And what will we do with that knowledge?" Savassan asked. Jake knew he did not expect an answer.

Telkar and many others among the Shelak had indeed

viewed the powerful crystals solely as weapons. It was only because Savassan was so respected that they had backed away from clamoring for better ways to kill their enemies—for a time at least.

"Our numbers decrease," Telkar had said. "We are being singled out by all the tribes. We need a way to defend ourselves, Savassan. And if these crystals will do so, then we must use them."

"A little more time," Savassan had pleaded. "We are the keepers of the relics. We need to understand them."

"If we are all slain to the last child by the other tribes," Telkar had shot back direly, "the relics will have no guardians at all."

They stepped up their pace. Both Jake and Savassan had had sufficient exposure that they were able to touch the crystals—Savassan had named them "khaydarin" crystals, which meant "Focuser of the heart"—and be quite comfortable with the resulting sensations. They progressed to being able to experience the sharing of emotions without touching the crystals at all, but simply by being in close proximity to them.

Too, as Savassan had suspected, they became more and more attuned to the relics. There were indeed stories here. They began to understand what some of the symbols in the artifacts meant. They were able to weave together something that allowed them to learn still other stories, uncover still more. Savassan was now engrossed in something he called a "mystery." Something that he was convinced would lead him still further along the trail of learning.

"There is more here . . . so very much more," he said to

Jake once. "And we are running out of time to grasp it all. It astonishes me, how ignorant we are. How far beyond us the Ihan-rii were."

More progress was made. They discovered that they no longer needed to use the crystals in order to sense one another's feelings as they had at the outset. At first it had been overwhelming, frightening, but now Jake found he felt enriched by the intensified contact. It felt right. It felt, as Savassan had theorized, as though it was something they had been meant to achieve. So now, Jake was bathed with the sense of awe and wonder that rolled softly off of his mentor like water over a smooth stone.

He sensed also Savassan's frustration. The kwah-kai, little primates who made their homes in the canopy, were known among the Shelak for their curiosity. They often figured in cautionary tales as to what could happen if young Shelak grew too curious.

"I always admired Little Hands," Savassan sent, and Jake sent back a wave of amusement. He, too, had admired the character Little Hands for his curiosity, even though the stories had been meant to warn him away from such traits rather than encourage him. Little Hands would be doing exactly what they were, he thought. As if to confirm this, one of the red-striped creatures suddenly landed on a branch near them, peered at them with bright yellow eyes, and chattered before leaping off to another branch and another adventure, its little hands . . . and little feet and little tail . . . bearing it securely on in its quest for more mischief.

Warm humor was shared between the two protoss. Although Jake was certain that anything they would uncover would have far greater ramifications than anything in any of the Little Hands stories.

If they had enough time to find it all.

Jake slept deeply, and he knew he slept, and he clung to that knowledge frantically, because this dream was the worst nightmare he had ever had.

He had been in caves, of course; he had even slept in the Cave of Relics, where the Shelak had placed all the artifacts from the Ihan-rii. But the cave in his dream was much different. He had never been so deep beneath the surface of Aiur before. So far away from the life-giving light that all protoss required. The darkness was cool and enveloping, but somehow Jake was not comforted at all. This was not the darkness he was used to, the darkness of the night, with the moon and stars above and the rustling of the wind and the familiar sounds of nocturnal creatures. This was a darkness that concealed rather than protected. He didn't know how he knew it, but he did.

Objects began to materialize to his vision in the darkness, images of certain specific artifacts. One was the obelisk. Except in the dream, it was not broken and damaged, with most of its once impressive height shattered and lost, but completely intact. This was what he had seen with his waking eyes, analyzed with his conscious mind. It soared upward, the flat black surface crawling with writing that Jake ached to read—

—Damn. I wish I could see this obelisk. I'd love to analyze it, see just how old it is, if I could make any sense of the writing myself. Darius was the linguist of the bunch; God, I miss him—

Others were there too: the shattered pillar they had found, whole and glorious; and what had only been broken chunks of stone now took on shape and hue and form. Still others appeared and faded out of Jake's vision, until he was so frustrated at the loss of knowledge that he forgot to be afraid.

In his frustration, he ceased to be a passive participant in the dream. A small piece of a stone tablet hovered just over his head, turning slowly end over end. Jake clutched at it. Long purple fingers closed over rough stone. Suddenly the thing had weight and he had to grab it quickly with his other hand to stop it from falling and shattering.

He brought it up, seeing the images as clearly as if the tablet had been made anew. There was no wearing away by time, no defacement by other angry protoss tribes, no stains or damage of any sort. Jake's eyes flew over it and he understood, he—

Jake bolted up from the sleeping furs, flailing. The only light came from the glowing crystals. Savassan was up instantly, having felt the blast of excitement from Jake's mind.

"I need tools to write!"

Savassan was the one obeying his student now, moving quickly to gather a sharpened stick from the fire and locating a cured hide while Jake laid his hands on the nearest crystal and caused the strength of its illumination to grow. Jake was on his feet, carrying one of the crystals with him as he went deeper into the Cave of Relics to locate the artifact he had seen in his dream. Savassan followed him silently, simply waiting and watching.

After a few moments of searching, Jake located the item he needed. He began to copy what he could see of it here, now, onto the parchment. Once had had done so, he closed his eyes. He again saw the tablet, whole and newly carved, and when he opened his eyes he methodically began to draw what he had seen. He didn't try to translate the symbols, not yet; he just wanted to capture them before the dream had faded so far that this insight was again lost to him.

"You saw these in the dream?" Savassan asked, gazing raptly down at the writing.

"Yes. This tablet and many others."

Savassan nodded. "I saw them too. The symbols fading in and out, too quickly for me to read them."

Jake said with some embarrassment, "I grew frustrated and grabbed this one. When I touched it, the symbols stopped disappearing."

Jake felt surprise, amusement, and admiration wash over him from Savassan. "Your impetuousness has gained us more than we perhaps know." His eyes moved quickly over the symbols. "This looks like a description of a place."

Jake shuddered. "Perhaps the cave we saw in the dream."

"I think that likely. But the description is incomplete yet. We will need to know more."

Now that Jake had discovered that in his dreams he could touch the artifacts, both he and Savassan were able to direct their dreams. They would awaken and scribble down every-

thing they had seen. At one point, as Savassan was perusing the symbols, he suddenly paled and sat back, shaking. Jake did not even need to ask, "What is it?" For clearly radiating from Savassan was the revelation:

"These are directions."

"Directions to what?"

"I do not know. But my heart swells at the thought."

They set out, following the directions that had come to Jake in the dream. It took two days, but finally they found the spot they were searching for. Disappointment surged through Jake. It seemed their goal was nothing more, and nothing less, than a large cluster of khaydarin crystals, jutting up like spears from the flat earth. The area was rocky and barren, and so it was no surprise that it had remained undisturbed and, fortunately, undamaged for so long.

Jake said hesitantly, "They are beautiful . . . but I thought we were to find the entrance to another cave."

Savassan's mental voice was resigned and yet still hopeful. "Let us touch these and see what they have to tell us."

Both protoss reached forward and laid respectful purple hands on the flat, cool surface of the crystals. Almost at once, information began imparting itself to them. Fragmented, difficult to comprehend, but information nonetheless. Jake released one and placed his hands on another. More, different information filled his mind. His head began to ache.

"We must touch them in a certain order," Savassan said, putting the last piece of the puzzle together.

"But . . . what is the correct order?" Jake look chagrined. There were literally hundreds of crystals here. Which ones were important? And how would they possibly know?

Jake looked at his mentor, then down at his hands. He saw the fingers, long and delicate, resting on the crystal. It was as if he saw them for the first time. The nails, the joints, the articulation in them. Three bones in each finger, each relating to one another in a certain way. The wind blew, and Jake's attention was diverted to the single tree that grew here and its leaves as they rustled and shifted.

"Yes!" Jake almost cheered. "He's so close!"

"He is. They are. This is a precious and powerful moment in our history," Zamara said.

"I wish I could reach back through time and tell him he's about to discover something wonderful."

He sensed dry humor from Zamara. "You have no idea how often I have felt such a thing myself. Regretfully, we can only observe. We cannot change. It can be . . ."

"Frustrating as hell."

Zamara agreed.

Beside him, Savassan was also looking at his hands and the leaves. Then he lifted the necklace of seashells that he wore and regarded them. The center shell was that of some sort of mollusk. It was beautiful, curving and pleasant to touch and look upon.

Then, to Jake's horror, he lifted the beautiful object and brought it smashing down on a rock. Jake stared aghast at the broken pieces. There was one particularly large chunk still intact, and Jake could see the chambers that the creature built for itself as it grew.

"Savassan!" Jake sent, horrified. *"That was an ancient necklace, one given to you with great honors. Why have you destroyed it?"*

Savassan turned lambent eyes on his student. "It is more than that," he sent, the words laced with an emotion so powerful it almost swept Temlaa away. It was awe, wonder, excitement, fear, joy, all mixed together in one extreme sensation. Jake almost cringed from it. *"It is a secret . . . a puzzle for us."*

"A puzzle. A secret. You remembered," Jake said to Zamara. "You remembered this moment. When the protoss figured out the Golden Mean. That's why you set up the door to the chamber that way."

"Yes," Zamara said. "We call it ara'dor, which means perfect ratio. They needed to think outside their own thoughts. They needed to turn to something larger than themselves . . . something unchanging and universal. As did you."

"You didn't expect me to come along and figure it out," Jake thought, grinning to himself.

"I did not," Zamara agreed bluntly. "I was terribly disappointed. I feared my one opportunity had been squandered."

He tried to read her thoughts, and sensed that she still had not decided if she had been right or wrong.

It was the same—the shell, the veins on the leaves, his own fingers. Each progressive section was slightly longer than the one before, and he narrowed his eyes at the precision, the beauty, of it.

"Wh-what does it mean?" Jake asked.

Savassan was busy unpacking the one large Ihan-rii tablet they always carried with them. This one had the most variety of markings on it, so it was useful in case they came across any other artifacts they needed to decipher. He placed it down, his hands shaking. The tablet was not a perfect square. Its width was not as long as its length . . . and the ratio was . . .

"It's the same," send Temlaa, almost reeling. "The Ihan-rii saw all this. They knew."

As one, the two protoss turned to the collection of crystals. Temlaa saw now that they were not arranged in a haphazard way. There was an order to them, a deliberateness that had escaped him.

He looked down at his hands, then up at Savassan.

Savassan's eyes closed in a half smile. "You do it, my student," he said. "The honor is yours."

Jake turned to the crystals, then looked again at the broken seashell. It seemed to originate in a spot slightly off center. It was as good a place as any to start.

Jake leaned forward and touched the crystal, then moved anti-sunwise, emulating the swirls in the seashell. One . . . one point six. He touched the next crystal and suddenly both crystals began to glow more strongly, emitting a faint hum. Each crystal had its own note, but they blended perfectly, caressing his ears.

"There's the humming."

"Yes. Here it is."

• • •

Jake jerked back, startled, and glanced wildly at Savassan. The older protoss, too, looked surprised, but more intrigued than alarmed. He nodded for Jake to continue.

One . . . one point six. A third lit up. Another note added to the melody. Jake's heart sped up with anticipation and not a little fear. He continued the process. The crystals he had touched now pulsated and the sound was incredibly beautiful, haunting and penetrating, shivering along his bones and into his blood and heart.

Finally, only one remained in the pattern. Jake glanced at Savassan, who nodded. Slowly, Jake reached out a hand and touched the last crystal.

The earth rumbled, and Jake and Savassan both leaped back. The crystals were singing now, their melody sweet and pure and intense. To Jake's utter astonishment, lines began to appear around the cluster of crystals, forming a rectangle. The ratio of the rectangle was, of course, one to one point six. The rectangle of earth slowly began to rise, lifting from the ground as surely as if it had been cut and raised by an unseen hand. It hovered above them, small clods of dirt the only thing to mar the perfection of the moment. Jake stared up at it wildly for a second, terrified that it would come crashing down upon them. Then, even though his fear was great, his curiosity was greater, and he looked down to see what the rectangle had revealed.

Below was not brown earth. Below was not even a cave in the truest sense. No naturally occurring cave was this perfect, this beautiful. The walls, while still clearly of earth and stone, were also somehow . . . more. Some kind of metal had been woven into it, like a bright golden thread in a dark

*brown blanket. It caught the dawn's light and reflected it
back. Steps had been cut into the earth so precisely that every
line was perfect. Crystals, embedded into the wall, lit the way
down into the heart of the ground.*

They stood at the entrance of the steps as if frozen in place.

*"This was what we were led to discover," said Savassan.
"This is our destiny, Temlaa. We cannot turn away from it
now."*

*Jake still stood for a long moment, emotions surging
inside him. Then slowly, carefully, the two protoss began to
enter the secret heart of the earth.*

"A cave, huh?"

"Yes. If they found the khaydarin crystals in one
accidentally, I wonder what they'll find in one that
came to them in a dream."

"Zamara should just tell you," Rosemary said. She
was ever the pragmatist. Sitting in the pilot's chair,
she reflected on the situation with Jake Ramsey. At
first, all she had cared about was that he housed information her employer would be happy to hear about.
When Jake had begun talking about his experience,
she'd just smiled and nodded. But now . . .

She'd never been much on learning about either
the protoss or the zerg, except insofar as they affected
business. She'd learned where to shoot to kill them
effectively, and where she was likely to encounter
them, but that was largely it. Now, however, she had
heard some things about them from Jake that
intrigued and actually fascinated her. She was think-

ing so hard that when the console started to beep she actually started. Jake jumped about a foot. They caught each other's eyes and laughed.

"We're in Dead Man's space," she said. "No word from Ethan, so I think it's clear of Dominion. Buckle up, Jake. The fun is about to begin."

CHAPTER 18

ROSEMARY SET THE POD DOWN IN A SMALL clearing about four kilometers outside the city limits. She landed the vessel deftly, guiding it with practiced ease into a niche beneath an overhanging rock. "Can't believe no one's taken my spot yet," she said, pleased. "This thing'll be completely hidden from the air. Looks like our luck may be turning around."

She shut everything down and went to ransack the weapons locker. She pulled out no fewer than five handheld pistol-type weapons and tossed him two. He caught one and dropped the other. She sighed.

Rosemary wavered between the AGR-14 gauss rifle that seemed to be a part of her and a shotgun. In the end, she selected the shotgun. "Lighter and every bit as effective at close range. If we ever need to use a weapon," she said, "frankly the handguns will be the best. It'll be an up-close-and-personal attack here. You know how to use these?"

He nodded, a bit sickened at the thought, and fastened the two handguns to the belt she gave him. She paused, eyeing him. "The lack of showering helps you," she said. "You look unconvincing enough as it is. Try not to look so worried, okay?"

"I'll attempt to be as grubby and menacing as possible," he said dryly.

"Just . . . stick close, okay? With any luck we won't be here for more than an hour. Ethan said I'd recognize the person who will be meeting us, and I know exactly where it's going to take place." She looked him up and down again. "Maybe you should stay here. I can come back for you."

"Like hell," he said.

"Just don't screw anything up, all right? Let me handle whatever comes."

"I'm completely fine with that."

With a smooth, practiced gesture, Rosemary slipped the shotgun around so that it hung over her back. "Then let's go to Paradise."

Jake had been on his share of wretched planets in his time, and though this place couldn't hold a candle to the misery of Gelgaris, it was bad enough. It was rocky and stark and the sky was a sick shade of red-brown. Fine dust of the same hue covered everything. The outskirts of Paradise were crowded with small shanties. Smells of cooking combined with the stench of oil, the acrid red dust, and the reek of unwashed bodies as Jake and Rosemary strode forward. He felt eyes boring into him, heard the sounds of rifles being chambered.

He and Rosemary walked side by side. Out of the corner of his eye, he realized that there were forms walking parallel to them. Jake kept his eyes forward and continued to walk. Suddenly he started and lifted his hand to his face. It came away wet and shiny with a gobbet of spit.

Rosemary whirled and fired the shotgun. The man who had spat on Jake stumbled, blood erupting from dozens of holes made by adamantine slugs, then fell. Jake stared.

Say nothing. Do nothing. The voice in his head brooked no disagreement.

Rosemary looked around, shotgun still at the ready. "Anyone else feeling the need to expectorate?" she challenged. Jake tore his gaze from the dead man. There was a handful of people, men and women both, who looked hard and angry and lethal. None of them was watching him now, though. Their attention was caught and held by the tiny girl with the blue-black, bobbed hair and the great big smoking gun.

"I didn't think so," Rosemary said. She turned and caught Jake's eye. "Kick the body," she said softly.

"What?" he whispered frantically.

"Do it."

Do so, Jacob.

Jake drew back his leg and kicked the body hard. It jerked, and he felt bile rise in his throat.

"Now turn and let's go. Look pissed off."

He did his best to obey. His back tingled as if he were being physically touched by the eyes boring into it.

"Probably for the best," R. M. said. "Word will go ahead and it's likely it'll be quiet for us." She looked up at him and grinned fleetingly. "Told you this was a tough place."

He did not reply.

The town itself was more of the same, but worse. Worse because it was crowded and loud and there were more buildings from which people could safely fire at them. Most of the buildings were standard-issue prefab, though they had all seen better days. Some were shored up with the stone that seemed to be the only building material available on the planet and pieces of debris from vessels. Jake knew that sometimes colonies fell prey to bad elements, little towns that once had churches and shops and family homes falling in disrepair. This was not a place that had once been anything other than what he now saw before him. It had only, ever, been this cesspool.

Rosemary looked around with sharp blue eyes. "I don't see anyone I know," she said, frowning a little. "But if there were any Dominion sniffing about it wouldn't be this calm. Come on, let's get off the street."

She took his arm and steered him toward a dilapidated building. He braced himself for raucous brawls and weapons fire. Instead, the silence was eerie as they approached. The door was old and battered. R. M. paused for a second. He looked at her, surprised, and before he realized what he was doing he'd read her thoughts.

Rosemary knew this place well. Too well. She'd

spent countless days here and was unhappy at the thought of being back. As she opened the door, a sickly scent rushed out, and he struggled to keep from coughing.

Their thoughts assaulted him. Chaotic, mad, angry, ecstatic, the thoughts and feelings wormed their way into his brain, twined around him, bathed him in softness and sensation, jabbed him with a delirium gone sickly wrong—

He staggered back a step, and Rosemary shot him an angry look.

Altered minds are disconcerting and sometimes difficult to manage, Zamara sent, oddly comforting. He felt her gently close out the unwanted, frightening images, inserting her presence between him and them like a protective shield. And he'd thought normal, everyday thoughts from sane and drug-unclouded minds were hard to handle.

He was shaking. Rosemary stepped close to unobtrusively steady him. He looked down at her, shocked. He vaguely remembered her saying that this was where she and Ethan had had their first "date." He recalled her craving for a cigarette, a slight hint of something else—

And then an understanding hit him. Rosemary Dahl was a recovering addict.

And she'd met Ethan Stewart in a drug den.

She frowned at him and gave him a slight shake. "Keep it together," she whispered fiercely, then turned to survey the room. Shakily, he emulated her.

There are no thoughts here you need to read, Jacob, sent Zamara. Again, though concern was laced through the words, Jake found them calming.

His eyes were growing accustomed to the dim lighting. There were no windows here, nor chairs, only soiled mattresses and pillows strewn all over on the floor. The addicts were splayed atop the filthy padding like dead bodies. Only the soft moans of pain or ecstasy and the subtle shifting indicated that they hadn't reached the end result of their addictions. Young women and men moved back and forth, carrying towels and buckets of water, washing up the mess that those who were too dazed to relieve themselves in the designated areas had left behind. In the faint glow provided only by cheap flashlights, Jake caught a glimpse of something glinting around their necks.

Were these people . . . *slaves*?

Before he could do anything other than stare, Rosemary was threading him through the room toward another door. "It's better in there," she said. "This is the room for the cheap stuff."

Inside the center room, it was quieter and cleaner. There were still moans and still people sprawled on the floor, still the reek of some kind of smoke, but there was not the stomach-turning scent of excrement and unwashed bodies. The floor was soft and carpeted, the pillows more lavish. And the . . . attendants here carried trays of the drugs of choice, not buckets and rags. Others sat at a bar, where they were offered beverages and smokes as well as other delicacies.

Jake hadn't realized such places existed. Rosemary looked completely unfazed. He turned to look at her, amazed that she had once joined those writhing on the floor of this hovel, amazed that she had been able to turn her back on this and become a master of a profession that required such intelligence, sharp reflexes, and skill.

She was scanning the room intently. Suddenly she grinned. "There's our ticket out," Rosemary whispered to him, nodding her head at a tall, muscular woman who had just entered the room. The woman looked nothing at all like Rosemary, and everything like her. They had the same posture, the same air about them, although this woman was almost as tall as Jake, and solid. Her hair had been shaved save for a long ponytail of golden blonde that hung past her waist. Her bare arms were black with a variety of tattoos that Jake couldn't make out in this dim lighting and was pretty sure he didn't want to. The woman saw Rosemary and nodded slightly. She made her way to the bar and stood beside them.

"Nice to see a familiar face," R. M. said, and added, "at least on someone who isn't stoned out of his mind."

The woman chuckled throatily. "Same here, R. M. You're looking good." Her eyes met Jake's. Jake fought the urge to quail. "This the guy?"

"He's our boy," R. M. said. "I imagine, though, that you're not here to buy us a drink or a stim-shot, Leeza."

"Not in this joint I ain't," Leeza replied in her husky voice. "Let's go."

She again looked at Jake, and something . . . shivered in him. Something was not right. He found his voice and was relieved that it sounded strong and relaxed. "How long you two know each other?"

"Six years," R. M. said. "We've been through a hell of a lot, eh Leez?"

Leeza grinned. "You can say that again. But the sooner we're out of here the better Ethan and I will like it. Let's go."

Zamara . . . ?

She dropped the barriers. Steeling himself for the onslaught of the drug-hazed thoughts and sensations, Jake focused his attention on Leeza.

Rosie ain't no fool. And Ethan'll be here any second. If I can't get this joker she's brought with her to move it's going to be too late and—

He stared at Leeza. She stared back. Rosemary glanced from one to the other. Jake shook his head "no." As Leeza moved her hand toward the holster of her handgun, R. M. whipped her own out and shot her former colleague right in the face.

Leeza's bold features were blown away in a spray of blood and bone and brain.

Jake started at the shot. Screams erupted.

"Damn it, Jake, you better have been sure about her," Rosemary cried as she shoved Jake toward the exit. Jake tripped over a sprawled body, trying not to throw up. He felt Zamara again erect the protective barriers and calmed somewhat. He scrambled to his feet and ran as fast as he could for the exit. Rosemary was firing as she went, and Jake had the strangely dispassionate thought that the poor slaves would have a lot more to clean up now than simple excrement.

"Stick close!" Rosemary yelled. Jake obeyed. They tore out the door and raced down the street. He felt Zamara shifting inside his mind, and the barriers were again lowered.

Focus, Jacob. Listen for the threat amid the fear and anger. Your lives depend upon this.

Jake thought fleetingly of Temlaa and Savassan, racing through the dark, misty rain forest of Aiur, minds alert for the thoughts of predators, animal or protoss. He clung to that image and tried to both focus and run.

—got a clear shot—

"On the left!" Jake shouted. Rosemary whirled sharply to the left and fired. There were no more thoughts from the left.

—don't know what's going on but I'm getting out of here—

Rosemary turned at the movement and Jake screamed, "No, he's just getting out of the way!"

The petite assassin hesitated, then lowered her weapon and kept running. Jake felt a flood of relief. In the midst of all this horror and slaughter, he'd just managed to save a life.

—Damn it, Trouble, what the hell do you think you're doing?

"Trouble"? Jake got a fleeting image of Rosemary lying in a bed, her black hair and pale skin contrasting vividly with the red sheet that was the only thing covering her, and—

Not his imagination, not this time. "Ethan!" he cried. "He's coming!"

Not a heartbeat later he heard the distinctive sound of approaching hover-cycles. Six of them appeared seemingly out of nowhere. Four whizzed past them, and Jake got a quick glimpse of armor and weapons firing. Two came to a sudden, abrupt stop in front of Jake and Rosemary.

The rider of the first bike was dressed in black. His skin was tan, his eyes were brown, his hair was black, and his very white teeth showed in a grin.

"Hello, Trouble. Greetings, Professor. Hop on, and hang on tight."

Jake and Rosemary hastened to obey. Rosemary leaped up behind Ethan—for it could have been no other—and wrapped her arms around him. Jake emulated her with the rider of the second bike, a large man who seemed to be made of solid muscle. Jake couldn't even see around him as they took off.

You require rest immediately, Zamara sent. *You have used up a great deal of energy in protecting yourself and in exploring the minds of others today. You did well.*

Zamara, I need to talk to this guy.

If you do not rest immediately your brain will be damaged. I cannot permit that to happen.

The scenery, if you could call it that, was a blur as it

rushed past. Jake began to feel slightly dizzy. Finally the bike slowed and stopped. He dismounted on rubbery legs, vaguely aware that there was a small, very new-looking vessel that he and Rosemary were supposed to board, vaguely aware that people were talking but that their words were gibberish, vaguely aware that the ground was rushing up to meet him with astonishing speed.

Hands grabbed him, and that was all he knew.

CHAPTER 19

THE WALLS WERE SMOOTH AT FIRST. AS THEY SLOWLY
went deeper, though, Jake noticed that the texture started to
change.

The hues were black and silver and gray, and thin, ropy
swirls gradually became apparent. Jake ran his fingers over
them. They were smooth, like vines, and for just a fraction of
an instant Jake could have sworn he felt . . . life in them.
Life? In a stone? How could such a thing be? But then
again—this was a thing of the Ihan-rii. Who knew what
was possible when they were involved? He shivered as they
continued their descent and it grew steadily colder.

Jake became aware of a faint, deep sound vibrating along
his bones. He now realized he'd been hearing it for a while,
but it was so like his own now rapid heartbeat that he
hadn't realized it was an external noise. The stairway
turned and then without warning suddenly opened up to
darkness. The light from the gems embedded in the curvy,
veiny walls seemed to stop here. Jake and Savassan came to
a halt. Jake felt air swirling gently around him and knew

that whatever lay ahead, it was in an area that was large and open. Open? So far below ground? How big was this place?

Savassan hesitated only for an instant, then put his foot down on the final step.

The light came up like a quickened dawn, soft white in contrast to the gemlike hues that had provided illumination on the stairs. The area that opened up before them was vast, the air cool and soft and clean. Stone formations jutted up from an artificially leveled floor, not ragged and bladelike but polished and carved. They were inlaid with small, blinking gems of a variety of colors. The ceiling itself was emitting the soft white illumination. It seemed to glow as if lit from within. Jake was deeply moved. All seemed balanced—the natural hue of stone and earth blending with metals, gems, and other substances that had clearly been placed there by the Ihan-rii. All had been perfectly preserved down here. Nothing had been exposed to wind or sand or water or the careless, hateful hands of protoss tribes determined to obliterate that which they could not understand. Jake thought of the world above the ground, the world that, until a few moments ago, had been the only one he had known. He thought with a flush of humility of the huts, little more than sticks held together with dried mud and covered with skins and leaves. He thought of their tools, their weapons, and the patterns they used to adorn their bodies. He thought of the necklaces of bone and shell and stones, carefully crafted by his people, and how once he had thought them beautiful. In a way they still were. But nothing he had ever seen above the ground, not even the sadly damaged relics of the Ihan-rii themselves, had prepared him for this. And somehow, Jake sensed that he had only seen a small fraction of the glories that were hidden here, tucked safely away, waiting. Waiting to be found once more by ones who would at least attempt to understand them.

He knew that he would never regard the world above-ground in quite the same way again.

Savassan moved forward now and stood by one of the pillars that had once been naturally occurring stone. He looked at the gems and motioned Jake over. Jake hurried to obey.

"Do you see?" Savassan asked his student.

Jake did, this time. There was a now familiar rectangle of gems in the pillar, all of them glowing faintly. He lifted his hand to tap out the ara'dor.

One to one point six. . . .

Each gem began to hum in a modified, softer rendition of the song the khaydarin crystals had played when he had stood aboveground. Jake touched the final gem. The song swelled and all the gems lit up for a moment, then subsided to their prior subdued glow.

A soft hum made the two protoss turn. A glowing line began to appear on the far wall, and Jake knew its proportions. The line moved rapidly, tracing a rectangle, flared, then vanished. An instant later, the outlined rectangle moved to the left with a deep grating noise and a flat platform slowly extended into the room.

Lying on the platform—shining, serpentine vines coiled around them and inside them—were six bodies. The beautiful world of dreams and humming and gleaming, shining perfection had just turned into a nightmare.

Revulsion and terror exploded from Jake, slamming into Savassan so fiercely that the other protoss stumbled. Jake himself fell hard on the stone floor and then started to scramble back to the stairs on all fours, back to the surface of the world he knew and understood, away from this secret that they never should have been able to find—

Savassan's hand on his ankle caused him to mentally shriek again, and it was several seconds before the older Shelak's calming thoughts penetrated Juke's fear-hazed brain.

"They are long dead, Temlaa; they will not harm us. Long dead, dry as grass. There is nothing to fear here."

Temlaa was not comforted. Why were there dead protoss here? He moved closer, slowly, nervously. The air in here, while breathable, was extremely dry. It was nothing like the moist air of the surface, or even that of a normal cave system. The unnatural lack of moisture meant that the protoss had not decomposed, but had rather desiccated. Jake thought that if he touched one, it would crumble to dust beneath his fingers.

They paused for a moment, honoring the dead. Savassan looked around and pointed. This one room, huge as it was, was not the only one. Oval tunnels, each perfect in its imperfection, led out in five different directions. Temlaa fumbled in the pouch at his side and found a stubby piece of charcoal. He knelt and drew a mark on the floor, then rose and looked at the tunnels.

"How do we know where to go?" Again, Jake marveled at the size and complexity and beauty of this place. Centuries it had sat here, untouched since the Wanderers from Afar

had left Aiur until this moment. No one knew. No one remembered. No one even guessed that it was here. Had any of the protoss even known? Was this a place forgotten, or discovered? How, indeed, would they know where to go?

Savassan looked at their options. "There are more mysteries here than we can begin to fathom in our lifetimes," he sent. "We have discovered one of them . . . the ara'dor. But my guess is that that is one of perhaps thousands of secrets held here. We should focus on this one. Follow the ara'dor, Temlaa."

Jake nodded. He looked at how the cavern was laid out and pointed at the tunnel that best seemed to fit the ratio. The two protoss emerged into another room that looked almost identical to the first. The only difference was that the throbbing-heartbeat sound increased. Jake made another mark on the floor. They looked around, saw more tunnels, and continued.

Jake made marks every few feet. He kept glancing back over his shoulder, as if the ghost of those long-dead protoss were following behind, smearing out the traces of their path so that the living interlopers would soon join the dead inhabitants.

Savassan glanced at him, mildly amused. "You are scaring yourself for no reason, Temlaa," he chided, and Jake ducked his head, ashamed.

The sound increased with each inward, spiraling choice they made, until at last they entered the final room. The ceiling arched above them in a demisphere. The twining vines that had enveloped the six desiccated bodies—

• • •

"Wires," Jake thought to Zamara. "Those are wires, but it looks like the stuff is somehow organic as well."

—now tangled high above them as well as around them. There were no bodies in here; the platforms were empty. But in the center, hovering and slowly moving up and down as it had no doubt done for millennia, was the largest, most perfect crystal Jake had ever seen. It pulsated as it moved languidly, and Jake realized that this was the source of the heartbeat sound. For a long moment he forgot his fear and simply gazed raptly at the object, seduced by its radiant beauty and perfection of form. He looked at the facets, at their perfect ratio, and felt like he and Savassan were kin to the long-departed Wanderers from Afar, the only ones on this abandoned world that comprehended at least some of their secrets. Or even comprehended that there were secrets at all.

Savassan was looking around intently, keeping his thoughts shielded from Jake. That, more than anything else he had beheld in this place, alarmed Jake.

"What is it, master?" he asked, using the old term of respect. He did not feel like Savassan's equal anymore, but very young and very ignorant as he looked up at the hovering, pulsating crystal.

"I think . . . I believe I understand," Savassan said quietly. "I believe the answers to . . . well, everything . . . lie right here."

Jake awoke sometime later and blinked up sleepily at the man standing beside him. *The man standing—*

Jake bolted upright, clutching the covers to his neck and staring wildly.

"Good afternoon, Professor," said the man. He was dressed in formal wear and looked to be about sixty-odd years old. His iron gray hair was perfectly styled, his blue eyes faded but clearly still sharp, his lips thin and barely moving as he spoke. "You're quite safe, I assure you. I'm Phillip Randall. I'll be your steward for the duration of your visit. Ethan Stewart has set up these quarters for you and hopes they are to your liking. If you'll excuse me, I'll notify him that you're awake. He's been most anxious to meet you."

Randall moved toward a large window and pulled back heavy curtains. Sunlight streamed in, and Jake closed his eyes for a moment at the brightness. Randall inclined his head slightly and stepped quietly out of the room. It was starting to come back to Jake now. The drug den . . . Leeza . . . the mad dash for survival . . . and Ethan Stewart, not a hair out of place, showing up just in time to rescue them. He wondered why he was so resentful of someone who'd obviously saved his life.

Whatever opinion he might hold of Stewart, Jake could not fault the man's taste. He looked around the room with something akin to awe. He had seen something this opulent only once before in his life, when he had met Valerian for a glass of port and a discussion about the discovery of wonder. That had been a glory of old weapons and armor, the glint of light on metal and the smell of cigars and leather. But it had also been austere in its own way. It was a room for study and training and reflection, indicative of the man who dwelt there. This room, perhaps also as indicative of its master, was all about the senses.

He sat up, supporting himself on overstuffed pillows. He lay on pale creamy sheets that were heavy and soft to the touch. The room had been painted a deep maroon color, and the gleam of copper was carried through from the bedposts to a padded bench at the foot of the bed.

The nightstand sported a bowl filled with fruit—grapes, pears, oranges, apples. Jake's mouth watered. Honest-to-God food. He seized an apple and bit into it, closing his eyes at the flavor.

"I thought you were going to sleep another full day." Jake's eyes flew open. Ethan Stewart lounged in the doorway, grinning. He was every bit as confident and good-looking as he had appeared to Jake on the hoverbike, and Jake did not like him any better than he did then.

"So you're the archeologist with an alien in his head. I'm Ethan Stewart. I don't know how much Rosemary's told you about me but I deny everything."

It took Jake a few seconds to realize that Ethan was joking, and then he laughed shakily.

"On a more serious note," Ethan continued, "she tells me that you two have been through quite a bit recently."

"That's an understatement," Jake said quietly. At once Ethan sobered.

"Yeah, I know. I've lost some friends myself to the marines and their handlers. Plus I'm sure you've had an interesting time with a bunch of protoss memories running through your head. By the way, I apologize profusely for the confusion with Leeza. She and I parted ways a few months ago and I hadn't heard from her since. I've found her contact here and have taken care of him. I'm only sorry Leeza had such a quick death. I don't much care for being used."

Using what he had learned thus far from Zamara, Jake carefully poked through Ethan's thoughts. He knew that R. M. trusted Ethan, but Jake wanted to know for himself. He still didn't fully understand what Zamara knew that was so important, he only knew that it was. And he had been through too much to simply turn around and offer himself up to Ethan Stewart like a lamb for sacrifice. He had to know— would this man betray them?

First and foremost, Ethan was indeed genuinely angry at Leeza. Everything he'd said was true, and Jake got a glimpse of how the source was "taken care of." He winced and immediately searched for other, distracting thoughts. He was surprised at the intensity of the feelings Ethan bore for Rosemary. It wasn't as tender as love, no, but it was powerful, and it was real. R. M. had been right when she said there had been a bond between them. It would take a lot for Ethan to decide to do anything to put R. M. in jeopardy.

The other thing that struck him was how strongly Ethan looked out for himself. Jake was an opportunity, nothing more. Ethan intended to use him. But Jake sensed nothing about betrayal or murder in Ethan's mind.

He supposed that was fair enough. R. M. was no angel, and Jake had suspected that Ethan ran his operations on the far side of anything resembling legality. Of course he'd want to see how he could use Jake's ability to turn a profit.

"Like what you're seeing inside my head?" drawled Ethan, grinning.

Jake started. "Um, I—"

"Let's cut the crap, Jake. You can read minds. R. M. turned you over to the marines the second she thought there'd be profit in it. And the only thing you know about me is that she likes going to bed with me. You wouldn't be human if you didn't mistrust me." Ethan grinned suddenly. "Then again, I guess there are some out there who would say you're already not human. Not entirely, at any rate."

"Um," Jake again said eloquently.

Ethan waited.

"You're right. I don't think there's anybody I can really trust right now. R. M. I trust because she's on the run like me at the moment." He thought about saying something else but the alien consciousness in his brain stirred and said, *The less said, the better.*

I've—we've—read his thoughts. He's not thinking about betraying either Rosemary or me.

At this moment, that is true, the presence acknowledged. *But thoughts change from moment to moment. And it is possible to lie in the telepathic link, if one understands how.*

Aw, shit, Jake thought, and he felt humor flutter from the protoss mind.

"Well, trust me, I have little love for anything resembling official channels," Ethan continued. "I admit, yes, I'm wondering how I can turn this situation to my advantage and make a bit of a profit. But I look at everything that way. Just my nature. It's what's gotten me all this."

Ethan raised his hands expansively and indicated the enormous, comfortable, expensive room that was, for the time being, Jake's. "So you can see, it has its bonuses."

"Indeed it does," Jake said.

"Look. Rosemary and I go way back. We're mercs, true enough, but right now, working with you, keeping you alive, and not turning you over to Val benefits all three of us. Put your trust in that."

Jake blinked at the usage of the nickname "Val" for Emperor Arcturus's son.

"At least put your doubts away long enough for a nice hot shower. There's a bathroom through there. Real water. I like my little luxuries, and I find those that I entertain do as well. You can resume interrogating me at dinner. Randall will escort you in when it's time."

Ethan winked and closed the door. Jake sat in bed for a moment, then, single-minded of purpose, rose and headed straight for the shower.

• • •

Jake emerged from the bathroom to find that someone had been in his room.

Someone sneaky and devious who had managed to come in and leave behind a tuxedo, shirt, cuff links, cummerbund, and a tie. The tuxedo waited for him patiently on a little hanging contraption next to the bed. Jake stood, dripping a little bit, the thick, plush towel wrapped around him, and stared.

Was this what it was like to be unspeakably, inconceivably, filthy rich?

The door opened and Randall entered, carrying a pair of shiny shoes that Jake knew would likely fit him perfectly. He nodded at Jake, clearly not at all taken aback to see him in a towel, and began laying out Jake's things for the evening. Jake stared at him, blinking, his mind still fuzzy.

The Professor has probably never even seen a tuxedo.

"I've worn a tuxedo twice," Jake blurted out, suddenly annoyed. Randall turned and lifted a gray eyebrow in mild surprise. "When I was nominated for Flinders Petrie Award for Archeological Distinction."

Nominated, but never won, he thought, surprised that even now, even in his current situation, the thought still vexed him. He was certain that wandering around with an alien in his head would get him something from the awards committee. Too bad he'd never get the chance to find out.

"Very good, sir."

"So . . . um yeah, thanks for dropping this off." He

smiled at the other man, and waited for him to bow and leave. Instead, Randall simply clasped his hands behind his back and stood patiently.

"Randall?"

"Yes, sir?"

Good Lord, what did one say to someone like this? Randall was intimidating the hell out of him. "Um . . . you may go now."

"The Professor does not wish assistance in dressing for dinner?"

"No, the Professor does not, and the Professor would also prefer it if you would stop referring to him in the third person." This current situation was almost as strange and alien-seeming to him as having the memories of a long-dead protoss blossoming in his mind every night as though he were actually living them.

But the impeccably dressed—he didn't even know the term. Butler? Valet? Servant? Gentleman's gentleman? Jeeves? He decided to just keep it simple and settled on Randall—Randall didn't bat an eyelash. He simply bowed slightly and said, "Very good, sir. Is there anything else you require, sir?"

Jake suddenly felt very weary, and sighed heavily. "My life back," he said quietly.

Randall didn't answer. He merely left and closed the door behind him.

Jake stared at the formal wear for a long time. Then he sighed, climbed into the clothes, used the provided shoehorn to wedge his feet into the perfectly sized, shiny shoes, and remembered that he was no good at tying a tie.

CHAPTER 20

RANDALL ARRIVED AN HOUR LATER TO ESCORT HIM to dinner. Jake followed him through several rooms as opulent as the one that he'd slept the day away in, their footsteps echoing on the dark green marble flooring. Jake hoped that Randall would return for him because he realized that if he had to negotiate his way back by himself he'd get hopelessly lost. Navigation was not one of his strong points and—

—left from the door, right, left, down stairs, left again, right—

Navigation, however, apparently *was* one of Zamara's strong points.

He was so distracted looking around that he almost ran into Randall when the older man stopped to open a set of mammoth doors. Jake ducked back with inches to spare and barely had time to compose himself before Randall was announcing in a tone of voice that sounded like fine old pewter looked, "Professor Jacob Jefferson Ramsey."

Jake's jaw dropped when he saw Rosemary.

She turned at the sound of his name, and met his eyes with a half smile. The blue eyes that had stared down the length of a gauss rifle were now offset with thick, sooty lashes and smoky eye makeup. Her skin was almost luminous in the candlelight that provided the only illumination. Her lips were dark red and slightly parted. The black bobbed hair had been washed, combed, and styled and looked sleek and silky. Light glinted from a diamond choker and the red strapless dress she wore plunged so low at the neckline and was slit so high in the leg that Jake thought he just might have a heart attack on the spot.

Rosemary was beautiful; he'd never not been aware of that. But he'd never seen her like this.

She lifted a raven eyebrow and her blue eyes ran up and down his body. "Well, Professor," she said, "You clean up rather nicely. Who'd have thought it?"

Jake glanced down at himself and managed a half chuckle. "Certainly not me."

Ethan had risen and indicated the only other seat at the table.

"Come join us. You're just in time for an aperitif. What would you like?"

"Whatever you're having," Jake mumbled. He almost missed the chair because the moment he was about to sit a hitherto unnoticed servant had pulled it out for him. He felt his cheeks flush as he sat down and scooted the chair up to the table. He was not permitted to take his own napkin; the servant was already folding it in his lap.

Ethan poured a red liquid into a tiny, elongated glass and handed it to Jake. Jake hesitated, then accepted the drink. If the man was going to kidnap or kill him, he'd have had an excellent chance earlier that day when Jake was dead to the world; he didn't need to try to drug him now. Jake took a cautious sip. The beverage smelled and tasted strongly of licorice and spices. He wasn't sure he liked it, so he took another sip to decide.

"I hope Randall meets with your approval," Ethan said. "Hiring him was one of the first things I did when I set up housekeeping here."

"It might please and surprise you to know, Jake, that all the lovely things here have been bought through legitimate investments," Rosemary said. At Jake's expression, she laughed. "Don't feel bad. Surprised me too."

"The black market was doing well enough, but about eight months ago my vessel crashed on a little backwater planet. In the two weeks it took for help to reach me I'd done some exploring and found myself an extremely pure source of vespene gas. Crime doesn't pay . . . as well as owning valuable resources does."

He grinned at Jake. "With regard to your situation, Rosemary's told me everything she knows." Ethan reached across the table to squeeze R. M.'s hand. Jake noted that despite the hired killer's new look, her hands were still very businesslike. The nails were short and unpolished and the fingers that twined around Ethan's bore calluses. Inwardly, Jake shuddered. Femme fatale, indeed, with emphasis on the "fatale."

He took another sip of the drink and discovered he had finished it. He still wasn't sure if he liked it. Ethan gestured to the servant, who began pouring wine.

"I've taken the liberty of pairing the wines with the courses," Ethan said. "I hope you don't mind."

Jake actually preferred cold beer, but he forced a smile. "I'm sure it will be delicious."

White wine splashed softly as Ethan continued. "So I've heard the nuts and bolts of the events. What I'd like to know is what you experienced. And your take as to why Val wants you so badly."

Jake took a sip of the wine as a small plate was set in front of him. What looked like raw fish drizzled with something purple and something green on a bed of something lettucelike challenged him to eat it. He picked up a fork and gave it a shot. It provided him a chance to collect his thoughts and was actually surprisingly tasty. He chewed, swallowed, and drank the dry white wine, stalling as long as he could.

"Sometime this century, Jake," Rosemary said. "Protoss may live practically forever, but Ethan's only got about forty more years."

"Sixty at least, my dear," Ethan said, and brought her hand to his lips. R. M. smiled, her lips parting.

Jake suppressed a totally irrational urge to punch Ethan in the face.

"Well . . . what do you want to know?"

Ethan squeezed Rosemary's hand and turned back to him. "Everything," he said.

Jake started at the beginning. He left nothing out. He knew that how well he fared with Ethan from this point on depended on how much Ethan thought he could use him. The second course came while he spoke, a thick, rich seafood bisque. Jake was momentarily distracted by how delicious it was and only when prodded did he pick up his story. He told them about the request to join the expedition, the meeting with Valerian.

"Ah, I've been in that room." R. M. nodded, lifting a spoonful of the creamy soup to her lips. "It's very intimidating."

At the moment Jake thought Rosemary very intimidating. He was more scared of her right now, in that red dress cut down to here and up to there, than he had been when she'd trained a gauss rifle on him. They'd moved to Jake's figuring out how to enter the chamber of the temple by the time the salad arrived.

The entrée, an exquisite roast bird drizzled with a berry sauce of some sort, was fantastic. After having existed on MREs for several days at this point, Jake was both ravenous for something that tasted like anything other than cardboard and at the same time discovering to his chagrin that his stomach had shrunk. He was already full. And the wine was beginning to have its effect. Nonetheless, he gamely kept shoveling down both food and drink.

"It was some kind of . . . time bubble she'd created,

a way to stay alive long enough for someone to find her. I still don't understand it. But there was a drop of blood that just hovered, and when I touched it, it sat there in my hand and then lost its cohesion. And then she . . . she started just . . . pouring all this information into my head. . . . It was the most . . . beautiful and overwhelming thing."

"What sort of information?" Ethan inquired. Jake blinked, trying to focus. Ethan looked exactly as he had when they sat down. Had he not had as much wine as Jake had, or was he just better at handling it? Jake didn't usually drink very much, and he'd had three glasses of wine and that weird licorice drink at the beginning.

"Um . . . I'm still working that out," he said with complete honesty, and wondered why Rosemary and Ethan found the comment so amusing. "At first it was just so overwhelming I couldn't make any sense of it. I mean . . . the protoss are so different from us, you know? Their minds are different."

Ethan had put down his fork and was watching him intently. Rosemary had her china blue eyes fixed on Jake. Jake stared back at her, suddenly mesmerized. He remembered getting a glimpse of her past when they had visited that awful place in the obscenely misnamed Paradise. He'd gotten the barest hint of what stim addiction did to those who weren't resoced, how strong one had to be to kick it. He'd seen her at what was arguably her best and worst— killing people with little emotion and great accuracy when they were about to kill her. She was so strong . . . and so beautiful.

She betrayed us, the voice in his head sent.

I don't care, Jake shot back. *At this moment, right here, right now, that doesn't mean a thing. Besides, you're the one who said she needed to come with us.*

You should not drink alcohol, the protoss part of him commented. *It clouds your judgment.*

Don't care about that either.

Fortunately I do, the protoss said.

What do you mean by that?

But it had slipped away, and he was glad of it, and he continued. "It was like trying to put a round peg in a square hole. She had to—shape my brain so it could handle the information. And while it was doing that I—I felt so many things I can't even begin to describe."

He stared down at the plate of half-eaten food. The servant approached as if to take it away, but out of the corner of his eye Jake saw Ethan wave him off. Neither Ethan nor R. M. said anything. They let him gather his thoughts in relative silence, the only sound being the clink of silver or crystal on china and the soothing murmur of classical music in the background.

Jake felt sweat begin to break out on his forehead. He willed himself to stay calm. *Keep it together, Jake. You're going to have to revisit this more than once in your life. Get ahold of it now.*

In a calmer tone of voice, he spoke of the desire to

kill, the almost overwhelming hate and rage that had seized him. "I was lucky I was unconscious," he said. "I don't know what I could have done if I hadn't been. I think it mirrored the protoss's own development as a race. I went through a lot of things and then it was done. I woke up and it was all there. But now—"

Jake. You should not tell them.

For some reason Jake was inclined to agree. But just then, Rosemary leaned forward and rested her chin on her hand. Her eyes caught the sparkle of the candlelight. "But now?" she asked.

Suddenly the voice in Jake's head urging caution was about as welcome as a rainstorm on a beach trip. R. M. knew the answer to this question; she and he had discussed every dream he'd had. This was for Ethan's benefit, not hers, and Jake knew it, and he didn't care.

"Now," he continued, holding her gaze, "it's as if all that information had been uploaded in a very compact form. And now, it's starting to play."

The scratching sound of Ethan's knife on the fine china plate caused R. M.'s eyes to dart to him. Jake sighed inwardly.

"Do you know if this is unusual? Granted, we haven't had that much contact with the protoss, but I've never heard of anything like this."

"You, my friend, are absolutely right," Jake barreled on. Zamara was growing slightly agitated at his stubborn refusal to be silent. "There was a terrible sense of urgency from the moment she reached out to me. She seemed to think it was very, very important that this knowledge be passed on, even if it was through what she clearly believed to be an imperfect medium."

Ethan looked at him thoughtfully as he chewed, swallowed, and pushed the plate away. "Really? So what's the information?"

Jake felt somewhat deflated. "I'm not sure," he said. "So far it's mostly been a single protoss's life story. Maybe there's some hidden meaning in it that I'm just not getting."

Ethan looked at him for a moment. The servant returned with a tray of three small crystal dishes of something that looked like purple ice cream and set a dish down in front of each of them. Jake assumed it was dessert.

"Maybe," Ethan agreed. "Jake . . . I'll level with you. I think you've got a fortune locked up in that head of yours. If Val was willing to put Rosemary on this assignment and then"—he paused, covered her hand proprietarily with his own, and squeezed—"was so willing to execute her, then you know something extremely valuable. Or dangerous. Which is the same thing to me."

He grinned wickedly and took a bite of the ice cream. Jake followed suit. It was cold and creamy and not quite ice cream, more like frozen ice, and the flavor was fruity and delicious, but he couldn't identify it. He was not the only one. Rosemary cocked her head and frowned. "I'm trying to place the sorbet's flavor, Ethan. Is it passion fruit?"

Passion fruit, Jake thought, The word conjured up images of engorged, dripping fruits, of lush tropical jungles and—

—the rain beating down on the trees, onto their skins, into their skins, a feeling of cool, soothed contentment. The rainy season was always better, even with the mud and the fact that nothing ever truly dried out. Because even in the rain, there was enough light to sustain them, and there was heavy fruit hanging from the tree, the outside black and knobby, the inside purple and fragrant, the perfect offering for the spirits of the animals who did not eat the flesh of others. Jake sliced one open with a knife, enjoying the aroma of the—

Ethan grinned. He had just opened his mouth to reply when Jake said quietly, "It's called sammuro fruit. It comes from Aiur."

Ethan turned, and for the first time since Jake had met him he looked caught off guard. He recovered quickly, the familiar grin settling into place on his features, but Jake knew he'd completely shocked the man. It made him feel good.

"The Professor is correct," Ethan said. "The sorbet is indeed made from the juice of the sammuro fruit of Aiur. Damned hard to find, even on the black market. This may be the only taste any terran may ever have of it. How did you recognize it, Jake? You couldn't possibly have had it before."

How *did* he know? He was looking at ice cream, not fruit. And protoss didn't eat, so it couldn't have been the flavor. Jake took another bite and smiled.

"The smell," he said. "I . . . the protoss . . . it recognized the smell."

"That makes sense," Ethan said, recovering his composure and finishing his sorbet. "Smell can be surprisingly useful for bringing on old memories. At least in humans."

Why does he know that? the protoss inside him asked. Jake felt a sudden chill. He reached out tentatively with his mind and again brushed that of Ethan. And again, he sensed a man who enjoyed the sensual aspects of life, who looked out for himself, who was highly intelligent, and who had definite plans for using Jake. Nothing more sinister than that. But Jake thought that was sinister enough.

But the question lingered. That was an odd fact for anyone to know. How was it that this mercenary with a love for physical pleasures knew so much about how the brain worked? Or was it just an offhand comment?

Before he could stop himself, he'd asked the question—and instantly regretted it. "I didn't know that. How do you know so much about it?"

He felt the entity within him wince at the blunder, and his stomach turned over. *Damn it . . . I should have played the fool. I'm good at that, because most of the time it isn't playing. . . .*

But Ethan smiled easily. If he had been unsettled earlier, any trace of it was now gone. Jake wondered if he'd imagined it in the first place.

"I make it my business to know a lot about a variety of subjects. You never know what bit of interesting trivia might come in handy one day."

The empty sorbet dishes were removed and replaced by a selection of cheeses. Jake wrinkled his nose at the smell of some of them and Rosemary, catching the gesture, laughed a little.

"What, the protoss doesn't like strong cheeses?" she said teasingly.

"No, I'm afraid that's entirely me," Jake said quite seriously. The other two laughed, and any tension that had lingered in the air dissipated. Jake was grateful. But Zamara stayed on high alert.

"So what do you think is so important then?" Ethan inquired as he spread a bit of Brie on a slice of apple.

Jake was now very, very sober. He realized what the protoss had meant by her earlier comment. Somehow, Zamara had cleared the alcohol from his system. That, he supposed, was a highly useful thing. He didn't need the silent urging from her to start fudging his answers. The hell with what Rosemary thought of him anyway. She'd been willing to kill him, and obviously would prefer Ethan to him no matter what.

"I have no clue," he said, although that wasn't entirely true. He was beginning to have his suspicions. "Maybe I haven't hit on the important stuff yet. Maybe everything I'm remembering is just . . . I don't know . . . a prologue to the real story."

Ethan nodded. "Makes sense. Tell it to hurry up the process though, okay?"

Jake laughed a little. "I'll be sure to do that."

It was time for coffee, rich and fragrant and black as night, and the actual dessert, a heavenly concoction of chocolate and cream accompanied by a generous dollop of sin. The sorbet, it turned out, had simply been a palate cleanser. As Jake forked the pastry into his mouth and let it dissolve, feeling the sugar hit his system like a drug, he felt very sorry for Zamara that she did not understand the concept of taste.

Ah, but we shall now. We understand it through you, Jacob Jefferson Ramsey. This is one of the things that you have given the protoss.

Jake was surprised, and absurdly pleased.

CHAPTER 21

OVER THE NEXT SEVERAL DAYS, SAVASSAN AND JAKE explored the underground rooms. It soon became apparent that it was larger even than they had imagined. Jake was convinced that practically every inch of their world covered this—

"—City!" Jake was excited. "It's a damn underground city. Hell, probably several cities. Look at this thing. The *Ihan-rii* have labs and highways and data storage all over the place down here. I wish I could get my hands on this—"

—place. No matter what else they stumbled upon, what else they thought they were learning, Savassan always returned to the crystal.

The dead protoss were no longer frightening to Jake's eyes, but he still wondered what had happened to them. Upon more careful examination, Jake realized that there was one representative from each of the six tribes among the dead. It did not appear that they had been injured, nor were there any obvious signs of illness. Of course, dried as the bodies were, it was hard to tell for certain.

Savassan would stand over the bodies for long minutes at a time, as if regarding them would coax them to reveal their secrets. He touched the vines that bound them, that penetrated their bodies at points, and glanced back at the crystal.

"They are heroes," said Savassan firmly in Jake's mind. "And that there is one from every protoss tribe—that cannot be coincidence."

Jake agreed. Nothing about this place spoke random happenstance. All was planned. "Do . . . you think they . . . were murdered?"

Savassan shook his head. "No. I cannot imagine the Ihan-rii murdering us. They nurtured us, guided us, cared for us. There must have been a reason for their deaths. A good reason."

He looked up at Jake with lambent eyes. "We must detach them from these vines," he told Jake.

Jake's eyes widened. "But . . . something might happen!" He glanced around at the huge chamber, still not entirely comfortable in its natural artifice.

"Such is my hope," said Savassan. "We have come so far toward unlocking their secrets, Temlaa. Will you stop now?"

Jake shook his head, although his heart raced frantically. Savassan nodded his approval. "If anything happens to me," he said, "go to the surface and find the rest of our people. What we have learned here must be preserved for generations to come. Do you understand?"

Jake nodded solemnly. Savassan returned his attention to

the corpses, calmed his mind, and stepped forward. With gentle, respectful fingers, he touched the vines, grasped one, and pulled it firmly from the dried corpse.

A light flashed on the gem-studded pillar. Jake's head whipped around.

"Did you see which one that was?" asked Savassan.

"Yes," Jake said, relieved that nothing more dire had happened.

"Watch them. Memorize the order," Savassan said, and continued. Jake kept his eyes on the lights as he was instructed. As the last vine was removed, the lights suddenly all brightened. Jake turned back to Savassan, and his eyes widened. The vines began to move. They looked like twining serpents, undulating and writhing with a soft shushing sound. The ends of the vines began to glow, softly, a radiant shade of blue, then as one they retreated into the stone and vanished. The vines still embedded in the bodies of the other five protoss did not move at all.

Savassan turned to Jake, and the thought he sent to the younger protoss made the blood pumping through Jake's veins seem cold.

"Master, you cannot!" Jake stared at Savassan, aghast.

"I must," Savassan said. "We have come too far to stop now." Even as he spoke, he was lifting the dried protoss corpse from the platform and laying it gently, reverently aside.

"But—this may be what killed them!"

"Quite possibly." The older protoss eased himself onto the platform. "Come, Temlaa. Enter the sequence."

"No." Jake's mental voice was firm. "I will not let you kill yourself."

Savassan's thoughts were gentle, kindly, but a bit exasperated. "You know I must do this."

Jake shielded his thoughts. They were too personal, too painful, to share. Besides, he suspected that Savassan knew well what he was feeling already. He steadied himself, then began to re-create in reverse the order in which the lights had flashed. The vines appeared from the wall, undulating slowly and gracefully and frighteningly. Each one moved toward Savassan as if with its own mind, fastening onto his body, wrapping around him, and Jake fought back the instinct to rush forward and grab Savassan and haul him to safety.

"Now the ara'dor," Savassan sent.

Jake closed his eyes, his finger hovering over the console. If he harmed Savassan . . .

One to one point six . . .

The giant, hovering crystal that so awed Jake and Savassan flared to glorious, radiant life. Jake cringed, shielding his eyes from the flash of magenta light, and winced as the heartbeat sound grew louder. Light started to envelop the prone form of Savassan. Jake stared. Where was it coming from? From Savassan himself?

Pain slammed into him.

Savassan's agony was so profound that it dropped Jake to his knees. It took him several precious seconds to recover sufficiently to get to his feet and head for the pillar with the glowing gems. He had to stop it! Even as he watched, Savassan's body began to wither. Jake realized that the desiccated corpses they had seen had not gotten that way through the ravages of time and a dry environment, but as a result of this thing, this abomination—

Frantically Jake entered the code again. Nothing. He couldn't stop it! He—

Then it came to him. He had to reverse the sequence. Quickly, focusing as he had never done before, Jake stabbed at the glowing gems.

The colors shifted. Instead of magenta, the crystal now began to glow blue. And instead of sensing crippling pain from Savassan, Jake now felt ecstasy.

He stared at Savassan. The older protoss's body was reversing the damage that had been done to it, and Savassan was now enveloped in soft blue light. Jake desperately tried to figure out what was going on. The best guess he could make was that whereas before the crystal was somehow draining energy from Savassan, it was now starting to pour energy into him.

He felt Savassan's thoughts brush his own and trembled from the joy he felt there.

"Yes," sent Savassan, "yes, it is nourishing me like the sun . . . sharing things with me . . . Oh, Temlaa, Temlaa, so beautiful, so healing. . . . I understand now. I understand!"

The crystal flared again, as bright as a sun, and then the radiance subsided. Its heartbeat sound faded to the background as it had before, and the light in the room resumed its normal soft white glow. Savassan's emotions calmed, became peaceful and joyful rather than wildly ecstatic. Jake quickly entered the sequence and the vines detached themselves and again retreated into the stone.

He hurried to his master, helping him sit up. Savassan was shielding something from him, and he begged to know what.

"I know what to do now," Savassan said. "I know the

path we need to follow. These centuries of hatred—it's wrong, Temlaa, so very wrong. We need to remember what we once had. We do not need the Xel'Naga, we need only each other!"

The term was strange, but Jake understood that this was the name the Ihan-rii used to refer to themselves . . . the name that had been forgotten.

Savassun slid off the platform. "We must go," sent Savassan firmly. The force of his thoughts was so strong Temlaa almost didn't object.

"But," he managed, "but this place . . . we can learn so much. We should stay here and explore!"

"—Oh please, please, stay here and explore, I'm never going to get the chance to see this place except through your memories, Temlaa—"

Savassan shook his head. "No. This can wait. We have a more important task."

"—damn it—"

"If it is meant to be, we will return and learn and study. But for now, we need to take this to our people."

"But—"

"Do you not understand?" The mental blast made Temlaa quail. "Temlaa—this is what we have been hoping for! Outside this place, our people are dying."

"The Shelak fight well. We are not in danger."

Savassan shook his head. "Temlaa. I refer to all protoss.

We are fighting and dying because of what? Because we hate each other. Why do we hate each other?"

"We hate the other tribes because they drove the Ihan-rii—the Xel'Naga away. And they hate us because we still honor them."

"No, Temlaa. That is what we have told ourselves. That is our excuse, because deep down inside, there is an ugly fear that we were forsaken because we were flawed. That we were not good enough to please them. Those long-ago protoss, who stood and raged and wept while the ones who made us forsook us—they did not originally hate one another. Each one hated himself, and that could not be borne. We were angry and afraid, and so we made one another into monsters. Different color skins, different ways of doing things—this does not a monster make. We are protoss. We are the same people. Tell me: If you could link your thoughts and emotions to an Ara—could you hate him?"

"I would feel his hatred of me."

Exasperated, Savassan waved a hand. "No, no, because he would be feeling you, sensing you, at the same time. You would know how deeply he loves his kash'lor, his children, how good it feels to have the sun on his skin, how joyfully he dances around the fires. You could not hate him, because you would become him!"

Temlaa stared. He started to form a thought and—

Jake bolted upright, sweating in the beautiful sheets. He ran a hand through his damp hair. Lord, he had a headache. Merging so completely with someone else—the thought terrified him.

He stumbled to the shower and let the water pour over him until he felt somewhat more human. It was then that he realized, standing under the stream as it plastered his hair to his head, that for the first time he'd been able to stop the dreams simply by willing it. Always before, it was as if Temlaa had been in control, and he, Jake, merely along for the ride. He wondered what that meant, and why, now, he had been able to exert that much control.

He nearly had a heart attack when he stepped out of the shower and almost collided with Randall.

"Good morning, Professor. I was just laying out your clothes for the day."

Jake caught his breath. "Okay, Randall, from now on, you don't come in without knocking."

"Very good, sir. Which outfit would the Professor"—Randall caught himself and smiled slightly—"would you prefer?"

The headache, chased away by soothing warm water, now came back with a vengeance. "Doesn't matter," Jake said, surrendering this battle. "Pick whichever you think is best. And uh, Randall . . . do you have anything for a hangover?"

Randall didn't bat an eye as he laid out trousers with a knife-sharp crease and a button-up shirt. He replied, debating which jacket went best with the outfit, "Of course, sir. The Master is quite used to guests overindulging on the first evening. I'll get you something directly."

Randall slipped out and Jake changed into the

clothes. He gazed at himself in the mirror, almost surprised to see a human visage looking back at him and not the smooth, mouthless face of a protoss.

He looked thinner, he thought. Somewhat haggard. He ran a hand over his just-shaven face, surprised at the hollows beneath the cheekbones. He gazed into his blue eyes and thought they looked . . . ancient.

"Damn it," he muttered, hating the peculiarity of the thought, and turned his attention to his hair. His hair had been blondish-brown on Nemaka. Now there was clearly some silver threaded in among the gold.

There was a knock on the door. "Come in."

Randall entered, holding a tray with a glass of greenish liquid on it. As Jake took it, he asked, "Think I could get a haircut while I'm here?"

"Of course, sir."

Jake followed Randall through the huge house, trotting behind the valet like an obedient puppy. He caught a glimpse of his reflection in a mirror at one point and paused, startled, and grinned. The haircut the multitalented Randall had given him looked fantastic. Even as he admitted that he was starting to enjoy this kind of lifestyle, he wondered what Ethan would ask in return for it.

"Damn, Jake, you look better each time I see you," came a sultry female voice.

Jake whirled, blushing that Rosemary had caught him preening in front of a mirror. His eyes widened. "I—would have to say the same."

Rosemary was wearing a brightly colored, casual dress that showed off her toned legs and arms to perfection. She had little or no makeup on, though Jake didn't know enough about such things to be able to tell, and wore a simple pair of sandals. Atop her hair was a large straw hat that should have looked ridiculous and oversized and instead looked utterly charming.

"How'd you sleep, Jake?" Ethan materialized seemingly from nowhere to slip his arm around Rosemary and give her a proprietary kiss.

"Busily," Jake answered.

"More dreams?"

"Indeed."

"Then you've probably worked up an appetite. Come on, let's eat outside."

A small table had been prepared, and Jake's stomach growled hungrily at the sight of juices, coffee, and lavish pastries. Randall's hangover cure had worked perfectly.

Ethan pulled out a chair for Rosemary, then sat down himself. Jake followed suit.

"I'd like to discuss ways in which we might use that alien brain to all our benefits," Ethan said. Jake reached out and brushed Ethan's thoughts, and found that the man had said exactly what he'd meant to. There were plans aplenty running around in Ethan's brain.

Jake didn't like any of the possibilities. He didn't like the thought of sitting at Ethan's side at "negotiations" and reading the minds of prospective partners. He didn't like the thought of mind-reading current partners who had betrayed Ethan. He didn't like the thought of planting suicidal or traitorous thoughts in decent people. But he smiled and nodded as if he did, murmured appropriate words during breakfast, avoided Rosemary's eyes, and thought the coffee bitter all of a sudden.

He pleaded tiredness and went back to his room. Once he got there, he sprawled on the bed and stared up at the canopy.

"Hey, Zamara," he said. "Where are you hiding?"

There was no response. Jake blinked. He tried again, mentally this time, closing his eyes to concentrate.

Zamara? What's going on? Are you . . . done?

No. But you are.

What? What do you mean?

This . . . this was a failure. Jake's heart contracted at the pain in Zamara's mental voice. *I had thought . . . had hoped . . . but you are refusing.*

Jake actually laughed aloud at that. *Refuse? Since when have I even had the option of refusing anything you've shoved into my brain?*

You always have, came the shocking response. *But you have never chosen to until now. That is the only reason I was able to tell you anything at all, to direct and bend and prepare you for this moment—you were willing to accept the knowledge.*

What about Marcus Wright?

That was not about accepting knowledge. That was about using it. There is a distinction.

Jake thought back to the initial contact he had had, when he had first found Zamara's body suspended in time in the temple. The sensations that had caused him to pass out. The flashbacks to a heart-stoppingly violent era in protoss history. The panicky loss of self. The guilt that still sat heavy upon his chest as if an incubus of old tales squatted on it. *That was acceptance?*

Yes.

Jake thought he'd hate to find out what coercion by the protoss was like, and felt a faint flicker of mirth that subsided again to that odd mournfulness and resignation.

But now, now you are not willing to go the final step. To learn the lesson that we learned then.

And Jake knew. He turned his face and buried it in the pillow, as if hiding from someone who was physically present. But he couldn't hide from the entity in his mind. Zamara was right. The lesson the protoss learned was that of unity. Of merging minds and feelings and thoughts and . . . souls? Did it go that deep? He decided that was too esoteric a question and simply refused to think about it.

The two protoss had left the Xel'Naga underground city unexplored to explore something else. To rediscover the ancient link that had bound them together as a unified people. To stop the hatred that served nothing save to degrade their souls and diminish their species. To take another's pain as their own, to fully share their joy with one whose mind was housed in another body.

To merge. To remember.

The bed was comfortable, the food magnificent, the shower glorious. But none of those things was worth doing what Ethan wanted him to do. Rosemary had said Ethan would protect her and Jake. Maybe protect them from Valerian—Jake believed that much—if it lined Ethan's pocket.

But Ethan would not protect Jake from turning his back on every moral code he'd come to believe in his years in this life. He'd be no better than Ethan—hell, no better than Rosemary, with her cold blue eyes and gauss rifle. He'd be used as a tool to hurt people.

We need to escape.

His face buried in the pillow, Jake nodded.

I can help you do that. But you must trust me.

Jake realized he was crying. *I am afraid, Zamara. I'm not a protoss. I don't have an ancient ancestral memory of being joined like that.*

I know. But you have accepted so much already. I believe your mind will be able to accommodate what I hope to share with you. This is the only way this knowledge will be saved. And . . . the only way you will be prepared to handle more knowledge. Knowledge that could save my people.

And if I refuse?

Ethan will ask things of you that will shatter your spirit. You will be condemned to do them, with no hope of escape. And it is possible that there are worse things that lie ahead, things you do not *know.*

Ah, shit.

Indeed.

Jake rolled over and wiped his face. "Let's do it," he said, and braced himself.

But before the onslaught there came a moment of gentle gratitude from Zamara, as soft as a breeze heavy with the scent of flowers. *Thank you, Jacob. Thank you.*

And then.

Information flooded him with such astonishing rapidity he whimpered and shut his eyes and ears in a futile, foolish attempt to block it out. It kept coming, of course, for this information, this knowledge, these sensations of unity, were not coming from his senses. At least . . . not the traditional five senses.

Emotions and sensations slammed into his head. Jake gasped soundlessly. And then, suddenly, as if he had been riding a runaway horse that had suddenly slowed to a comfortable canter, Jake was processing it all.

No. Not Jake, not Jacob Jefferson Ramsey.

And not Zamara, nor Temlaa.

All.

All of them were working together, almost in a dance, catching the information and sensation, registering it, integrating it, and moving on. The supreme confidence of Randall, walking down a corridor somewhere. The master chef, writing out the menu and sending an assistant to harvest herbs. And oh, Jake didn't want to see but he couldn't help it, couldn't ignore it, could only see and integrate Rosemary's warm feelings of sexual satiety and momentary content. Dozens of people, hundreds of thoughts and feelings, crowding upon Jake and Zamara, and they were juggling them deftly.

Until they stumbled across one thought.

Somewhere, in this massive complex that was part mansion and part laboratory and part training facility, someone had a thought that caught Jake and Zamara like a punch in the gut. It was a fleeting thought, a butterfly wing–light thought, crowded out at once by more pressing thoughts of food and a hot shower.

Wonder what kind of bonus we'll get from Mr. V for the mind reader.

CHAPTER 22

HOW WAS THIS POSSIBLE?

Jake had been reading minds since the minute he got here. Nothing, no one, had indicated that Ethan had planned to betray him. Quickly, without even thinking about it, Jake located Ethan and dove into his head.

Nothing. There was nothing there about betraying Jake. How was that possible? Was that nobody, that . . . workaday mechanic in Ethan's employ simply mistaken? But how the hell are you "mistaken" about business dealings with the son of an emperor?

Easily, hardly even thinking about it, Jake slipped into Rosemary's thoughts, searching for any sign that she knew about it, was in on it. Nothing. She was as in the dark as he was.

In the dark. . . .

Jake closed his eyes, but still saw. He again went as Temlaa down the winding stairs into the caverns, beheld the glowing gems and the smooth stone that perhaps wasn't completely stone, saw the hovering crystal and what it did for both good and ill to the willing Savassan—

That was it.

Jake understood exactly what had happened.

Ethan sat alone in his private quarters. The lights were dim, the only sound that of water flowing gently from a delicate fountain. His breathing was smooth and controlled, his gaze soft as he regarded the flickering candle flames in front of him. Forty candles, bound together; forty tiny flames burning brightly. All he saw was the flame, all he thought of was the flame, all he was was the flame. He let it fill his thoughts, then drew back his right hand.

Ethan snapped it forward, bringing it swiftly to the flame in a punching motion, almost but not quite burning his knuckles.

The candles went out. Smoke wafted upward, gray and curling. Ethan closed his eyes and breathed deeply.

He was not at all psychic. But he had learned to train and discipline his mind so that it obeyed him. Part of what extinguished the candles was air, doing nothing but following its natural movement. But part of it wasn't.

He rose, lithe and powerful, his body forced to the same rigorous standards and discipline as his mind, and went to the mirror. Ethan regarded his cleanly shaven head and reached for the psi-screen.

It was a deceptively delicate collection of wires and chips, and he placed it on his head as he might have a crown. It slid down into position, and he felt a tingle that he knew was not a physical sensation. These things were next to impossible to find on the black market, worth a not-very-small fortune if one managed to do so, and Ethan Stewart owned two of them. Goodwill gifts from his employer. He wore one; his most trusted and lethal assassin wore the other.

Amazing, that something so little could do so much. The screens in general prevented telepaths from reading his mind. This one had been extensively modified to allow certain surface thoughts to be read. Thoughts completely created and controlled by Ethan Stewart, who had mastered such things. It had come in handy many times in the past while conducting business. Right now, it was invaluable.

He moved the psi-screen into place, fastening it to his scalp with small pieces of tape, and then donned and secured the wig. The result was that both psi-screen and wig were undetectable. Even Rosemary had not noticed that his hair was false. Ethan snapped the wrist unit on, taped it down, and pulled on a long-sleeved shirt. He made a mental note of the time; it would not do to wear this equipment overly long. He'd been warned about the consequences—memories erased, paranoia, and eventual insanity.

He was deep in thought as he left his exquisitely decorated quarters and went to the elevator.

Jake Ramsey had bookish intelligence. A lot of it.

But Jake didn't have "smarts." And smarts was what had gotten Ethan where he was.

Rosemary Dahl, now . . . she had smarts. But she also put too much faith in what she and Ethan had shared over the years together. Ethan stopped whistling and frowned to himself. That was the one thing he truly regretted about this whole thing. He liked Rosemary. He had done everything he could to prevent having to turn her over to Valerian, but there'd been no way around it. All or nothing, Valerian had said when they conversed. Both the professor and the assassin. The one had the information, the other by this point undoubtedly knew too much and could be a liability.

"Don't worry, we won't kill her. She's too valuable," Valerian had said. "We'll just do a little bit of resoc on her once we've determined what she knows."

Ethan had wanted to believe that. And because Ethan always got what he wanted, he had convinced himself.

He was a bit sorry he couldn't follow through on some of the lies he'd held in his head as he had spoken to Jake at luncheon that day. It would have been handy to have had his own personal mind reader on call.

But in the end, there hadn't really been the option of refusal. Ethan owed Val far too much at this point. This way, everyone got what they wanted.

Well. Everyone except Jake and Rosemary.

The elevator came to a stop on the bottom floor. The doors opened, but Ethan didn't get out. Instead, he hit in a code. The doors closed and the elevator continued to descend, past what all but a handful of people here believed was the last floor of the complex, past the laboratories, into the secret heart of a secret place.

The doors opened.

Ethan stepped out into a cool, stony area. It had been cost-effective to work with the cave structure that riddled the heart of the planet. Most of the underground laboratory was "unfinished," as Randall might have phrased it, and there were more bare stone walls than artificially erected ones. The cooler temperatures benefited the vast array of sophisticated technology that Ethan had ordered set up. The money went into the equipment and the people, not the décor. Ethan went down here only infrequently. He liked his luxuries more immediately available, in the form of food, drink, and tactile and visual comforts.

Dr. Reginald Morris was waiting for him. "Good day, Mr. Stewart. Right on time, as usual."

Tall, slender, bespectacled, with thinning, graying hair and a white coat, Morris looked avuncular and harmless. Ethan thought the man rather like Jake. Morris's passion was his work, and he found it inconceivable that others didn't find it as fascinating as he did. Ethan did, actually. It was why he had faked Morris's death and hired him away from the government, where Morris had specialized in training Ghosts.

Morris extended a hand and waved Ethan to the familiar chair. He fiddled with the equipment and asked, "Any problems, Mr. Stewart?"

With long, gentle fingers, Morris touched Ethan's face, turning it this way and that and looking at it intently.

"None so far. I'd say your theory has passed the ultimate test."

Morris moved the chair and began to examine the back of Ethan's head. He tilted it and angled it slightly. "Hold it right there, please," Morris murmured as he turned to find the proper instrument. "I'm so very excited about getting a chance to meet Professor Ramsey in person and examining him for myself. I wish I could have had a peek at him earlier today."

"You'll have a chance soon enough. Patience is a virtue, they say." Ethan's voice was warm with humor, and Morris chuckled along with him.

"I don't apologize for my enthusiasm." Morris selected a scanning device and ran it in slow, thorough motions over Ethan's head. A holographic image of Ethan's brain appeared on a table to Morris's left. He watched it intently as he continued to run the scanner.

"Don't worry, I promise I'll let you have a crack at him before I turn him over to Valerian's people."

"As I said, I simply can't wait." They went through this every time Ethan donned the psi-screen and every time he removed it. Careful maintenance of brain activity was the first sign of overusage of the equipment. "So far so good, Mr. Stewart. You continue to impress me. You're startlingly mentally disciplined for a non–psi subject."

Ethan smiled. "Discipline is remembering what you want," he said. Since he was a teenager, Ethan had always known what he'd wanted, and pursued it with a single-mindedness of purpose that unfailingly stunned his allies and devastated his enemies.

Morris pursed his lips and nodded, then switched off the scanner. "Everything looks quite satisfactory," he said. "When do I get to get my hands on the Professor's delightfully modified brain?"

"This evening," Ethan said. "Valerian's people should be arriving in just a few hours."

Thanks to his union with Zamara, Jake had been able to bypass Ethan's hitherto perfect psi-screen and learned that this evening, he would be turned over to a walking, talking cliché of a mad scientist. He couldn't run. This whole place was a beautiful trap, baited with food and comforts. His only consolation was that his enemy had fed him well and permitted him to rest. But that was small consolation indeed.

He turned to the only friend he had now—Zamara.

What do we do?

We must escape. What I know—and now what you know—must not be permitted to fall into the hands of people such as Valerian or Ethan. It is protoss history, protoss knowledge. It is for us. We will decide if, when, and how we will share it.

Jake rolled his eyes.

Sounds great to me. Only one problem. How the hell do we get out of here?

Do you trust me, Jacob Jefferson Ramsey?

Jake nodded. He had taken that step already, by permitting himself to merge with her. *You know I do.*

Yes. I do. But . . . I wanted you to be certain.

I am. So what do we do?

There is one who will aid us. One who I knew would be important to the ultimate success of my endeavor. We must convince Rosemary Dahl of what we know.

Rosemary lingered in the shower. It was her second one of the day, as she'd told herself she had gotten too hot and sweaty outside and needed to refresh herself. It was a complete and utter lie, and she knew it, and she didn't give a rat's ass. She was going to enjoy every minute of Ethan's hospitality.

She wrapped her hair in a towel and reached for the thick, soft robe, grinning as she recalled last night's romp in bed. God, she'd missed that. She'd missed Ethan, and only now that she was with him again did she realize just how much. They were two of a kind, scoundrels both, and she had more fun with him than she'd ever had with anyone else. The only thing that could make this better was if they were facing certain death together, as they used to on a fairly regular basis.

She stepped into her room, sighing wistfully.

"Rosemary?"

Rosemary whirled and barely stopped herself from leaping onto the intruder.

"Damn it, Jake, what the hell are you doing in here?"

And hello to you too, came the distinct voice in her head.

Rosemary gasped. "Get out of my head," she snapped. "I didn't know you could do that."

Let you read my thoughts?

"Yeah. Cut it out. Oh, and get the hell out of my private quarters while I'm standing here dressed in nothing but a robe."

The image that hit her brain from Jake's thoughts at that comment made her wish she had, indeed, sprung on him—and not in a way he would have enjoyed, either. Hard on the heels of that thought was one of utter mortification, and despite herself Rosemary chuckled.

"You must have a reason for being here. Out with it."

He hesitated, and spoke with words. "You're not going to like it. But you're going to have to believe it."

She felt the smile ebb. "Go on."

Thoughts that were not words but something deeper, more profound than words, more complex than visions, filled her mind.

Jake Ramsey was right. She didn't like it.

"Nice try, Jake. I get that you might not like playing on the dirty side of things, but it's your only chance to stay alive. Feeding me this crap isn't going to suddenly make me stop trusting Ethan."

He stared at her. "But—you read my thoughts. I told you what I know!"

"Jake—this could be utter bullshit you're sending me. And probably is. I've known Ethan for almost a decade. I know what he will and won't do, and there's no reason to turn you over. We weren't traced, and soon he's going to take us away from here and on a variety of missions that'll have us hopping all over the sector."

Jake seemed stunned. She smirked a bit. "What, did you think all you had to do was send me a fake thought and I'd turn my back on the one person I trust? Give me more credit than that."

"Normally I'd admire your loyalty, but—Rosemary, I swear, this is the truth! We've got to get out of here!"

"You're so certain? Then we can dig up some proof." She raised a raven eyebrow at him. "Got you there, do I?"

"What kind of proof?"

"If he's been talking with Valerian, there will be records of the conversation. This is Ethan's castle. He'd feel completely safe keeping records, and he'd want to have them handy in case he's double-crossed. See? Told you I know how his mind works."

Jake looked completely shaken. "How do we find them?"

"Hey, innocent until proven guilty, burden of proof and all that. Your job, not mine."

"Rosemary, you know I don't have the skills to hack into a holographic comm system, let alone a complicated security system like Ethan's got! Come on—if there's no proof, then you're right. You turn me over to Ethan and he kicks me until he feels better. But if there is, we have to find it *now*. They'll be here in just a few hours. Please!"

Jake Ramsey wasn't a deceptive man. Maybe the thing inside him had taught him how to dissemble, but he looked like his worry was completely genuine at the moment. She narrowed her eyes, regarding him thoughtfully.

If they were caught, Ethan would be very upset with her. But Jake was right. It would be easy to direct Ethan's anger toward Jake and not her. Besides, Rosemary liked a good challenge. And if, God forbid, Jake was right . . .

"All right. I'll help you out; I can use the practice. And when you can't find anything on Ethan I'm going to laugh my head off at you."

He nodded. "If I can't find anything, you'll have that right."

Again, his certainty seemed absolute. A shiver passed through her. Annoyed for no reason she could articulate, she decided to rattle him, and dropped the robe. She heard him make a little sound of embarrassment as he turned away. She reached for a fresh sundress, then paused. Ingrained in her was the deep need to always be prepared for the worst. She fished out her old uniform, noticing that it had been cleaned. The leather smell hit her strongly, reminding her of the countless times she'd donned this outfit and ended up with blood on it, usually someone else's. She pulled on her boots, turned, and tapped him on the shoulder.

"Let's go," she said coldly. "I'm looking forward to seeing how you look with egg on your face."

"Rosemary," he said with quiet earnest, "I wish to God I was wrong."

CHAPTER 23

JAKE HAD THOUGHT THAT IT WOULD BE AN uncomfortable adjustment, sharing himself with an alien consciousness at so deep a level. It was just the opposite. While Jake was utterly unfamiliar with such bondings, Zamara was well accustomed to it, and took a gentle lead. Instead of losing his identity, Jake felt himself . . . augmented. It was like being in a dance that Zamara knew well, and she guided Jake easily through the steps. She knew when to step back and let Jake come to the fore, and when to move forward and put her centuries of knowledge to good use. She did so now, and Jake, lost in the machinations of politics and games that all ended with someone dying, gladly let her.

Jake closed his eyes, shutting out the distractions of visual input in order to focus on the mental voices and sensations. Jake would have been lost in the overwhelming cascade of images and sensations, but Zamara navigated them as smoothly as an experienced rafter does a river. He swiftly isolated those with information and began to probe their thoughts.

"Prof? Ready to go here. . . ."

His eyes still closed, Jake held up a finger for silence. There. That was the one. The woman in charge of security for the entire compound. Quickly Zamara/Jake scanned her thoughts. Jake almost laughed aloud as he realized that Zamara had an eidetic memory.

"I've got a map now," he said to R. M., and he realized that his voice sounded slightly different—more confident, less frightened. "Alison Lassiter is the security chief. I know exactly where the communications room is now. There are some codes . . . hang on . . ."

He heard her whistle appreciatively. "You know, if you're not putting me on, you and I should go into business for ourselves when we get out of here, Jake."

Jake ignored her while Zamara quickly memorized each code. "Okay, I've got them. I think Zamara will be able to misdirect any security we run into."

"Let's do this thing. Ethan is fond of tea in the afternoon and I'm getting hungry."

He rose. "One more thing. Zamara's going to be much better at this than I am. I'm going to let her be in charge for a bit."

"What does that mean? You got a split personality now, Prof?"

Jake hesitated. "Nothing so dramatic. Just . . . if I try to do this, it'll take that much longer for things to happen. You might not notice any difference. We're kind of . . . joined now."

"I want to get this over with as soon as possible. By all means, let the gray-skinned alien drive."

"Her skin's purple," Jake said absently, and stepped aside. Zamara moved forward in his consciousness, and Jake suddenly felt . . . different in his skin. He recalled the dreams in which he had felt comfortable in a protoss skin, and upon waking felt disoriented at being in a human body. Zamara's reaction was almost identical, and both watched and felt simultaneously as Zamara adjusted to it much more quickly than Jake had.

"Let us go," Zamara/Jake said.

Rosemary lifted an eyebrow.

They went.

It was easier than they had thought. Jake permitted himself to hope that stealing a ship would be a piece of cake too, but Zamara was dubious.

The first obstacle was simply a matter of obtaining codes and adjusting thoughts, she told Jake. *The vessels are much more carefully guarded. We will require things other than simple codes to commandeer a craft.*

Oh, Jake thought, dispirited.

Rosemary was good at this sort of thing, and after a few moments Zamara relaxed and let her take the lead. R. M. actually knew some of the people they encountered and was able to quickly put them at ease. A few asked to see security passes, at which point Rosemary turned her smile on Zamara. The protoss gently planted the idea that they had seen the proper clearances and the two were waved through.

It was at the door to the communications room that they ran into trouble. Zamara pointed a stubby human digit and quickly entered the code. The door irised open.

Three guards stood there, with rifles pointed at them.

Rosemary kept playing the part. She glowered and batted one of the rifles away from her body. "Don't point that thing at me!" she snapped.

The security guard was unfazed. "We got a report that there were some violations of security areas. Stand over there with your hands on your head, please. Both of you."

Rosemary's blue eyes flickered to Zamara's/Jake's. A communication passed between them and, as in a harmony born of years of training together, they sprang. Lithe as a cat, Rosemary darted under the gun pointing at her head, grasped it, and slammed the guard in the jaw with the butt of his rifle. Completely unprepared for such an attack, he staggered back. Rosemary leaped on him and quickly wrapped an arm around his throat, choking him. The guard dropped the gun. His hands dug into Rosemary's arms, but to no avail. He blacked out and fell heavily. She turned to give Jake a hand.

It was not needed.

Zamara acted with a knowledge of how to fight that Jake did not possess. It was with great effort that she restrained herself from killing the two guards. Until Rosemary was convinced, killing Ethan's people would only serve to upset her and delay them.

"Damn," Jake said as he looked at the two bodies lying on the floor. Zamara had given him back control for the moment.

"Hell, Jake, where'd you learn to do that?" Rosemary helped him tie up the guards, cinching their own belts tight around their wrists.

"That was Zamara," Jake replied. His hands were shaking.

"Ethan's going to want to marry you when he sees this," Rosemary said. Jake did not reply, merely rose and entered the code that would seal the doors shut. He glanced back at Rosemary.

"Your turn," he said. "We got here . . . what, a day and a half ago?"

She had slipped into one of the chairs, and her fingers were flying as she nodded. "About that. What's the code?"

He gave it to her, and she entered it. Jake suddenly realized that one of the guards had gotten in a good blow before he'd gone down. He realized this when he tasted blood. Crap.

"All right, I've accessed the databank. It's encoded too."

Jake rattled off another code and she entered it, her eyes focused. He watched her closely, and saw her suddenly tense.

"Aw . . . aw no, no," she murmured.

"What is it?"

She punched a button and the space above the flat black surface to her right shimmered and took on color and form.

"Valerian," Jake murmured. He'd known he was right, but still . . .

Rosemary cleared her throat. "Five communications from Ethan to Valerian. The first one the day we escaped from the *Gray Tiger.*"

Ethan's voice was recorded, but his image was not captured. Cool, smooth, familiar to Rosemary and now Jake, Ethan's voice asked, "Well, well, wanting an update on your investment?"

The small representation of Valerian smiled. "Partially. Let's say I'm calling in a favor. I have a job I want you to do."

"Name it."

"Two people have escaped imprisonment aboard one of my vessels. One of them is a scientist who has information I need. The other is helping him. Someone you know—Rosemary Dahl. Given your previous relationship, I think it likely she'll contact you for help. When she does, I want you to notify me at once and detain them."

"The scientist, of course; but what do you need with R. M.? Doesn't she already work for you?"

"She does. And don't worry, I know you're fond of her. I am, too. We'll just see what she knows, resoc her, and send her back to you."

"I—I don't like this. You're sure you need her?"

Valerian's tiny, patrician face looked stern. "I wouldn't say so if I didn't, Ethan. And it isn't exactly wise of you to try to thwart me on this."

"I just don't want her damaged, that's all. You can

have this scientist, of course, I don't care about that crap—but Rosemary's mine. I want her back when you're done with her."

Valerian smiled thinly. "Of course."

The hologram had more to say, but Rosemary punched the button with a stiff finger. Jake looked at her sympathetically. Her color was high, but she didn't meet his gaze.

"We should listen to the rest of them," Jake said quietly. "We need to know everything."

"Yeah," Rosemary said. The steadiness of her voice surprised Jake. She selected the next several messages, all of which were brief and brutally to the point.

"The ship has departed," said the mini-Valerian on the last communication. "It should arrive in about twelve hours. Rest assured that you are doing the wise thing. Ramsey might be handy to have around, and Dahl might be . . . amusing, but the security of your own little empire ought to be paramount. And I promise, if you cooperate, you will be safe. I've spent a lot of money on you over the years, Ethan. And I hate the thought of having invested unwisely."

Rosemary stared at the holographic image, feeling like she'd been gut-punched. She slammed her hand down on the console, and the image disappeared.

"Rosemary?" She felt Jake's—or was it Zamara's—mind probing hers gently, wanting to offer comfort.

She thought for certain she'd explode. Instead she said quietly, "Get out of my head for a few, okay?"

She felt him . . . them . . . retreating respectfully and heard Jake cough and shift his position. Her face averted, her mind her own for the moment, Rosemary Dahl placed a steadying hand on the console, closed her eyes, and let the hurt wash over her.

Ethan.

How could he have done this to her? After all they had been through. After he had found her in squalor in Paradise, had gotten her out of there and off the drugs, had been the first lover who'd ever cared about her pleasure. Had saved her life more than once, had told her she was the best trouble he'd ever had. . . .

She should have known the minute she saw this obscenely lavish complex. *"Wise investing" my ass,* she thought. Valerian had set him up with all this. After all his grandstanding about never working for the Dominion, Ethan had sold out. He'd been in Valerian's pocket for years, if the Heir Apparent's comment was to be believed. At least she hadn't lied about the dirty work she was hired to do.

She heard a soft gasp of pain escape her and bit her lower lip hard. She didn't want Jake to know how badly this betrayal had wounded her. Although, of course, at some point, if they made it out of here alive, Jake would again read her thoughts and know what she was feeling. Would, if she was correct, *feel* how shattered she was by the betrayal.

She decided she could live with his knowing that. When they were on a ship out of here.

"All right," Rosemary said, her voice calm and

under her control again. "Sounds like we've got about an hour, maybe less. We don't want to be seen, so let's shut down these cameras and sensors."

She called up a display of the whole complex. Jake leaned in, looking at the map.

"We're here," he said, pointing at one spot. "The ships are docked here."

Rosemary narrowed her blue eyes. "The shortest route isn't always the best," she said. Her short-nailed fingers flew over the console. "There. These corridors are for transporting freight—they're less populated." She began shutting down cameras one by one.

"Why don't you just shut them all down?" Jake asked. Rosemary could all but feel his pity, and it angered her. She didn't want it, and she didn't need it.

"Because that would alert someone right away. No sense in alarming those who don't need to be alarmed. Let them eat their sandwiches in ignorance. All right, there we go. So what's needed to get that ship to launch?"

Jake sighed. "Retinal scans and voice and genetic recognition patterns."

Her blue eyes flickered to his, and she saw him literally cringe at the coldness he must have seen in them.

"Whose?"

He swallowed hard. "There are ten people authorized to do it. But some of them aren't on site, and uh . . ."

"Ethan's one of the ten, of course?"

Jake nodded.

Rosemary let her lips curve in a smile that had no warmth in it. "Piece of cake," she said.

She rose and went to the still-unconscious guards. She picked up one rifle, checked it, then tossed it to Jake. She was not surprised when he caught it smoothly. She searched the other two as well, finding a small pistol on one of them. She took the pistol and a rifle, checked them both, tucked the pistol away, and rested the rifle comfortably, familiarly, in her arms.

"Let's go find him."

Rosemary appeared out of nowhere, and Ethan started backward.

"Hey," she said, grinning up at him.

"Hey yourself, Trouble," he replied. He nodded to his companion, one of many who came to give him updated reports each day, and the slender, nondescript young man nodded and slipped away. Ethan moved toward Rosemary and took her into his arms, bending his head to kiss her passionately and possessively. She responded, her arms snaking around his neck.

"Mm . . . looks like someone missed me," he murmured against the soft skin of her throat.

"Aw," she said, mock-sadly. "Guess I can't fool you."

He pulled back and ran a hand through her short, silky black hair. "Come on. Let's go to my room."

Rosemary grinned at him. "I have a better idea. I have a confession to make. I've been a bad girl."

"Oh? Do I need to spank you?"

"Hm . . . I'll let you be the judge of that. I've hacked into your systems."

He tensed slightly. "What? Why?" Damn it . . . had she suddenly gotten wind of what he was planning?

"I wanted to make sure I hadn't lost my touch. And I found a nice little spot I wanted to . . . share with you. So I turned the cameras and sensors off."

She trailed a finger over his lips as he spoke, and he bit it lightly. "Naughty little Trouble," he said, but couldn't help grinning.

Rosemary tugged on his shirt and growled softly. "Come on."

He followed her, still smiling.

He was not smiling as he rounded a corner and felt something cold and hard and definitely not sexy digging into his ribs.

"After nine years, you're going to find out just how appropriate the nickname 'Trouble' is."

Ethan forced himself to remain calm. "What do you think you know?" he asked. For answer, the small gun she'd somehow gotten ahold of dug into his ribs. He had stopped walking, but now he continued, his mind racing.

"Enough," she said shortly. Despite the direness of the situation, he admired her professionalism. She wasn't going to go on an angry rant and jeopardize whatever her plan was.

"Oh, come on, Trouble, if I don't know what you know—"

"You can't bluff your way out of it. One more word out of you and I'll put a hole through you."

"If that were true you'd have done so al—"

The pain as she fired through his arm was excruciating and utterly unexpected. Blood flowed down his arm, and he almost fell.

"Rosemary! What are you doing?"

The voice was high with alarm, and Ethan recognized it as belonging to Jake. Ethan blinked and tried to focus.

"Shutting him up," R. M. muttered. She shoved Ethan roughly from behind, and he stumbled forward. "Don't worry, he won't faint. I know what I'm doing."

And indeed she did. The wound hurt like mad, but she hadn't severed or broken anything. Then again, she had been careless, because if he dripped blood there'd be a trail that—

"Train your weapon on him, Jake, while I tie this up."

Damn it.

Jake looked uncertain, but obeyed. Rosemary stepped in front of Ethan and calmly reached to tear his shirt. Once, that would have been a prelude to passion. Now she was only interested in binding his wounds—not to help him, to ease his pain, but simply to stop an inconvenient dripping on the floor. He considered his options as she expertly tied the rag around the wound. They weren't very good.

"Listen, Trouble," Ethan said. Without batting an eye she pressed her thumb on the wound, and he saw stars for an instant. He gritted his teeth and continued. "You think I meant what I told Val? That I'd give you over to him along with Jake?"

Blue eyes, cold as ice chips, flickered up at him, then down to her task. "Absolutely."

"Come on, love, you know me better than that. Why would I do that?"

"I don't have time to list the reasons. And there's only one reason you wouldn't, and that's if you gave a rat's ass about me. Which I know you don't."

There was an instant he could have taken her as she stepped back and reached again for her weapon. It was a good bet that Jake wouldn't fire at Ethan if he lunged for Rosemary. But the muzzle of the gauss rifle was about a foot away from Ethan's chest, and while it was a good bet, it wasn't *that* good. Rosemary had responded to him, even though he knew she knew better. That meant she wasn't as unmoved by his betrayal as she wanted him to think. And that meant a chance.

"We'll leave Jake here for them and you and I'll take off together," Ethan continued. "Jake's the one with an alien in his head, not you. They'll give chase for a bit and then give up. Trust me."

For a fraction of a heartbeat, he saw doubt in the china blue eyes. Then Jake said, "He's lying, Rosemary. He knows that if he doesn't hold up his part of the deal Valerian won't stop hunting him till he's dead."

Ethan's head whipped around, and he stared at Jake. *You can read even my mind, bastard? Even with the psi-screen, huh? Then read this.*

Jake winced.

"I know that, Jake. Keep moving, Ethan." Rosemary had retrieved a rifle from where she and Jake had stashed them, and gestured with it. "You do what we ask and there's a good chance I might let you keep your . . . equipment."

Ethan couldn't read minds, but he didn't have to to know that Rosemary wasn't bluffing.

He lowered his head and went where she directed him. He knew where they were going. His vessels were the only way off the planet. Rosemary was a jack-of-all-trades, and she knew how to pilot as well as she knew how to hack into systems, as well as she knew how to kill, as well as she knew how to—do other things. Even having a stumblebum like Jake as her only crew wouldn't be too much of a handicap for her, and who knew but that the protoss inside Jake's skull knew even more about such things than R. M did.

There came a slight crackle from Ethan's right front pocket. Jake looked confused, but Rosemary knew what it was. They paused.

"Boss?"

Rosemary's eyes narrowed. "Answer it. And be smart, Ethan."

His hand crept up and pressed a button. "Yeah, Steve, what is it?" Rosemary nodded at the casual tone of his voice. He felt Jake's eyes on him intently and knew that if he tried to warn Steve, Jake would know. Damn it. He should have just clapped the bastard in the equivalent of irons the minute he got here.

"We got some communications systems down. We lost the vidfeed in areas 9, 47, and 43."

Rosemary mouthed, "Don't send them to the communications room." He nodded slightly.

"Roger that, Steve. That's my pet's doing." He smirked a bit at the irritation on her face at the condescending term. "She wanted some private time, if you know what I mean."

Tinny-sounding laughter came through. "I do. You're a lucky man, boss. She's a hot little number."

Ethan grinned. "That she is." Rosemary prodded him with the tip of the rifle, and his stomach muscles tensed. "Anything else?"

"Negative, sir. Have fun."

"I will, Steve, I will." He turned off the device and quirked an eyebrow at her.

"Good job," Rosemary drawled. "Now all we need is one of those sleek little vessels of yours and we'll be on our merry way."

Randall knocked on the door to Professor Ramsey's room. "Sir?"

Silence. Randall sighed. The Professor had made clear his dislike of Randall's entering unannounced. But Randall *had* announced himself. If the Professor was sleeping, the door would be locked. Randall had the code, of course; he had all the codes to all the rooms. But he would respect the Master's guest's decision. He tried the door. It opened easily.

Randall stepped inside, thinking to simply hang the clothes he'd brought with him, and then paused. The Professor was usually a very tidy person, he had observed. Most guests took advantage of the luxury of being waited on hand and foot. But the Professor was different; he always put his clothes away and made his own bed. Today, however, the bedclothes were in disarray, and Randall saw that pillows lay on the floor.

He frowned. He had not gotten to be where he was in life without trusting his instincts, and right now, he suspected that something was gravely out of order.

He spoke into his radio. "Elyssa? Is Miss Dahl in her room?"

"One moment, sir," said Randall's female counterpart. Randall pursed his lips and looked over the disarray. "Negative, Mr. Randall."

"Thank you."

Randall turned and strode the short distance to Rosemary Dahl's room. Elyssa was hanging a full-length ball gown and dropped him a curtsy. Randall frowned a bit. Elyssa was too efficient—she had already begun to straighten. He would have liked to see the room as it had been.

"Anything wrong, sir?" the tall, elegant blonde Elyssa asked.

"Nothing. You may go, Elyssa. I'll take care of the room."

Elyssa didn't bat an eye, merely nodded and left immediately, closing the door quietly behind her. Randall went through the room meticulously, his concern growing by the minute. He realized the fawn-colored leather pants and vest Rosemary had worn upon arrival were missing. Why had she chosen to put them on?

He activated his radio yet again. "Mr. O'Toole," he said, formally, "can you tell me if there are any security devices that have been disabled in the complex?"

"Damn, you're a sharp one, Randall," Steve O'Toole said. "Yeah, matter of fact. Boss's little hottie wanted some private time in sections 9, 47, and 43."

Randall closed his eyes briefly. Idiots. He was surrounded by idiots. He forced a dry chuckle. "I . . . see. I take it then that she and Mr. Stewart are in that location at the moment?"

"Yep."

"Where is Professor Ramsey?"

A pause. "Hey, he's with them. Boss is probably pissed as hell that he ran across him." Steve laughed.

"Yes, quite," Randall said. "Thank you, Mr. O'Toole."

He said nothing of the danger he feared his employer was in. While the Professor possessed no dangerous weapons whatsoever other than his telepathic abilities, which the good Dr. Morris had developed a method to block, Rosemary Dahl was quite deadly indeed. He'd read up on her to be prepared for just such an occasion as this. Mr. Stewart had a crack security team, of course, but Randall doubted they'd be a match for Miss Dahl in the present situation.

He removed his jacket and cuff links, then rolled up his shirtsleeves, in preparation for demonstrating his primary reason for being in Mr. Stewart's employ.

CHAPTER 24

JAKE BEGAN TO BELIEVE THEY MIGHT ACTUALLY pull this off.

It was all due to Rosemary, of course. And to Zamara, sitting quietly inside his consciousness and watching everything. But with each step they took that didn't prompt twenty guards to start firing at them, he was heartened.

They reached a door at the end of the corridor, and Rosemary prodded Ethan. He grinned down at her with a trace of superiority. "Stop with the empty threats. You need me alive, R. M."

"True," she said, nodding to Jake to indicate that he should drop and stash the rifle. When he'd done so, she did likewise, making sure Jake kept the pistol aimed at Ethan. "But I could cut off your hand for the genetic scan ID. That would make me smile."

Ethan's own smile faded somewhat, and he placed his hand onto the black square on the right side of the heavy metal door. Sensors came to life and the square started to glow. Red light moved slowly down from top to bottom, scanning Ethan's right hand, and a message appeared on the screen directly above the handprint: *Initial Identification confirmed. Genetic match approved for Ethan Paul Stewart. Proceeding to secondary confirmation: Vocal recognition.*

"Ethan Paul Stewart," Ethan said, leaning into the microphone embedded in the wall.

Again, the message flashed. *Secondary Identification confirmed. Vocal recognition approved for Ethan Paul Stewart. Proceeding to tertiary confirmation: Retinal mapping.*

Ethan moved to the left side of the door. A small camera emerged and he placed his right eye over it. He kept his eyes open while a blue light shone gently.

Tertiary Identification confirmed. Retinal mapping approved for Ethan Paul Stewart. Admission to hangar granted.

The huge door swung inward. Jake was startled for just a moment as he realized that he was looking directly into a cave. A cave that, like the long-ago underground complex into which Temlaa and Savassan had stumbled, blended technology with nature. Except that terrans weren't quite as good at it as the Xel'Naga were. The merging looked forced rather than natural, clumsy rather than graceful. Large gray pieces of equipment with aggressively blinking lights were shoved into niches that had been carelessly hewn from the rock. While there was a lot of equipment sitting around apparently waiting to have something done with it, Jake didn't see many personnel milling about; it looked like they'd caught a break. At the far end, the cave opened up to blue sky for easy launching of the ships. There was a glass and metal control center in the middle of the large cavern. One man, balding and slightly pudgy, was there at his station. He had his feet up on the console, reading something that didn't look particularly edifying to Jake and occasionally reached for a cup of what was probably coffee.

The ships, four of them at the current moment, sat lined up sullenly, their noses pointing toward the blue sky. One of them was the escape pod from the *Gray Tiger*. Jake thought it looked terribly small and beat up, now that he saw it next to its sleek and well-maintained neighbors. Jake didn't know enough about ships to know what they were called, but Rosemary would. That was all that—

Jake's skin prickled. Inside him, the part that was Zamara was instantly alert.

Ethan was in the lead, walking quickly but not too quickly toward the nearest ship. Rosemary was close behind him, the pistol, out of view but every bit as lethal as it had ever been, pointing at his back.

Jake's pulse quickened. He looked around. Something was amiss. For no good reason he understood he hurried over to Rosemary.

Up there—

Jake surged forward, blocking Rosemary's body from—what, he still didn't know. "Look out!" he yelped.

The tiny darts—three of them—struck him in the throat. He thought that whatever drug they were laced with must have been kicking in right away when he looked up to see Randall crouching above them on the gray stone, lowering his hand, a small contraption on his wrist. But no, this was real. It really *had* been the valet who had attacked him. Randall gathered himself and leaped down with feline grace.

Rosemary whirled as Randall hit the ground, swinging around her pistol to fire at this new threat.

"Good help is worth every credit," came Ethan's smooth voice as he lunged for Rosemary's weapon.

Jake crumpled. He stared up, watching with dimming vision as Randall straightened and ran to assist Ethan. Jake had two thoughts as he started to go unconscious.

One, entirely his own: *Damn, I hope I can move like that when I'm sixty-five.*

The other was pure Zamara: *Jake—get out of the way.*

He did.

Zamara surged to the forefront of his brain. As she had done when Jake had overindulged on wine that first night, Zamara chased the drug out of Jake's body for the moment. His vision cleared. Randall was almost upon him now, about to step over the prone body of the man he'd shot. Zamara bolted upright, grabbed Randall's leg, and pulled. Randall stumbled and almost fell, catching himself at the last minute and pulling himself free with a sharp twist. The sec-

ond had given Zamara a chance to get to her feet—
Jake's feet. She settled again into Jake's body, forcing
herself to quickly get accustomed to the short, oddly
balanced stature of the human male, to the clumsi-
ness of wearing another's body like an ill-fitting gar-
ment. She stood in the attack formation she had been
taught since childhood, moving lightly back and forth
on her feet, center of gravity low to the ground, arms
out for balance, silent and alert. Ready to attack.

Randall's pale blue eyes registered only the barest
hint of surprise. Then he quirked his lips in amusement. Randall dropped into a fighter's stance, moving
lightly on the balls of his feet. Zamara realized at once
from the pure ease and fluidity of the movement that
he was up against a master. The guards he'd taken
down earlier were no doubt sharpshooters, but
Randall needed no such encumbrances. The small
toxic darts had been his first line of attack. But if they
failed, it was obvious to Zamara that Randall needed
nothing but his hands to kill. Randall might not have
had the physical strength he'd possessed when he was
a young and no doubt highly successful assassin, but
he had forty-some years' worth of knowledge.

All this went through Zamara's mind in the fraction
of a second's grace she had before Randall feinted
with his right fist, then brought his left in with shocking speed.

He struck empty air. Zamara leaped upward, turning a full, graceful circle in the air, then dropped to
the ground, kicking out with a sure sweep of her leg

to simultaneously knock Randall off balance and pull him forward.

Randall struck the ground hard with a grunt, and Zamara heard a crack. The valet got to his feet, blood oozing from a cut on his cheek. He narrowed his eyes as he spoke.

"You're full of surprises, Professor." His look indicated that he wouldn't underestimate Zamara again. And sure enough, scarcely had the words left his lips than Randall had sprung again with deadly efficiency. Zamara was barely able to parry, to protect the human's fragile face as Randall, his eyes blazing, struck at her again and again and again, the blows coming down like a downpour in the rainy season. Zamara felt this body beginning to tire; its muscles were not used to moving in protoss mannerisms and they were protesting.

Randall was too good, too powerful, too trained in the art of hand-to-hand combat for Zamara, unused to moving in this body, to stand against him much longer. It was all she could do to simply block, her arms stinging and aching, unable to press an attack, feeling herself being pushed back. Randall was done playing with her. He was closing in for the kill.

It had come to this. She had not wanted to do this, had not been certain even if she would be able to. Jake had some protoss memories, yes. Jake's brain had been rewired. To attempt this, however, could result in failure or even damage Jake's brain. But she had no other choice.

Zamara surged forward instead of retreating. Randall had not been expecting such a movement and was, for a heartbeat, slightly off balance. It was the opportunity Zamara needed. She leaped and kicked hard, then dove backward and brought her hands together tightly for just an instant.

She pulled them apart. Glowing blue energy hovered between her palms.

Holy hell! Jake thought.

Randall's blue eyes widened.

For a long second the two opponents stood regarding each other. The orb hovered, turning, its eerie light casting Jake's features into sharp relief. Both combatants were bloody, bruised, and sweating. Both were breathing heavily. Neither was about to back down.

Randall charged.

The ball exploded. Hundreds of shards erupted, each one moving forward like a blade toward Zamara's enemy. A sound like the hum of a thousand angry bees filled the air and Randall gasped as the psionic energy struck him. He arched in pain as each of the glowing blue shards seared him, ate through his flesh like acid. Two more balls formed in Zamara's hands and hurtled directly toward Randall's chest.

Randall dropped to his knees. Zamara leaped over him, landed lightly, and whirled, fingers splayed, more psionic energy forming at her fingertips.

Randall fell, his body twisting around to look at her. She could smell burning flesh. She stood, ready to attack again if need be.

He managed, somehow, to prop himself up on his elbows. For a few seconds they looked into each other's eyes. As Randall stared up at Zamara, the protoss somehow knew that the valet understood completely what had transpired. Blood began to drip from Randall's mouth, thick and crimson, falling off his chin to splash on the floor.

Randall smiled. He looked . . . pleased. The valet nodded slightly in respect.

Zamara let the energy fade. The humming sound died. She lowered her arms as Phillip Randall crumpled, lifeless, to the stone floor.

Ethan was good.

But this time Rosemary was better.

The injury to Ethan's arm cost him dearly. He grabbed for the gun the second Rosemary's attention was diverted and even managed to close his hands on the weapon. Rosemary immediately brought up her knee to his groin. He'd anticipated the movement. Grunting, he brought the butt of the gun down on her knee, and she gasped in pain. Gritting her teeth, Rosemary slammed her foot down hard on his instep, then hooked her leg around his and yanked. At the same time, she released one hand from the rifle, found the injury on his arm, and squeezed it with all her might.

Ethan cried out in a most satisfactory way and started to fall. Instinctively, he let go of the weapon to catch himself. He tried to fall on his shoulder and roll, but Rosemary didn't give him the chance. She gripped the rifle firmly and slammed the butt down into his solar plexus. Ethan curled up into a ball, writhing, gasping for breath like a fish.

Rosemary turned to aid Jake, and blinked when she saw him standing, panting only a little, over Randall's prone form.

As Zamara relinquished control of his mind, Jake started to tremble.

I've killed a man. God help me I've killed a man.

"Damn, Jake," Rosemary said, her voice laced with admiration. He looked up at her, agonized. Rosemary stood over the whimpering form of Ethan, her hair only slightly messed up by the fight. She had the gun back, and it was trained on her former lover. Rosemary glanced back down at Ethan, and prodded him with a foot. "Get up."

Jake caught movement out of the corner of his eye. He jerked his head around and saw that the guard in the booth was staring at him, slack-jawed. Their eyes met, and faster than Jake would have expected from such a rotund personage, the guard ducked beneath his desk.

Rosemary had followed Jake's gaze. She swore and fired a shot. The glass shattered.

"That bought us some time, but not much. Come on." She gestured to the first vessel, and Ethan started to move toward it.

"Faster, you bastard," Rosemary growled, and

Ethan picked up the pace to a trot. Rosemary grimaced, and Jake noticed she was favoring one leg, though still keeping pace. "Stay close to him," she called to Jake. "If any shooters come in they won't fire at us if they think they might hit him."

Rosemary let Jake scurry up the ramp first. "Strap yourself in—we're going to have a rough liftoff."

Jake nodded, then paused at the door, looking back at Ethan standing on the ramp. He'd clearly gotten the worse end of the fight. His face was a mask of blood, the wound on his arm had reopened, and he kept his balance only with a great effort.

"I guess we have to take him with us," Jake said, wishing there were another alternative. "If we leave him here, Valerian will kill him."

Rosemary stepped into the ship and stood beside Jake. She regarded Ethan pensively and shook her dark head.

"No. Valerian isn't going to kill him. I am."

She fired.

Crimson blossomed on Ethan's crisply starched, perfectly white shirt. Ethan stared at his former lover, completely taken by surprise, then slowly toppled off the ramp. His body struck the stone floor with a crumpled-sounding *thump*. Rosemary thumbed a button. The bloodstained ramp began to retract as the doors closed. She slipped into the pilot's seat, buckled up, and started hitting controls.

Jake stared at her. She looked up at him, a thin line of annoyance marring her brow.

"I said strap yourself in."

"Damn it, Rosemary, you just shot him in cold blood!"

She turned back to what she was doing. "I did what I had to, Jake. If I'd let him live he and Valerian would be following us to the end of the universe."

Rosemary is not incorrect, Zamara said inside his mind. *He would have been a tenacious pursuer. His death will aid my mission.*

There seem to be a lot of deaths associated with your mission, Jake thought heatedly. *A lot of human deaths.*

It is regrettable, but necessary. Soon, you will understand.

Jake wasn't so sure.

There was a faint hum as the ship powered up. Jake started to feel very weak and stumbled to a seat. He realized that while Zamara had been able to mitigate the drug, or the poison, or the whatever it was, she had not eliminated it entirely from his system. Shaking, he leaned his head against the glass, looking at the small room with the shattered glass and the frightened guard. As he watched, he saw a hand emerge from the safety of below the desk. It fumbled around, then hit a button. A Klaxon started to shriek.

"Great," muttered Rosemary. Jake turned his suddenly heavy head to the cockpit, seeing that Rosemary was aiming the ship right for the blue oval that promised freedom. But there was something wrong about it. Jake blinked, wondering if it was the effect of whatever the now deceased Randall had injected him with. But no, it was there—

"Rosemary, it's a force field!"

She snorted, and the ship moved slightly to the left. "You know what the nice thing about being right where we are is, Jake?"

He muttered something along the lines of "What?"

"We're on the inside. Where the controls are."

She lined up on a large gray metal panel on a side wall, touched a button, and it exploded. Rosemary permitted herself a whoop and then turned the ship's nose to the blue sky.

Jake's stomach dropped to his ankles. He did not like flying at the best of times, and now was definitely not the best of times. He fought to hold on to his lunch as Rosemary yanked the little vessel upward at astonishing speed.

He could fight the drug coursing through his system no longer. Jake's eyes closed and his head fell backward. The memories came in waves, in a rush now. Dimly, before he lost consciousness, Jake wondered why—if it was because his brain finally, finally was able to comprehend at a swift enough pace, or if this, the final story of Temlaa and Savassan, had to be told quickly, before it was too late. . . .

CHAPTER 25

SAVASSAN HAD CHANGED. HE HAD ALWAYS BEEN A puzzlement to the other protoss, but when he returned with Jake in tow they understood him even less. It had taken Jake a long time to grasp what Savassan was trying to get across; it took the Shelak tribe even longer. But Savassan persisted.

First, Savassan spoke of the crystals. He and Jake demonstrated how to touch them, how to prepare oneself for the merging, the loss of self and gain of other that would come in a wave which would sweep one away if one was not careful. He watched with pride as one by one they took those first tentative steps into something large and beautiful and profound. They learned to work with the crystals, and with each other, and the experience bound them together even more tightly.

But Savassan was not content . . . not yet. . . .

Rosemary glanced quickly over her shoulder. Jake was out like a light. It was probably the best thing for both of them.

Luck had been with them, in that Ethan had had a

system runner. This blocky, ungraceful vessel was the only ship its size that had the engine power to make a warp-jump. Black marketers loved the things. You didn't need a large crew, there was a goodly amount of room for cargo storage, and you could give pursuit the slip with ease. While she'd have loved to have had the firepower of a Wraith or other fighter, right now the ability to outrun was more valuable than the ability to outfight. Ethan's other two ships, Wraiths that were augmented startlingly far beyond what the government permitted, were right behind her. The system runner rocked violently as one of them got in a good shot. They'd try to cripple the ship now, while there was still a chance of forcing her to land. Once in space, she'd have a much better chance of escaping. The goal was to capture her and Jake, not blow them out of the skies.

At least, she was sure that was what Valerian wanted. She had to hope that Ethan's thugs knew it—

The ship lurched violently, and Rosemary smelled smoke. She swore, unbuckled herself, and flipped the extinguisher switch. The acrid smell of burning wires and plastic mixed with the chemical reek of the extinguishing foam.

Jake kept on sleeping.

"We need . . . a way to be in this place," Savassan said to Temlaa. "A way to bring order. There must be guidelines for how to navigate this unity in which we find ourselves. We must strive, each of us, to be good, and pure, and sacred, so

that what we bring to the whole makes it that much more profound and powerful."

"But how are we to bring the others? How can we get them to understand the powers of the crystal? I cannot simply walk into an encampment and invite them to join us."

"No, you cannot. But perhaps I can."

"Damn, damn . . ." Rosemary swore as six bright spots appeared on her computer screen. One Valkyrie and five Wraiths. Apparently somewhere along the line, Valerian had decided to send more than one ship to pick up a scientist and an assassin. Valerian was nothing if not intelligent. The zippy little vessels were now closing in on her. They weren't firing on her, and even Ethan's ships had now called off the attack. Rosemary knew what they were trying to do—pen her in so she couldn't make the warp-jump. Her fingers flew, trying to simultaneously figure out where in the universe she wanted to go and to pilot the ship out of this trap, to flee like a wounded deer chased by a pack of wolves—

"Bad analogy," she muttered to herself, abandoned an attempt to plot a course, hit the controls, and dove.

Savassan had not revealed even to Jake what he planned. All he would tell them was that the tribe was to gather right as dawn was stretching pink and golden fingers across the purple sky. Each of them selected a crystal, and bore it reverently out into the damp earth. Savassan looked at each of them in turn.

"What we are about to do," he said, "will, I hope, be long remembered as a turning point in the history of our people. I have been touched by the Xel'Naga, and in turn, I have shared what I have learned with you, my tribe. But it must not stop here. Sit. Hold the crystal in front of you. And when I tell you to, each one of us will touch his crystal, close his eyes, and open his mind and heart to those protoss out there who hunger for this—who hunger and thirst for something they do not even know exists. We are not creating anything new. We are discovering something ancient. We are remembering that which has been forgotten."

Jake shivered. Slowly, he sat beside his master. Without even touching the crystal, he was already linked with them on one level, sensing their worry, their hope. Their fear.

"Touch the crystals," said Savassan, "and call to our brothers and sisters."

Jake gasped as the sensations flooded through him. He could do nothing save let it all wash through him with a brain that had been redesigned so it could process such a wave.

Zamara all but sang inside him.

Do you understand, Jacob Jefferson Ramsey? Zamara exulted in his mind, in his blood, in his very cells. *Savassan awakened something we had not known for eons. And through me, that moment will never die. I am a Preserver. I have the memories of all protoss who have ever lived. My mind is one of only a handful even among the protoss that can bear such knowledge. As long as my consciousness lives—in you, Jacob—this moment will live. And be re-created, when you pass this on to another, as I have done with you. You are experiencing what we did: the instant, the connection that changed us forever. You are now a Preserver. You are now a keeper of that which is sacred and which will continue to shape all those it touches as long as there is a Preserver to hold that knowledge.*

I . . . I understand . . . , Jake thought, still drifting in that vast sea of connection and interweaving.

The images that came were sweet ones. After Savassan had sent out the call to his fellow protoss, they cautiously came to him. They were frightened and defensive, but they could not argue with what they had experienced.

The mystic Savassan taught them what he had learned. How to link minds and thoughts and work with the energy created. How to focus and direct thoughts, respecting those of others while blending them into a whole that was so harmonious, the protoss were almost a single, radiant, beautiful mind.

"This is a path of order," said Savassan. Savassan, whose name would be lost to everyone but Zamara and now Jake. Savassan, who would be known as "He Who Brings Order," as . . .

Today, he goes by the name of Khas. We revere him, and honor his memory. He united us under the Khala . . . a system of order. The "Path of Ascension." It is what pulled us out of the Aeon of Strife. Without it, without this knowledge of how deeply we are one, we would have destroyed ourselves.

Jake remembered the hatred the protoss had

toward one another, how the tribes were being destroyed not by an external enemy, but by their own kind. And he had been in Temlaa's skin when these pivotal moments in history occurred. Tears filled his eyes, and he wiped at them.

Do not be ashamed that this moves you, Zamara said. *If it did not, it would mean I had failed.*

This is healing . . . this . . . Even in this link that bound him so tightly with thousands of long-dead protoss, Jake knew he was in his present. And that he was in extreme physical danger. What he was experiencing called to him; he was loath to leave, but an idea was stirring inside him.

This moment had given the protoss pause at a point in their existence when they tore each other apart with their bare hands. It had saved them. What could it do—

Jacob—this is not for them. . . .

It can be—

And before a stunned Zamara could even try to intervene, Jake had thought it, and in the thinking, it was done.

Rosemary Dahl froze. She could do nothing but surrender to what suddenly flowed into her . . . nor could the captain of the Valkyrie *Anglia* . . . or the mechanic on his first deep-space mission . . . or Elyssa, or Steve, or the frightened guard in the launching bay, or all the others who had served Ethan and Valerian.

It hurt, it blazed, it purified, and it stretched them wider than they had ever been stretched before as their limited, unaltered human minds did what pathetically little they could to grasp it all.

We.

Are.

ONE.

Rosemary felt Ted Samsa's heart beating in her chest. She relived Elyssa Harper's first kiss. Steve O'Toole's first kill. A bite of ice cream. The bark of a beloved pet. The cry of a newborn. The smell of that newborn's skin. Every memory, every feeling, every sense of *being* that hundreds of people felt and sensed and remembered sang through her mind. The joys that made them laugh were hers. The tragedies that made them weep were hers. The stings, the slights, the smiles, the wonder, the boredom. All of the things that go to make up a life, an identity, a sense of self flooded her. And she knew that they were tasting her life as she was savoring theirs.

While there was hate, and fear, and prejudice, because people hated and feared and prejudged, it could not possibly, possibly be directed at anyone in this link, this circle, this deep and profound pool of unity. For who could hate his right hand? *Your hand is my hand.* Who could hate his left eye? *For your eye is my eye.*

For a timeless moment, caught in this never-before-experienced state of ecstatic union, the captain could not speak the order to attack. Rosemary could not enter the jump coordinates.

The ships drifted. The moment stretched on.

• • •

Jake wanted nothing more than to stay here, drifting in this unspeakable sense of unity and peace and sensation. But he slowly detached himself from it and floated back to the reality of his present. Jake blinked his eyes, not at all surprised to find tears still wet on his face. He felt empty and horribly alone.

He struggled with the seat belt and stumbled to Rosemary. Her eyes were wide and glazed, her lips softly moving, an expression of almost childlike delight on her face. Hating himself, Jake extended his thoughts into her mind. He had to read her thoughts in order to know what to do to make the jump. He sifted through the thousands of minds that were interconnected in this moment and found the glowing, brilliant thread that was Rosemary Dahl in this glorious tapestry of union.

"Oh," he breathed, softly. He felt her pain, shocking and keen and achingly lonely. Her bitterness, her disillusionment. Brief flashes of her history, of cruelty and squalor and horrific violence, of determination and grit and a will that pulsed strong and true and powerful.

This, then, was what Zamara had sensed about Rosemary. The protoss had dived in past the walls that a broken soul had erected to protect herself. She had found the Rosemary inside the R. M., the woman inside the killer, and deemed her worthy. Jake had seen only the vaguest glimpses of something other than a coldhearted killer, someone who used every tool at her disposal to further her own goals. Now he could see *her*, could feel *her*, could—

He leaned forward and kissed her forehead, gently, without passion, as he might have a child.

No matter what she did, he could never hate Rosemary Dahl again.

Now he pulled out of that connection, searching for the information. Rosemary was going on blind luck here. There was no telling where they would emerge, or even if they would emerge intact. Jake didn't know a great deal about interstellar travel, but he did know that if you didn't plot a jump with great care and precision, you could end up A) dead, B) dead, C) so far away from wherever you wanted to be you'd never get back, or D) all of the above.

He found the information he needed, bent over the console, entered it . . . and hesitated before he pushed the button. There was a good chance this wouldn't work, and, as he was ever curious, there was something he had to know.

Zamara?

Yes, Jacob?

This changed the protoss. What will it do to us?

That moment was never intended to be shared beyond our own species. The Khala is for us, not you, and it is sacred, not a toy.

She was angry with him, but she could not argue with the results. At least, the initial ones. He sensed her softening.

I must admit . . . you chose wisely, this time. Truly, Jacob,

I do not know what will happen. Your species is . . . young yet to grasp the true significance. Most likely, most of those who experienced it will discount it, scoff at it and dismiss it as a momentary fancy.

But . . . not all?

No. Not all.

Jake could live with that.

He pushed the button.

The Dark Templar saga will continue in
Shadow Hunters

AWARD-WINNING AUTHOR CHRISTIE GOLDEN has written twenty-eight novels and several short stories in the fields of science fiction, fantasy, and horror.

Golden launched the TSR *Ravenloft* line in 1991 with her first novel, the highly successful *Vampire of the Mists*, which introduced elven vampire Jander Sunstar. *Vampire of the Mists* was reprinted in trade paperback as *The Ravenloft Covenant: Vampire of the Mists* in September 2006, fifteen years to the month after its initial publication.

She is the author of several original fantasy novels, including *On Fire's Wings* and *In Stone's Clasp*, the first two in her multi-book fantasy series from LUNA Books. *In Stone's Clasp* won the Colorado Author's League Award for Best Genre Novel of 2005, the second of Golden's novels to win the award.

Among other projects are over a dozen *Star Trek* novels, including *The Murdered Sun*, *Marooned*, and *Seven of Nine*. She's authored the *Dark Matters* trilogy, the duology *Homecoming* and *The Farther Shore*, released in June and July of 2003, and the duology *Spirit Walk: Old Wounds* and *Enemy of My Enemy*.

An avid player of Blizzard Entertainment's *World of Warcraft* MMORPG, Golden has written two novels for the game, *Lord of the Clans* and *Rise of the Horde*. And no, she won't tell you her characters' names.

Golden has had the remarkable opportunity of writing much of this current trilogy in a place that to her feels alien indeed—Flinders Island, Tasmania. In her more sedate life, she lives in Colorado.

Look for these **WARCRAFT** novels
by *New York Times* bestselling author

CHRISTIE GOLDEN

WARCRAFT: LORD OF THE CLANS

WORLD OF WARCRAFT: RISE OF THE HORDE

Available wherever books are sold or at www.simonsays.com.

POCKET BOOKS
A Division of Simon & Schuster
A CBS COMPANY

SCDT1a

WORLD OF
STARCRAFT®

ORIGINAL NOVELS BASED ON
THE HIT VIDEO GAME!

Available wherever books are sold or at www.simonsays.com.

POCKET BOOKS
A Division of Simon & Schuster
A CBS COMPANY

SCDT1b